Filaree

A Novel
of an American Life

Sincerely,
Marguerite Noble

Illustration by Glen T. Strock

Filaree
A Novel
of an
American Life

Marguerite Noble

University of New Mexico Press
Albuquerque

Library of Congress Cataloging In Publication Data

Noble, Marguerite, 1910–
    Filaree: a novel of an American Life.

    Reprint. Originally published: 1st ed. New York: Random House,
c1979.
    1. Title.
PS3564.026F5   1985   813'.54   85-1130
ISBN 0-8263-0825-2 (pbk.)

University of New Mexico Press paperback edition
reprinted 1985 by arrangement with Marguerite Noble
and International Creative Management

Fourth printing, University of New Mexico Press, 1991

To those pioneer women
who survived
in a life of suppression

I am a parcel of vain strivings tied by a chance bond together.

—Henry David Thoreau

I

1. The woman sat silent in the spring wagon, her back rigid. The springs under the board seat did little to cushion the jarring to her pregnant body. With an effort she shifted her heavy weight to the far side of the open wagon, widening the space between herself and her husband. She had no liking to sit near him.

She pulled her sunbonnet lower to block the glare of the winter sun—and the sight of the man. It helped her to forget for a moment that she was trapped in this land with him. Her glance fell on her distended stomach, and the thought came: *bloated as a dead cow.* Rage enveloped her.

The woman was past her thirty-first birthday, but she looked younger. She had a finely chiseled nose, a strong chin, and expressive lips. But it was her eyes that people noticed. Sometimes changing from green to gray, they seemed almost too large for her oval face. Work and childbearing had failed to take away her freshness. Though she had often heard it said that you lost a tooth for every child you bore, the woman still had all of hers. Except for the awkwardness of her protruding abdomen, her body was lithe and well-shaped, the flesh firm. And yet the woman felt prematurely old, aged by too many years of unrequited living.

It was a day in January, 1910. That morning at dawn the couple had set out from their Filaree Ranch. They were headed for the midwife at the Roosevelt Dam settlement and had long hours to travel before reaching the town of tents, buildings, wagons, and a saloon—thrown together for the construction of the new dam. The road was marked by two ruts: Wagon wheels had exposed the rocks and ground the dust as fine as the flour the woman made biscuits with.

Again the wagon threw the woman's cumbersome body toward the man. Righting herself quickly, she gripped her hands over her distended stomach, trying to keep her balance. A forewarning labor pain momentarily paralyzed her.

'Spose I start birthing this 'fore we get to Roosevelt?

Breathing between the pains brought on by the bumping wagon, she fastened her eyes on the miles of sere country in the Arizona Territory that the ranch folk called "The Mesa." The woman saw it as a landscape entombed in a desolate growth of mesquite and palo verde trees, greasewood and cat-claw bushes, and cactus. But she recalled that in a wet spring the filaree turned the earth green, and the plants blossomed with purple flowers.

Maybe the child will die a-borning.

The man pushed up the brim of his sweat-ringed hat, and from habit scanned the sky over the Sierra Anchas and the Mazatzals. He spat to clear his throat of the dust. "Nary a cloud. Damn sure need rain *now* to bring up the filaree."

The woman ignored the man. Her thoughts were of The Mesa. It was an unpredictable country. In drouth times, the land battled the aridity. Some plants died, and others adapted, like the cactus. Some resisted and survived—like the filaree. The nerves and spirits of The Mesa people became as tattered and frayed as the dessicated plants. They swore at the land, and some fulfilled their threat to move on—or to go back where they came from.

But when the rains came, the woman had seen her husband ride down a draw with the filaree belly-high to his horse, and his stirrups brushing the mariposa lilies. In such years, The Mesa folk recovered and forgot.

But 1910 was not a rain year, and the man in the wagon was beginning to be afraid. He remembered the drouth five years earlier which had "damn nigh wiped him outa the cow business." The rotting carcasses of his dead cattle had filled the air with a stench for miles. The buzzards had settled to tear at the decaying flesh—"To feed themselves on my misfortune, the puking bastards." The man told himself it was to blot out these recollections that he occasionally sought out the Tonto Saloon. "A man had oughta be able to take a drink once in a while with his neighbors."

The isolation of the country had brought to the woman a torturing loneliness. She had a hunger for something more than six children, a husband she did not love, and days of monotonous drudgery, with few escapes for pleasure or change. When the family had left Texas six years earlier, she had hoped to find a fuller life in the Arizona Territory. But each year in this new land, so recently clear of the Apache Indians, had diminished her hope to a dull yearning. She blinked her eyes now to clear away the dust that lifted from the wagon wheels.

Perhaps, someday . . .

The man slapped the reins on the horses' rumps and pulled his hat deep over his eyes. It was gray felt, with four dents to peak the crown: "Texas style," he called it. On The Mesa most men creased their hats down the middle, with the dents on two sides of the crown.

He was heavily built, his belly straining at the twilled cotton shirt, the belt fitting below the bulge. His clean gray work pants were tucked inside his boot tops—Texas style like his hat. The man was eighteen years older than the woman, but he did not protest the passing of time as she did. At least his cow ranch gave some satisfaction to his life.

The man reached work-stiffened fingers into his shirt pocket for a square of tobacco marked "Battle Ax Plug." With his side teeth he wrenched loose a formidable bite. In his mouth he worked on the chaw like fresh fuel, as if feeding mesquite limbs into a campfire. He leaned over the side of the wagon and hissed forth a stream of brown juice. The spittle plopped in the road and splattered and rolled like filthy raindrops. The woman turned away.

"Damn dry," the man repeated.

The woman's tone betrayed no interest. "Always need rain in this godforgotten place. But it weren't no better in Texas."

"Leastways in Texas we had water in the Navasota River."

"Don't you recollect in Stone Springs that the dampness gave you the catarrh bad? You had spells of feelin' poorly. What's frettin' me now is the younguns alone back there at the ranch. That Hannah has a heap of responsibility. And I worry about the lamp gittin' afire."

"Damnation, woman! You're always frothin' at the mouth." He jammed the tobacco cud to the other side of his cheek. "That girl's fifteen past. She kin take care o' that outfit good as a man."

"Ain't fair, though, her taking care o' that passel o' younguns —and the stock."

"You'd complain if you's goin' be hung with a new rope."

She thought: *If I was hung, I leastways wouldn't be bornin' no more younguns.* And promised herself: *This is the last baby. There'll never be another one.*

Before the wagon had pulled out, the woman had told her oldest daughter, "Hannah, you're to mind the little ones while I'm birthin' this baby." The child's eyes had grown serious, and she had nodded. The woman wanted to block out the vision she had of the ranch with Hannah cooking, washing, herding the children to the one-room schoolhouse, mediating quarrels, and caring for the chickens and feeding the horses in the corral.

She thought, too, of Mary Belle, fourteen, the one who "riled her ma the most." She had told the second-born, "You aggervate me plumb to death." To her younger sister, Shug Holman, the woman had confided, "I marked Mary Belle when I was a-carrying her. Ben was drinkin' then. I was rebellious. That youngun's got the defiance of the devil. She causes the ruckuses with the others."

She now said to the man, "I told Annie to help Mary Belle with the dishes. Annie's the only one can git along with the rebel. I threatened to lick Mary Belle if she teased Annie 'bout her stutterin'.''

The man brandished the whip, the horses strained and let out gas. The man sluiced brown spittle over the side of the wagon. "Did you tell Stockton about feedin' that dogie calf in the back corral? That boy'll go chasin' bugs and fergit his own name. That nickname 'Spider' fits him right."

The mother answered. "Spider'll do his chores. That boy may grow up to be a science man. I hope Carter'll shut the henhouse door at night. Them varmints—"

"That Carter ain't worth the powder it'd take to blow him to hell."

The woman kicked at the satchel under her feet. "Ain't right you talk o' the younguns like that. You expect too much. He's only twelve. You're takin' out your grudge on him when it's the no-rain that's gallin' you."

"Carter's showin' your family's blood in him—bad blood—Holman blood."

The woman bristled. "I told Hannah to go to Ma's if she needed help."

The man snorted. "You couldn't a-give her worse advice."

"You're bullheaded when it comes to my folks. Mebbe Pa never had as much git-up-and-go as he shoulda, but"—she lifted her head high and looked at her husband—"you kin choose your friends, but God gives you your people. You shoulda let Shug stay with the children."

"I don't want that Shug around them. And goin' by the name of Holman after all the husbands she had—and run off. Hannah don't need no help from that sister of yours. Anyhows, Hannah done a right good job a-drivin' that team from Texas, didn't she?"

The woman had remorseful recollection. Hannah, ten at the time, drove the buckboard across the endless plains of the Llano Estacado. She pictured the child's fragile freckled skin assaulted by the sun, and the small hands jerking at the heavy

reins. The tarpaulin over the ribs of bodark wood was insuffi-
cient cover for the three-month journey. The woman's brother
had made the trip with them. "Good thing Jimso was there to
spell Hannah on the drivin'," she said.

"Jimso, hell! Always a-suckin' on the hind tit."

The woman fell silent and turned her back to him again. He
was so different from the lean cowboy back in Texas who had
come "sparkin' " her when she was fifteen years old.

Her thoughts went on to their first year of marriage and the
baby, born too soon and buried under a mound of river rock,
with neither cross nor headstone to mark the spot. She recalled
her husband's grief at the death of the son who carried his
name, and she had a flash of sympathy for this man whose sense
of loss had equaled her own.

She reached to push back her hair, her long hair that years
ago in Texas he had described as "brown as jerky gravy." She
resented her long hair now, a burden whose weight, she believed, gave her frequent headaches. The man refused to permit her to cut it. He had said, "No lady cuts her hair." She
claimed that it was the cause of the headaches which sometimes forced her to lie for hours in a darkened room.

The man wiped the back of his hand across his mustache,
which was stained with tobacco spittle. He said, " 'Pears like
a mite o' clouds gatherin'. Still 'tain't too late for filaree. Ol'
Man Burns told me that when he come here in the seventies
there weren't no filaree. Said when them fellers from California
brung in sheep, the seeds was in the wool. He heard tell they
was 'sposed to come from Australia."

"I heard it was from Europe."

"Gov'ment feller told Burns the word was Spanish. They call
it different, like 'al-fil-a-ria.' It growed so rank with that water
from the spring on the El Bar outfit that Ike Talbott done cut
it and raked it into stacks like hay." The man shook his head.
"Mebbe he had to, 'cause being foreman he does what the boss
says. But I can't never be no farmer hand."

In good years the filaree had filled her yard; she had taken to calling her home the Filaree Ranch. The name had stuck. In drouth, the plant hugged the earth and waited—and survived in its tenacity. She thought of herself in the same way: waiting for the rain, waiting for life to give her something— something to fulfill her destiny.

Now it was winter, and the purple blossoms had dried, the leaves had shrunk, and the spearlike seeds had turned brown and curled. When touched by moisture, the seed would unfold to make a spike which would burrow into the earth to regenerate. The woman often amused herself by placing one of the tiny sabers in her palm and spitting on it to watch the spike untwist. Last spring she had pressed the lacy leaves in The Sears, Roebuck Catalogue, labeling on a scrap of old envelope: "From Dreamy Draw in Lonesome Gulch," where she had gathered the plant. A growth of filaree, like a patchwork quilt of green, could soften the austerity of The Mesa.

She felt the movement of the child within her, still protesting. She had thought Benjy, now six, would be the last. She swayed with the wagon, waiting and hating. She did not respond to the man's announcement that they had reached Ash Creek, and that it was time to water the horses, to get a bite of grub.

The man spat out tobacco juice and raised his voice. "Hear me? We'll stop at Ash Creek. Hear me, Missus Baker?"

"Yes, I heard you, Mr. Baker."

She had called him "Mr. Baker" since their courting days. It was the custom in Texas. In turn, the man called his wife "Missus Baker." He had not used her first name, "Melissa," since Texas. Nor did the woman call him "Ben." To the children she spoke of "your papa," while he spoke of "your mammy."

The midday sun was cutting vertical shadows when the man drove the team to the banks of Ash Creek. Although it was not the custom of Ben Baker to help his wife from the wagon, he now held his hand out to assist her heavy descent. Then he unhitched the team from the wagon and tied the animals to a hackberry limb. With a shovel he dug in the sandy bottom of the dry creek. A seepage of moisture came up; gradually water collected in a small depression. When the sand had settled, Ben Baker led the horses to the small water hole. After the horses had finished drinking, he fed them oats from a pan, fettered their front feet with hobbles of twisted rope, and released them to graze on the sparse dried grass of the flat.

Melissa heard him humming the mournful fragments of a song: "Old Texas . . . the state where I was born . . . in the county of Llano, down by Llano town . . ." For a moment she could understand the loneliness in the man.

Waddling into the mesquite thicket by the roadside, she stepped with caution through the burrs that clawed at her skirts and her ribbed cotton stockings. She had to reach down over her abdomen to dislodge a nettle stinging her leg. She looked for a cleared space. Gathering up her long skirts, she squatted carefully. To balance her heaviness, she reached out her hand to grasp a stump. A few minutes later, she came out from behind the thicket.

Ben Baker observed the woman's awkward body. "Why don't you set a spell on this tarp?" he asked. "You look a mite peaked. I'll git a fire goin'."

But she only resented the solicitous tone of his voice and thought, *You're a few years too late, Ben Baker, with your consideration.* She shook her head. "No. Just git down the grub box for me."

He piled twigs into a pyramid and lit them. He helped the blaze along by fanning his hat across the fire.

Filling a blackened can with water from the canteen hanging on the side of the wagon, the woman set a coffee pot on the fire. When the water boiled, she dropped in a handful of coffee, and then a cup of cold water to settle the grounds. She filled her husband's tin plate with biscuits and fried beef prepared that morning at the ranch. He saw her standing with a cup of coffee in her hand, sipping slowly. "Ain't you goin' eat? Want I should git you something to set on?"

The woman shook her head. "I ain't hungry. My back's achin'. I got one of my headaches comin' on."

At that moment they heard horse's hoofs, and an unexpected rider appeared suddenly from the growth of hackberry trees in the dry creek bed. As he rode closer, she saw him grin and noted that one tooth was missing in front. The sun glinted on the silver-colored badge exposed on his shirt where he had opened his coat.

Her husband, still squatting on the ground with coffee cupped in his hands, focused his gaze on the rider. "Ted Neeson," he muttered. "Damn sneaky bastard. Comin' outa nowheres. Tooth's gone where Ike Talbott whipped him in the ruckus they had."

The rider, still grinning, forced his horse near. He halted the animal and made a motion toward lifting his large-brimmed hat. "Howdy, Ben. Howdy, Miz Baker."

She acknowledged him with a slight movement of her head. Her husband did not rise. He nodded, his face impassive. The horse made a restless kick at the ground, and the dust rose slowly. The rider spoke again. "I been missin' a calf or two. Was out lookin'. Seen yore horses up the draw. Figgered maybe you mighta spotted some critturs with my brand on 'em."

"No. Ain't seen none o' yore stock, Neeson."

The rider hesitated, with a longing glance at the coffee pot on the fire. "Guess I'll mosey along." He turned, taking his yellowed grin with him.

Melissa Baker watched the retreating figure. "He ain't got the manners of a hog. Ridin' his horse so close to camp that the dust come onto the food. Guess he expected an invite to grub, leastwise a cup o' coffee."

"I wouldn't give Ted Neeson the time o' day from a broken watch. Lookin' fer cattle. He's a bigger thief than any man

what ever rode into or outa The Mesa. Hides behind that
deputy badge he's sportin', and damn careful everybody sees
it."

When her husband had finished eating, Melissa scraped the
remaining bits of food on the ground and lumbered to the
creek bed to scrub the dishes with sand. Back at the wagon,
she rationed a cup of water from the canteen and rinsed them.
She held up her head. A familiar sound came to her. Gambel
quail. At the Filaree Ranch the quail came to feed with her
chickens. Her mouth softened. Melissa saw a lone quail, his
black-tasseled head bobbing, perched on a mesquite limb. The
bird made a sound like the gurgle of water rippling over rocks.
She heard the man harnessing the horses.

2.

It was late in the afternoon when the wagon reached
the straggle of houses and tents at the Roosevelt Dam. Baker
reined his team in front of an unpainted building. On the
weathered boards, faded black letters said TONTO SALOON. "I
wanta see a feller," he told Melissa. "Won't be long." He
climbed down and led the team to a watering trough.
"Horses'll be all right. I got some business in here. Then we'll
go to that midwife's house."

Melissa watched her husband clump onto the board sidewalk
and through the swinging doors of the saloon. Her back
slumped against the wooden seat. She watched men with their
weather-whipped flesh, in rough, grimed clothes, walk down
the street. Some turned to enter the door that had closed
behind Ben Baker.

She took off her bonnet, loosed the bone hairpins and let her
hair tumble to her waist. Melissa noted the rancid odor. It
mingled with the street smells of dust and horse manure. She
had always saved rain water to wash her hair with, but the

barrel under the eaves had been dry for weeks. The hard water of The Mesa only caused soaps to curdle, gumming the strands, and she had finally resorted to rubbing in dry cornmeal and brushing it out. The cornmeal had removed some of the oil, but the smell lingered. So she had given up. Her head was throbbing now.

She turned to watch two Apache Indian women, their uncombed black hair falling down their backs. They plodded down the street, their voluminous skirts of flowered calico sweeping the dust. She knew them to be "them Apache squaws camped in their wickiups outside the settlement." On The Mesa Martha Brownell had told her in hushed tones that some white men visited the squaws in their brush huts and paid them money. Though her spine stiffened with distaste, she harbored a wish that her husband would visit the wickiups and leave her alone. Anything rather than bear another child.

The tired horses stomped their feet, shifted their weight, switched tails across their rumps at the flies that were trying for the last bites before dark. The woman stood in the wagon and stretched her muscles. A man came out of the door of the Tonto Saloon. It was not Ben Baker. Melissa put her hands against her aching temples; she could not push out the thumping.

The swinging door opened again and Melissa recognized the burly form of Ted Neeson, outlined in the light. She frowned. *He got here in a hasty hurry from huntin' his cattle.* Aware of Neeson's quickness to quarrel, especially when drinking, she wondered what sort of accusations he had spread inside. Neeson ran cattle on the country adjoining the El Bar where Ike Talbott was foreman: He had lost his front tooth as a result of hinting too broadly that Ike had been rustling. Melissa watched him sway and disappear into the deepening shadows.

The street grew quiet—except for the jangle of piano notes that came from the saloon. A woman's brassy voice sang

". . . bet on the gray . . ." She heard loud laughter. Shivering, she reached into the back of the wagon, pulled out a knitted shawl and wrapped it close around her shoulders. The horses tossed their heads. Melissa sagged lower on the seat, searching for a comfortable position. The light winged away like a buzzard sailing slowly and lazily out of sight. It grew dark. And still she waited.

3.

The next morning Melissa Baker sat on the porch of Samantha Cote's boardinghouse with her landlady. Aunt Samantha swayed back and forth in her rocking chair, her knitting needles clicking in rhythm. Mrs. Cote was not anyone's aunt, but had taken on the title as women in this countryside often did when they passed middle age. Aunt Samantha's husband had died in Arkansas before she came to Roosevelt with her son Jobe. She looked at the figure of Melissa sitting erect in a straight-backed chair, trying to ease the strain on her back. Her voice was kind. "Miz Baker, I know yore restless for yore time to come. It don't hurry none fer you to fret. I've done a heap o' midwifin' and I'm gonna take keer o' you."

Melissa was glad to have someone to confide in at last. "I cain't sleep at night," she said. "Cain't turn over. Have to lie on my back. Bones and muscles git cramped somethin' fierce. Numbs me. Legs and arms go to sleep on me. I have to fight to git breath."

"I know. Won't be long till that's over with. Could be comin' any time now."

The two women looked across the valley. The hills were dull with winter shrubs blotting the chalk soil. Dust rose where men and mule teams, tearing at the earth, disgorged boulders and spewed up dirt, and moved lumber like ants tugging at seeds.

Melissa shifted her bulk to the edge of the chair. "Aunt Samantha, we're grateful you could take us in."

Samantha Cote did not break the beat of her knitting. "Glad to have you. I ain't got nary ol' man. I gotta make a livin' fer me and my boy Jobe."

Across the canyon a dog howled. Melissa said, "Reminds me of the way the train whistle sounded back in Texas."

Samantha said, "Miz Baker, you spoke 'bout 'back in Texas.' How did you folks happen to come to this country?"

Melissa breathed deeply, feeling the constraint imposed by the pressure of the unborn child. "Everybody was comin' West, and my folks was already out here, writin' back to come join them. We had a good ranch at Stone Springs, but my husband had the catarrh-asthma bad there, with the dampness of the Navasota River."

"I come out here 'cause I heard I might find a job cookin' for the dam builders," Aunt Samantha said. "How long you Bakers been in this country?"

"We settled at the Filaree Ranch on The Mesa six years ago. It taken us three months to come from Texas to Arizona. Left Stone Springs the second day of February and landed in Globe City the fourth of May."

"Did jist yore own family come out?"

"Our neighbor Ol' Man Wattle drove one wagon, and my brother Jimso rode his saddle mare. We had three wagons. We brought our buggy. Six horses. Two spans of mules."

"Yore pa and ma already out here?"

"They come five years before. Our oldest girl, Hannah, she was ten then, and she drove one wagon. I spelled her some, and Jimso traded off."

"Musta been wearisome for you to be cookin' fer all that tribe on campfires."

"It was a long tiresome trip. Spent a powerful lot of time packin' and unpackin'. Some days we didn't make more'n ten miles in a day. After it rained, we stayed three days at Alamo Creek a-dryin' the quilts on the bushes."

"I've done a heap o' travelin' myself, and I know what the wimmenfolk go through."

"Carter—that's my oldest boy—he was six then. He took down with the fever and crampin' in the stomach. He liketa cough himself to death."

"It's the wimmen what worry about sickness in the young-uns—not the menfolk."

"The rest o' the younguns took down. Didn't have nothin' to doctor them with but coal oil, turpentine, and sugar. Took lots o' cookin' keep them all fed. Ran outa fresh meat the first week out. Sometimes Ben and Jimso couldn't find nothin' to shoot. Sometimes they got rabbits or quail. In the rain, couldn't find no dry wood."

"Didn't you hit lot of dry country?"

"On the Texas plains and comin' through New Mexico. Dirt. No way to wash clothes. Days was the same—burden-some. I got headaches all the time. I could feel a spell comin' on. It's my hair gives me the headaches. My man won't allow me to cut it. Says it ain't fittin' nor proper."

"Wimmen take the hardship and the tribulation. Men is spared the worry of the younguns and the cookin'. Has this country helped yore man's catarrh?"

"He don't have no more spells."

"What'd yore folks do when they come out?"

"My younger sister Shug—oh, everybody likes Shug—well, she and her husband—that was her first one—brung Angora goats to the Arivaipa country in south Arizona. You see, Ed-wards County was big on the mohair business. Shug and her man come in ninety-eight." Melissa put her fingers to her vibrating temples.

"I've seen 'em comin' here without hide ner hair way to make a livin'."

"My man sold our ranch in Stone Springs, and we had cash

to travel on. We heard 'bout the buildin' of the Roosevelt Dam, and Mr. Baker brung his mule teams to hire out. If I do say so, he's got good spans. That big mule, Jumbo, is the workingest mule ever pulled a fresno scraper, so my man says."

"You's lucky to have yore folks here to help you git started."

"Ben Baker don't cotton to my folks. The Holmans. Never did. Said my sister was wild as a mustang. Goin' to dances in the schoolhouse. Playin' cards. He don't hold to this. His pa was a Baptist minister, helpin' to organize the Primitive Predestinarian church back home."

"Some men is hard on their families. Don't hold to friv'lous goings-on."

"I was hungry to see my folks out here. They wrote back about the new 'Territory of Arizona.' Once when he was a young feller, my husband had come out to Arizona on a trail drive."

"Some men is like yours. In Arkansas our neighbor whipped his boys with a halter strap."

"My husband ain't like that. He just cusses them younguns. He didn't want my brother Jimso to come with us from Texas. But we had to have another man along. Ben Baker claims my folks is flighty—always movin' from one place to another." Melissa's eyes narrowed. "'Tain't so. My folks is the laughin' kind. Pa never harangued us younguns. He's, well, easygoin'. Likes his pranks. Pa was a homebody—staying close to his family. 'Course Ma done a heap of the work of makin' the living."

Aunt Samantha looked up, put down her knitting to stare out across the valley. "I've seen men spend the money in the saloon, and their wives didn't have clothes enough to cover their nakedness."

"Pa was never a drinkin' man," Melissa Baker continued. "One place comin' out from Texas we had to buy water. Way out in this stretch of dry country we seen one house. Just scrub brush. An old sign said 'Indian Wells.' We seen a bucket and a rope hangin' on the well. The shack wasn't big enough to skin a cat in. Roof slantin' down. Porch lean-to, sagging. A puny rosebush, tryin' to live, by the corner of the porch. When I seen that rosebush, I knowed there was a woman around."

"Wimmenfolks always try to bring out a purty or two. We brought a yellow rosebush, with all them stickers."

"Yes, a woman's got to have somethin' purty to take away what's ugly—and lonely—and the orneriness of her man."

"Did you see the woman at the house?"

"She come out holdin' a dishpan against her apron. Law! she was dirty. Guess there was no way to wash much. She looked vacant-like. Poured the water on the rosebush and backed into the house. Her man come out, a big rough-lookin' man. He give us a long look and then come toward us."

"What did yore menfolks do?"

"My husband said howdy and could we water the animals. The man told us it'd cost five cents a bucket. Said there was no place to water fer fifteen miles. We had to pay."

"Weren't you tuckered out?"

"Hannah looked mighty peaked. She always helped me good at camp. I depended on her—guess that's why I've always called her Sister. She would just lean up against a mesquite tree, her face white and the freckles standing out like coppers. When she looked like that, the other younguns would start to call her Turkey Egg. I said, 'Sister, are you sick?' She didn't answer. I told her I'd drive and she could lie on a pallet in the back of the wagon."

"Miz Baker, pains me bad to hear about the pore little youngun."

"I think the child was still ailin' from when we come through El Paso and met the train. It was her first sight of one. She was drivin' the team when the train came around a hill, with fearsome black smoke pourin' out. It whistled and was on us 'fore we knowed it. Hannah dropped the reins and jumped outa the wagon. She run under a barbed wire fence. Ripped her arm. There was blood all over her."

Aunt Samantha stopped knitting again. "Pore little thing. Ain't Hannah the one you said stuttered?"

"No, that's Annie. She's younger. The men likes to bait younguns and belittle them. Jimso began laughin' at Hannah. Slapped his thigh. Told her, 'Turkey Egg, you run faster'n a roadrunner. Did you think that train was goin' come eat you?' "

Aunt Samantha jabbed her knitting needles into the brown wool. "That riles me to hear you tell it."

"Riled me. I said, 'Jimso Holman, leave that youngun be!' He seen I was madder'n a wet hen. He slunk away like a egg-suckin' dog."

"I'm glad you got yore spunk up."

"Oh, my sister Shug is the one who gets her spunk up. She don't kowtow to no man. One night I was feerful Benjy was goin' to die," Melissa continued. "He was three months old then. We camped on the desert. Benjy was sick. His wheezin' woke me up in the night. He'd done taken the whoopin' cough."

"I tell you mare's milk is good for the whoopin' cough."

"That baby couldn't hardly git his breath. I gits a blanket and puts it over a turned-up chair and makes a little tent beside my bed. Put a lamp in it to warm it, and stuck the baby inside. I set up all night long. 'Fraid the lamp might tip over. To keep awake, I bit my hands till the blood come. My husband slept on—snorin'."

"Menfolks don't get fearsome over a sick youngun."

"The tent was smellin' bad. Stinkin' feet. Sweaty underwear. Coal oil stink. Benjy wheezed all night. Come mornin' though, he was breathin' a mite easier."

For Melissa, there had been little release from the unending work—and her headaches. She remembered stopping at one creek to do the family's washing. The stench of dirty clothes offended her. The towels, stuffed away damp, had soured, as had the men's socks, worn weeks on sweating feet. The baby's didies reeked of old urine and rotting fecal matter. She had wanted to retch.

She had set her washtub under the trees. Taking the rub-board, she scrubbed her husband's denim pants, heavy with axle grease, mud, sweat, and manure. The harsh soap, made from rendered pig fat, ashes and lye, burned her hands. Rubbing the clothes across the ripple of the washboard skinned her knuckles, leaving them raw and stinging. Her back ached. She twisted out the water, her frail wrists hurting. Then she hung the clothes on the bushes to dry.

At camp Hannah was in charge of the baby. Melissa dragged herself to the wagon and crept inside its dark interior. Her head pulsed. She pulled out the hairpins and let the heavy mass of her hair fall down. She loathed the burden and longed to get a butcher knife and cut it off, to destroy it at the roots. Or maybe destroy herself? Or her husband? She shut her eyes, seeking to close out the pounding, and fell into the oblivion of sleep.

4. Jobe Cote, Aunt Samantha's son, stood uncertainly inside the Tonto Saloon. The boy, unfamiliar with the interior, hesitated until he saw Ben Baker at the bar. Then he walked over to him and touched his shoulder. "Your wife wants you should come. My ma says she's near birthin'."

In the house at the edge of the settlement, Samantha Cote and Melissa moved their chairs closer to the stove. Outside, the wind beat against the frame house where the woman awaited the baby she did not want. Gusts of air made dives down the stovepipe, forcing out the smoke under the stove lids. The drafts pried at the windows, craftily sliding under the frames.

Samantha rose to stir the fire. Melissa did not move, only listened to the cry of the wind, which seemed to echo her own desolation and despair. The front door opened. Light from the lamp escaped to the dark outside. Jobe Cote shut the door behind him. He rubbed his hands and blew breath on his numbed fingers.

"Miz Baker," he said, "I found yore man at the Tonto. He said he'd be along directly."

Melissa closed her eyes as if to shut out fact. Her pains were increasing. Her face contorted, her body twitched, moisture appeared on her lips. She stood up, pressing her hands against her abdomen, and began to walk.

The midwife took her arm. "I'll help you walk, Miz Baker." The women moved across the room and back again. Samantha nodded toward her son. "Jobe, when you warm up a mite, git in a heap of that mesquite wood. Build up the fire and then go tell Mr. Baker to make haste. She's nigh."

She strived to comfort the woman. "Don't worry none. I've born many a youngun. The first time I was only fifteen years old."

Melissa felt wetness on her inner thighs, her legs, her feet, her gown. She looked at the puddle on the floor.

"Yore water's broke," the midwife said. "Shouldn't be long now. You want to lie down? Try to save yore strength."

Melissa lay down on a bed and pulled the comforter over her head. She felt she could not endure the pain, and she wished for death. The hours passed. Night shaded to the grayness of dawn and into the lightness of early morning. Still Ben Baker did not appear.

The midwife, alone with the woman, watched her suffering. Melissa screamed. Rushing to the bedside, Samantha bent over and felt the throbbing, pumping abdomen. "Push, Miz Baker, push—hard. Everything's gonna be all right." She tried to make her voice sound confident.

Melissa screamed again. The midwife reached down between the woman's gaping thighs and pulled at the protruding head of the baby. It seemed to fight against entering the world. The midwife pulled, and still the child resisted. Finally it

yielded to a determined yank as Melissa's body forced out the
unwanted birth.

Samantha held the baby upside down and spanked its bottom. She took her fingers and wiped mucus from the child's
mouth. Wrapping it in a flannel cloth, she laid the bundle by
the mother's side. "Miz Baker, rest now. I'll come back and
clean up." Almost as an afterthought, she turned to say, "It's
a girl."

The mother did not look at the baby. Released from the
strain that lacerated her body and tormented her thoughts, she
set her eyes on the cobwebs hanging from the ceiling rafters.
Then she fell asleep.

The midwife slumped in the rocking chair, her arms lifeless
and dangling impotently at her side. Weariness deepened the
wrinkles in her face. Her breath was labored. Her head fell
dejectedly against the back of the chair. Her guttural snores
mingled with the dying cackles of the fire. The room was dense
with the breathing, the smoke, the steam, the burning wood,
and the smell of human blood.

The sun was high when Ben Baker pushed open the door,
his stolid body swaying. He looked around, accustoming his
eyes to the dim light. Finally, clumping to the bed he stood
over the form under the comforter.

The midwife, aroused by the man's entrance, forced her
body up from the chair. She rubbed her hand across her eyes,
not so much to wake herself up as to erase the harrowing night.
Her voice was low with contained anger. "Yore missus is
asleep."

But the woman, covered by the comforter, was not asleep.
She did not speak nor move but lay inflexible in her vacant
world, consumed with hate.

5.

Melissa's parents, the Holmans, were in the yard of their home, a few miles from the Baker ranch. Sarah Holman had just come out from the kitchen, where she had put a black cast-iron pot of dried beans to cook.

She looked at her husband in the chair tilted against the wall of the porch in the place that got the most shade. Her voice was sharp. "Silas, you better git movin' and water that garden, so's we can git to the crossroads and meet the new baby."

Silas Holman, holding a small piece of pine wood, made no action except to open his jackknife and run the edge against the wood. "Directly," he said.

"Silas, in the forty years since you come from Georgia, you've whittled enough shavin's to cover the Four Peaks." His wife spat a sluice of snuff onto the bare ground.

Sarah Holman was a slight woman, thin-bodied and thin-legged, with a bent back and a browned and wrinkled face. She scurried about the yard like one of her Rhode Island Red hens bustling from seed to bug to manure pile, scratching, digging, cleaning. She tried to rouse her husband again. "Their wagon's apt to be comin' 'fore I git my chores done. I'm aimin' to invite them to supper. Mebbe Ben'll stop long enough for us to see the baby."

Silas Holman ignored his wife as she scurried by. He squinted his eye on the open blade of the jackknife and slowly drew it across his open palm. "Just lay off yore naggin'. We'll git her done."

"We?" Sarah Holman turned her eyes on her husband, and then hurried on to remove the clothes from the bushes where they were drying. It was conceded by The Mesa folk that Silas Holman contributed little to the livelihood of the household. But people's reaction was tolerant. They "cottoned to the old scalawag," and overlooked his indolence. He was a genial, witty, entertaining man, who spoke grudgingly of no one and never caused any trouble.

The Holmans lived an hour's wagon drive from the Filaree Ranch, but they seldom visited with the Bakers. They were aware that their son-in-law "had little use for the likes o' them." Now, though, they hoped that the new baby would be an occasion for Ben Baker to stop and visit.

Folks on The Mesa called them "Ol' Lady Holman" and "Ol' Man Holman," although neither had reached sixty-five. The lot of earning a living had fallen to Sarah early in their marriage, and they depended on her cow, chickens, and garden. She admitted that she sometimes "managed mighty poorly."

This morning Ol' Lady Holman was cleaning the chimneys of the kerosene lamps. She crumpled pages from an old Sears, Roebuck Catalogue and pushed her hand inside the globes. Then she scissored away the charred wicks, careful to straighten the threads so they would not flame and smoke the glass. She spit a stream of snuff drippings into a tin can.

The old man continued his whittling. He scrutinized the shining blade. Slowly he shaved a thin slice of fiber from his whittling wood. He cut a delicate spiral chip as translucent as a membranous onion skin with the light shining through. Silas Holman cut only soft wood such as the cottonwood that grew by Tonto Creek, soft so his blade would not be nicked, never suffering it to hard mesquite or ironwood. His knife was a fine instrument, bone-handled with two blades that he kept as sharp as the razor by the mirror in the bedroom.

The Mesa folk knew that the Holmans had a history of "movin' on." It was said that when the old man was a young buck, he had come to Texas one step ahead of the sheriff. The rumor went that he had killed a man in Georgia. In Texas he had met Sarah, small and fragile, barely out of childhood and filled with the yearnings of young womanhood. Sarah's father disapproved of "that wanderin' feller from Georgia." But once Sarah had seen Silas, with his long, slender build, striding through the wild pecan grove near her house, she blocked out her father's admonitions. When she was fourteen, she ran away with him. The couple inveigled a young preacher, a friend, to marry them on a large rock in the middle of the river that separated two counties.

Sarah's father followed them with the sheriff. At the river's edge, the sheriff said, "My jurisdiction ends here. The river is the boundary." The bride and groom started westward. They would never see him again.

On the journey, their routine became established. No sooner would they be settled in one shack than they moved on. Sarah, early in her marriage, managed to buy, or trade for, a cow, to raise chickens, and to put in a garden. By selling butter and eggs, or doing seamstress work, she managed to provide for them—and for the children who began to arrive with un-wanted regularity now. They remained in Texas until Melissa's marriage, and then moved on to New Mexico and Arizona. By this time Sarah had borne and raised five children, and she was weary. Pressure and poverty had aged her, changing her dispo-sition and her appearance. She had long ago lost any illusions she had once entertained about "that long-limbed fellow from Georgia." But her real regret was that all her children seemed destined to repeat their parents' bleak history. With a pang, she thought of Melissa, coming home now with her new baby.

The old man got up to wash his face. The wash basin rested on a tree stump outside the back door. A flour-sack towel hung on a nail. On the stump was a celluloid comb with three teeth missing. With a flourish the old man doused his head, face, and goatee with water. Holding a forefinger against the side of his bulbous nose, he alternately closed the other nostril and noisily blew the accumulation on the ground. Then he sat back in the tilted chair to wait for his wife's call to "come and git it." He folded his pocket knife and kicked aside a pile of shavings.

6.

Melissa stayed with Aunt Samantha a week. One morning Ben Baker drove up, his wagon loaded with supplies, and the two set out for the ranch, the bundle of the baby like a barrier on the seat between them. It had no name yet.

The wagon jolted down the ruts. The road was a long brown rope, twisting, coiling, stretching, encircling the hills and valleys and flat lands that led to The Mesa and the Filaree Ranch at the foot of the Sierra Ancha mountains.

The man made small attempts at talking, but the woman refused to answer. The dull quiet of the desert was broken only by the sharp sound of the horses' hoofs striking the rocks in the pathway.

The infant uttered a plaintive squeak, a thin complaint. The woman did not touch it, but looked a long time at the tiny face resting in a thin nest of black hair. *I will never, never born another child,* she vowed to herself, staring with defiant eyes at the man. Then she focused her attention on the interminable road ahead.

The sight of the baby brought her thoughts back to the children at the ranch. "Hope Hannah didn't have no trouble while we were gone," she said, breaking her silence at last. "I'm always fearful that coal oil lamp will git afire."

The man's face relaxed. He was glad to hear her voice again; she had hardly spoken since the baby's birth. He wanted to tell her how lonely he felt—how he thought constantly of Texas, how he feared that the rain wouldn't come—or that loco weed would drive his animals crazy if they got hold of it. He wanted to tell her he was sorry for the Tonto Saloon and his absence while the baby was being born. But the words would not come.

The woman had another reason that prompted her to speak. She hoped that her husband would stop for the Holmans to see the new baby. "Ma said she and Pa would meet us at the turnoff. I'm plumb lonesome to see them. And they wanta see the new baby."

The man stopped humming. "We're better off not associatin' with yore kinfolks."

"Ma will have us some vittles to take home. They've got word by now when we'll be drivin' by. Jimso stopped off to see me at Missus Cote's." Seeking to alter the depression she felt and to ease her legs, which ached from the wagon's jolting, she said, "Kin we stop? I need to git out."

The man jerked on the leather reins, and the woman got down from the wagon. She walked across to the brush-hidden roadside. When she returned, she lifted the baby and opened the front of her dress. Without looking at the child, she directed its questing mouth to her breast.

The road edged along a creek lined with sycamore trees, and the woman lapsed into reverie. The winter trees, denuded of foliage, reached out gaunt arms of skeletal whiteness. She recalled the many colors of the leaves last fall. They had descended like gaily painted ships, she thought. Or like women released from subjugation, flirting with the ripples of the moving stream, bobbing coquettishly before they were snagged and entrapped in the mud. Melissa likened their fate to her own.

Dark came and the Bakers pitched camp at Sycamore Creek. As they ate, Melissa again mentioned her desire to see her parents. "We ought to reach Ma and Pa by midmorning or noon. I bet she'll have tomato preserves and watermelon pickles for us to take home."

Ben Baker flung the remains of coffee into the bushes and said nothing.

She tried again. "Wouldn't take long. I ain't seen my folks in so long! I'm sick to see them."

The man whirled and walked away. The woman called after him, "They wanta see the new baby."

Ben Baker turned around. Reaching hardened fingers into

his shirt pocket, he extracted a plug of brown chewing tobacco. "We'll stop at the schoolhouse on the way home. Tell the younguns we're back." Melissa noted the finality in his voice.

7.

The wagon reached the schoolhouse before midday. Ben Baker reined the horses to the shade of a mesquite tree near the door. The metal grated as he pulled back on the brake. Hearing the sound of their arrival, the children of The Mesa rushed out the door and hurried toward the wagon, boys in worn overalls and girls in long-sleeved dresses. Melissa searched for her own children. She saw Hannah's thin face and freckled nose and Mary Belle's red head. Stockton stood apart, and she noted that his hair needed a good "scissorin'." Carter grinned, displaying a split in his lower lip. Pushed aside by the older children, Benjy was calling, "Lemme see the ba-bee." Annie was the first to climb onto the wagon and pull back the afghan that covered the tiny form.

A clamor of voices surrounded them. "Miz Baker, can I take a look at the new youngun? What is it? A filly? A colt? Mama, I ain't had no chance to see."

Hannah held up her hand. "All you younguns git in line. You gotta take turns. Annie, you stay there and be first, then climb down."

Annie stared at the baby in the apple box. "It's so little. So funny looking." She turned to her mother. "Mama, is it a boy or girl?"

"A girl baby."

"What's her name?"

"Name? We ain't . . . It has no name yet."

Annie smiled. "I saw first and I get claim first. Mama, can I name her?"

The woman's voice was apathetic. "Why, I 'spose so."

Annie's smile spread. "I'll name her Velma Marjorie. The teacher read us a story. The girl's name was Velma Marjorie. She was beautiful. Lived in a castle. Clothes was silk. Gold necklace." She stopped for breath and leaned closer to the baby, "I love you, Velma Marjorie."

The teacher came out the front door and walked to the wagon. "How are you, Missus Baker? We've been waiting for the new baby."

"I'm fine, Miss Hobbs. I do hope our younguns studied their lessons."

"The Baker children are always good scholars. Missus Holman sent word they would wait for you at the crossroads."

"Thank you. I'm gettin' fidgety to see my folks." Melissa fastened her eyes on the teacher and thought that the young woman looked wan. "Miss Hobbs, are you beginnin' to get used to The Mesa?"

"I don't mean to complain, but times I do get lonesome," the teacher said.

Melissa Baker nodded in understanding. "I know. I suffer myself from the loneliness, and I got all my family with me. Wish we could help you more."

Ben Baker returned from the horse trough, where he had gone to splash water on his face. Drying it with a blue bandana handkerchief, he said, "You younguns have had a look. Now it's time to move on. We gotta git for home."

The teacher went inside the school building and came out with a bell in her hand. Standing on the steps, she rang the bell. The children stopped talking and came to line up in front of her. She said, "Today we have been honored by having a new baby. This calls for a celebration. School is dismissed for the day."

Delighted cries filled the schoolyard. The children rushed into the schoolroom, and emerged laden with coats, hats, lunch pails, books. Hurrying to their horses, they saddled and started down the path. Those who walked were already on the way.

The Baker children took another look at the baby before they saddled their animals.

Baker took his place on the wagon seat, slapped the reins, and turned the horses onto the road home. Melissa's thoughts returned to the teacher. Miss Hobbs had awakened a spark in Mary Belle, who had never been a scholar and whose low grades were marked with disgrace by the Baker family. Mary Belle had come home early in the year and related that the teacher had told her about a wonderful "cyclopedic book," bigger than a dictionary, and had shown the class pictures of the Taj Mahal. The child had declared, "I ain't never gonna marry and I ain't never gonna have no babies. I'm gonna work and buy me a cyclopedic book and go to India and see the Taj Mahal."

Melissa said to her husband, "I wish we could find something to take away the loneliness of Miss Hobbs. I don't want her to leave, like the other teachers. She's so pretty, them blue eyes and that white skin. And her hair's got gold lights when the sun shines on it."

"I cain't see nothin' wrong with her life," Ben Baker said. "She's here to teach the younguns."

"What she needs is companionship," Melissa said. "Wonder that Ike Talbott hasn't took a fancy to her. He's single and plenty good-looking." She thought about the tall cowboy foreman from the El Bar, with the laugh that rang from the Sierra Anchas to the Mazatzals. Sometimes he would stop by the Filaree or she would see him at the local camp meetings. He had a way of bowing slightly and looking deep into her eyes as he asked, "And how are you today, Missus Baker?" Now she felt her heart increase in beat, and a strange embarrassment came over her.

Her husband abruptly changed the subject.

"Those younguns'll be home 'fore we are. Hope they git after the chores." Ben Baker clacked at the horses.

Melissa strained her eyes on the road ahead. She was looking for the turnoff that led to the Holman place. In the distance she saw two figures hurrying down the road. "That's Ma and Pa! I can tell Ma's red sunbonnet far as I can see it."

The horses drew closer to the figures, and the woman waved at them. Her husband made no motion to hurry the horses. The Holmans reached the fork in the road. As the team pulled near, Silas Holman hurled his battered hat high in the air. "Hallelujah! Glory be! Welcome. Drive down to our house. Dinner's waitin'."

Sarah Holman's face was covered by the long narrow slats of her bonnet. She took it off and waved it aloft, swinging it by the strings as a banner. The horses moved on in a walk, but Baker did not pull on the reins to halt the animals. The hatless old man and the woman swinging the red sunbonnet ran alongside the wagon, breathing hard as they tried to touch the boards.

Melissa stood up in the seat, the baby in her arms, but the man still did not brake the wagon. The woman cried out.

"Mr. Baker! Stop! For the love of God, I beg of you. Stop this wagon!"

Her husband lashed at the horses with the leather whip. The grandparents hastened their steps to keep up with the wagon. Ben Baker brought down the whip.

The animals lunged forward, throwing the woman to the seat. His voice roared, "Gittup, Baldy!" Again he raised the whip, and the animals broke into a gallop, leaving the old man and old woman faltering in their steps, the dust rising around them.

With each flash of the whip, the animals increased the distance between the woman in the wagon seat and the two figures in the road. Her mother continued to wave her bonnet as if the frantic movement would slow the horses and signal them to return.

Melissa Baker kept her head turned backward, watching until the red sunbonnet disappeared behind a crest in the road.

Then she turned to stare ahead, drawing her face within her own bonnet. Her eyes were dry, the tears imprisoned within.

8.

The Baker children watched their parents' wagon pull out from the schoolyard, and then they left on their horses, taking the shortcut to the ranch. Much of the trail was rocky and interrupted with brush. They used caution in riding through the rocks, the rough territory, and the cholla cactus, watching for gopher holes where a horse could "damn well cripple hisself." The children did not fear being thrown or hurt. The catastrophe would be in injuring the horse.

But once they reached a long stretch of loamy sand, they loosened their reins, kicked their ponies in the ribs and flanks, threatening the animals with willow switches. Their father had warned them, "I don't hold none to runnin' the horses. Don't chouse those ol' ponies." Ben Baker knew that his children did not heed his orders. As he told his neighbor, John Brownwell, "There never was a youngun but what run his horse soon's he was outa sight o' the house. I recollect good my pa warnin' me."

Back at the ranch, the children busied themselves with the evening's chores as they waited for their parents' arrival with the new baby. Carter watered the stock and examined a wire cut on the colt's shoulder. Mary Belle fed the chickens, and Hannah built a fire in the cookstove. "Spider," she reprimanded Stockton, "you-all put that lizard down and git me a fresh bucket o' water." Then they stationed themselves on top of the small hill that rose beyond their backyard.

The clarity of the air made the wagon visible when it was still a long way off. They ran down the hill to meet it. Hannah struggled to open the barbed wire gate. The wagon passed through and stopped at the house.

Melissa went to work the moment she was inside. She mixed corn bread, poured it into an iron skillet, and set it in the oven. She cut slices of steak from a beef quarter that her parents had brought during her absence in Roosevelt. She salted and peppered the pieces, and with the edge of a saucer beat the beef until she felt the fibers break. The meat sizzled in a skillet of hot grease, the aroma filling the kitchen.

Spider dumped a load of wood into the box behind the stove. "I'm hungry as a she-bear with suckin' cubs. Hannah didn't cook good like you, Mama."

"You men would starve plumb to death if it weren't for wimmen to git yore vittles. Hannah done fine."

Hannah put crockery plates on the oilcloth-covered table. "I done what you said. I boiled the beans every day so they wouldn't spoil. I didn't let no one light the lamps but me. Made Spider and Carter wash their hands 'fore they ate."

Mary Belle wrinkled her nose. "I done the dishes every meal. I done most of the hard work. Annie never done nothin'— much. Spider said a bad word. He said—"

"Hush, Mary Belle. You don't need to say the word. You're meddlesome."

"I washed Spider's mouth out with soap." Hannah laid the knives on the table. "Mary Belle fought with the boys and hit Benjy. I slapped her. She said she's gonna tell on me." Hannah stopped suddenly, as if she had completed her report and the burden was removed from her narrow shoulders.

"I tol' you-uns to mind Hannah while I's gone. Don't know how I'd a-managed without her."

Mary Belle, turning her back to her mother, stuck out her tongue at Hannah and waggled it snakelike. Hannah walked past her and put spoons and forks on the table.

In the corner Annie held the baby in her arms, rocking her gently. She made small noises at the infant. "Velma is my darling," she sang.

Mary Belle swaggered to the corner, feet apart and hands on her hips. "How come, Annie Baker, that you don't stutter when you sing? It's my time to hold the baby. You hold her so's you don't have to work."

Annie turned her eyes upward, appealing to Mary Belle, "P-p-please let me hold her l-l-longer."

"Stop stuttering, Annie. You know Mama tol' you to 'Stop and think before you talk.' Gimme that baby. You got to name her 'cause you hollered first."

"Velma Marjorie," Annie crooned.

Mary Belle's voice rose. "Velma Marjorie? What an ugly name. I'd rather call her Baby than that ol' name. Baby, baby, baby," she repeated.

Melissa took the corn bread from the oven. "Spider, call yore papa to supper."

After the meal was finished, the woman took the food scraps and went out the back door. She called, "Here ya, Red." A redbone hound, long ears nearly touching the ground, slunk from under the porch. The woman tossed a piece of corn bread in the air. The dog jumped, catching the bread. Behind the hound came Marble, the Australian shepherd, whose name came from the one blue eye and one brown eye. She threw the remaining bread on the ground and walked away from the yard into open land.

Evening was Melissa's magic time, elevating her spirits and arousing her fantasies. She walked to the barn. In the impending dusk, she saw the corral dust darken to olive, and the breeze carried the smell of manure and sweated hide. Her nostrils twitched but she was not offended: This was part of her outdoors.

Mourning doves foraged in the corral, pecking at grain bits and animal droppings. One of them ceased eating to menace another with flapping wings. Did she give in too often? She wondered. Should she, like the bird, fly up and fight?

Inhaling deeply, she caught the tanginess of greasewood.

She broke off a branch of the varnish-coated leaves and held it to her nose. Somewhere she heard the call of a coyote, and the dogs answering from the yard. Again the coyote called, a primeval howl.

Back in the house, Melissa wet the wood, putting it in a jar of water. The pungency of the damp leaves floated out and spread through the kitchen. "If that don't beat all," her husband said. "Yore a queer one. What-all you wanta bring that dang stinkin' greasewood in the house fer?"

The children grouped themselves around the kitchen table studying, while their father leaned a chair against the wall behind the stove and listened. "Did you-uns git yore lessons good while yore ma and pa was gone?" He knew the answer but it pleased him to hear the affirmative response. Ben Baker set much store by learning. His own lack of education had left a wound that remained open. He struggled to make sure that his "younguns got schoolin'." In a life compounded of drouth, wormy cattle, thieving coyotes, calf-killing cougars, and the friendless emptiness of ranching, he tried to fill some of the void with his children's education. Melissa, too, had little schooling, and she shared the man's goal. Sometimes it seemed as though it was the only tether that held them together.

"You git on with yore books," Ben Baker said. "I hear some trompin' outside." He left.

A lantern on top of the stove cast a faint and flickering light on the children, whose heads were bent over their books. In the center of the table was a kerosene lamp whose glow yellowed the children's faces. "Mama, I cain't see too good. The light ain't—"

Melissa went to the other room and returned with another lamp. "Mebbe this'll help. Ain't much coal oil left and the wick's jagged, but it'll do till you finish." She pulled a chair to the table, turning her attention to the children's studies.

Annie looked up and screamed. "F-f-f-fire! L-la-lamp!"

Melissa jumped to the stove, and grabbing the blazing lamp,

ran toward the back door. From the smoking chimney, flames licked out around her hand. She rushed through the door with the lamp held high and threw it as far as she could into the yard. As the glass shattered, the flames followed a trail of kerosene into the darkness.

She pushed the children back into the house. Her heart beat in rapid throbs, and she was aware of pain. The skin of her right hand was seared, showing red flesh under the soot. She plunged it into a basin of cold water. "Sister," she called to Hannah, "bring me the baking soda and a clean rag." She slumped to the floor, her hand held aloft. Hannah ran to help raise her mother to a chair.

The man strode into the kitchen. "What the hell? I seen the fire in the yard. I'd been down at the pasture. What—?"

While Melissa walked around the room, trying to soothe the agony with the wet cloth, he exploded: "Damn fool thing to let the lamp burn up. Coulda set the house on fire. Carelessness. Plumb orneriness." Then he stalked outside.

The woman turned to the children. "Younguns, you'd best git to bed," she said.

"Mama, kin I do anything for you?" Hannah's narrow shoulders shook and she wiped her hand across her eyes. "I'll put the baby to bed."

"Thank you. I'll just set up till this burning stops a little. Mebbe I'll put a little grease on it. You younguns always watch them lamps. That one ran outa oil. I plumb fergot it, I was so wrapped up in studying with you-all. When you fill the lamps, be powerful careful not to spill any oil outside."

The children walked quietly into their bedrooms. The woman, stepping to the window, stared into the dark night of The Mesa. She nursed the burning in her hand and the rage still within her which pictured a red sunbonnet waving in the road.

II

1. Melissa's days varied little in monotony—the changing of soiled didies for Baby, the cleaning of chicken manure from the steps where the hens hunted shade, the sweating over the flatirons on the cookstove. It was a never-ending battle against the dirt, the cobwebs, the flies, and the barrenness of the countryside. She tried to confide her anger to her friend Martha Brownell when the neighbor woman came to sit and quilt with her. "Menfolks takes us just as if we ain't flesh and blood —ain't got no feelin's. Ben Baker used to court me with smiles and honey words. Now he's got no time ner thought fer nothin' but hisself—and talkin' 'bout his Texas. He thinks only 'bout the cows and the horses and the feed. When he has trouble, he goes to the saloon. Us wimmen cain't git rid of our problems that way. All we can do is git tired and old and ugly."

Like the filly snubbed to the post in the Baker corral, Melissa struggled to break away. She concealed her fretting, festering inwardly but dutifully fulfilling the responsibilities expected of her. She refused to be subdued.

Melissa's yearnings remained unsatisfied, including her most compelling hunger, a desire for education. "Martha, I got me a gnawin' fer book larnin'," she told her friend. "At night I dream of readin'. Do you—?"

Martha Brownell, who found deciphering the printing on the flour sacks a strain, nodded, but Melissa could tell that it was more out of politeness than understanding.

She participated in the nightly ceremony for the "younguns to git to their books." When the supper dishes were washed and put away, the oilcloth on the kitchen table scrubbed and dried, lessons were spread out. In the center of the table the coal oil lamp presided, its chimney reflecting clean to give out responsive light. Melissa hung her husband's lantern from a rafter of the ceiling. When her husband carried the lantern to the barn or corral or privy, she thought that it cast rays of urine-colored light. When the children studied by it, she thought that the lantern shed golden beams.

She told the children she had gone to the third grade in school, which meant that she had attended three or four months for three years in the frontier schoolhouse on the Texas plains. Now Hannah and Mary Belle taught her the seventh- and eighth-grade lessons they had learned that day. She did ciphering with them on their slates, and spelling in the blue-backed book, and reading. Melissa would recite, "Oh, Tiber! Father Tiber!/To whom the Romans pray . . ." and look to the children for approbation. In her enthusiasm, she dismissed the exhaustion of the day's labors.

The fall before Baby was born, a change had come about in Melissa's schooling. Annie, ever perceptive of other people's needs, noted it. Her mother seemed to tire more easily. In evening study, enmeshed with a strange lethargy, Melissa found it difficult to keep awake with the children. She sometimes went to bed before they left the study table. It was then that Annie learned that her mother was "with child," or as she heard it whispered at school, "in the family way."

Melissa first missed studying with the children when Benjy took down with the croup and she rode to the Brownell Ranch for mare's milk to feed him. The following nights she walked the floor, holding the boy to soften the coughing. Melissa missed more lessons. In the next weeks, she became heavier in body. Her cricketlike movements slackened.

One afternoon when they were alone, Melissa spoke to Annie. "I've got behind in my lessons with yore older sisters. I cain't keep up with them." She turned away her head, and Annie heard the constriction in her mother's voice. "I wonder, Annie, I wonder—" and the tightened words failed. "I wonder, Annie, if I could study with you?"

Annie was only eleven, but at that moment she felt older than her mother. She looked at Melissa's tired gray eyes and felt somehow that she had no right to see into the privacy of an adult's fractured hopes. Annie sensed that to survive, her mother had to clutch to the hope of learning.

Melissa absorbed knowledge that came her way as the filaree sucked up the sporadic rain of The Mesa. Sometimes she found a newspaper left at the ranch by a passing rider, or she pored over a discarded magazine or the mail-order catalogue, or read the instructions on the bottles and cans of tomatoes and corn. There were no books at the Filaree Ranch, besides the Bible and a worn copy of a *McGuffey's Reader* which she had brought with her from Texas. She liked to quote the morals contained in the reader to her children, and to admonish them about the virtues of goodness and kindness and generosity and tolerance.

Melissa filled the isolation of her days with dreaming and questioning. "I hanker to know the names of all the grasses that grow on The Mesa," she told Martha Brownell, "and why the colors change with the sunset over the Four Peaks, and what makes the horses go crazy when they eat of the loco weed, and what are them little red balls on the scrub oak trees?"

"Well, Melissa, it's just that way. No one can explain it. Grass is grass. Some's good fer cattle to eat and some ain't. Colors has always been changing since Creation. I don't never see them red balls you talk about. I guess it's jist thataway— according to God's way."

Martha Brownell had satisfied herself, but restlessness stirred within Melissa.

She showed Martha the white mariposa lily she had found in the spring and had pressed between the pages of the Bible, and she read the verse she had written to accompany the flower. Martha Brownell shook her head and later at home confided to her husband John that she was "powerful fond of

Melissa Baker, but the woman gives me the nervousness with her funny ideas."

Martha was as unlike Melissa as the desert gourd was unlike the mariposa lily—though the two plants grew together, nourished by the same soil and weather. Martha's body frame was coarse and serviceable; Melissa's as delicate as the flower and as crushable.

"Sakes alive, Melissa Baker, yore a handsome woman. You don't no way look like you've born younguns. Many a young girl cain't hold a candle to you. But you are a mite too thin—skinny as a fence post." The Brownell woman looked at her own broad hips, flabby waist, and dropped bosom. But she was contented. Her husband filled her need. Except for Silas Holman, John Brownell was about the only man on The Mesa who had no closeness for drink. Martha's son William was as unimaginative as she and caused her no concern.

"Men gives us bruises and hurts that don't never heal," Melissa burst out. "Menfolks say words that cut a woman with their meanness. They give us tears that scald us bad as the bilin' wash pot. Nighttime we gotta lie down with them that has said and done us pain."

"Melissa, the men has got their problems too. Now, my man John says—"

But the woman of the Filaree Ranch was not listening. "Martha, sometimes Ben Baker smells like a hog. Long underwear he don't never change. Sleepin' in the sweat and dirt. Tobacco on his breath, on his teeth. There's no place fer a woman to go. The children don't git kindness—" She stopped and thought about William Brownell, Martha's boy, and how his parents gave no encouragement to his schooling. "Martha, I got one thing to be grateful for—and I do give credit to Ben Baker: He has a heap o' carin' that his younguns go to school."

2. The children waved as they rode down the trail toward school, and Melissa waved back. She looked at the filaree covering the yard. The rains had come generously at last, and it had responded. The land everywhere was layered with the plant and stippled with its blossoms, as if quilted in a green-and-purple fabric—a fabric fastened by the giant pins of the saguaro cactus. She thought for a moment of Miss Hobbs. It was late spring, and soon school would be out for the summer; the lonely teacher could return to her home and to her family. Melissa wished she could do something to help Miss Hobbs.

At the schoolhouse, William Brownell had come early to sweep the room before class. Miss Hobbs had come early too. They were alone. The teacher looked at the strong young figure, taller than she, and at fifteen more man than boy. The morning light caught his sinewy arms making great sweeps with the broom.

Slowly, as though compelled, she walked to the boy. She put her arms on his shoulders. Surprise made the boy drop the broom. She pressed her body tight against his, and kissed him.

William Brownell jumped back, loosening the teacher's arms. Then he ran toward the door and out into the freedom of the yard. He fled to the arroyo nearby and hid until his hard breathing eased. Then he started for home.

The other children met William leaving as they arrived. They wondered at his running. At the schoolhouse door, Miss Hobbs told them that she would start class a little late that morning, and that meanwhile they could go play. They wondered if she were ill, because her face was red and she trembled.

William Brownell did not return to school that year. Later Martha told Melissa, "I do declare, that boy came runnin' home from school, said it was near the end anyway, and he thought he orta help his pa build fence. Always before Willie said fence-building was a squatter's job, not a cowboy's. John was glad to keep him home. He needed help, and Willie's got to be big and strong this past year. But it do beat all. I don't know what come over that boy."

At the end of the week, Miss Hobbs appeared at Melissa's door. "Missus Baker, I could not leave without seeing you. I've come to say goodbye. I'm leaving in the morning. My sister is sick, and I've got to go. I've given the children their grades and closed the schoolroom. It won't make much difference, the term is nearly over. You've always been my one friend here. You've understood my loneliness." The teacher hurried her words as if she wanted to get out the whole story. She put her arms around Melissa. "Goodbye, my dear, dear friend."

3. The next fall Ben Baker, who was a member of the school board, hired a replacement for Miss Hobbs; the new teacher's name was Eustace Blackmere. From the first morning of the school year, he ordered his pupils to address him as "Professor," but before long they referred to him as "Old Stoneface." His countenance was at all times grimly rigid. But the children could tell when he was angry; the vein in his temple would become enlarged and pulsate. Mr. Blackmere was a monochrome of gray: his face, his hair, and his one suit of soiled twill, with the short sleeves exposing his wrist bones and his gangling hands.

He regarded teaching as much an infliction for himself as for the children. As Mary Belle reported to Melissa, "Mr. Blackmere don't appear to like teaching us. He seems to be hurting all the time. We're scared of him."

He had special ways of punishment. If the culprit was a girl, he would draw a small ring on the blackboard, forcing her to stand on tiptoe with her nose inside the chalked ring. A boy who misbehaved could expect a more painful object lesson. Mr. Blackmere would storm without warning to the offender, grasp him by the hair and shake him until his eyes bulged and his teeth clicked.

The Baker children gave him no reason for such violent correction. They adhered to their parents' creed that the teacher was right and that they were "in school to git larnin'." Hannah, who was the best scholar in the school, made sure that her brothers and sisters stayed in line.

The Mesa school had no clock. Mr. Blackmere used his own timepiece, a large thick silver watch, the cover engraved with a train snorting smoke and rimmed with a scroll of flowers. Each morning, the teacher took out the watch, popped open the cover, and laid the timepiece on his desk. He referred to it at noon, recess, and for class recitation. To the children the best moment of the day came when he glanced at the silver watch and announced that school was dismissed.

One morning Carter, who was William Brownell's replacement, had come to school early to build a fire, and Professor Blackmere arrived shortly after him. He hurried in erratic strides to his desk, and when he assembled the pupils, the vein in his temple was pulsating ominously. His gray face was darker than usual, and he focused a glare on them.

"One of you is a thief," he announced. "Someone stole my watch. Last night I left it on the desk. I didn't miss it until I went to bed. It was too late to return here. This morning the watch is gone. I order the thief to walk up and put my watch on the desk."

No child spoke and no child moved. They watched his Adam's apple move up and down in his scrawny neck. His words fell on the silence like an ax smacking a chopping block as it beheaded a chicken. "Since the criminal refuses to give up the watch, I shall name him. Carter Baker!" The class exhaled a communal breath. The executioner's voice bellowed.

"Carter, you were the only one in this room, building a fire. Thief, bring me my watch—and get out!"

The boy remained at his desk as if paralysis chained him, his face white. Old Stoneface galloped across the room and yanked him out of his seat, holding him up by his hair.

Carter pulled away and stumbled toward the door. He stopped and turned, his face red and contorted. "I ain't no thief. I didn't steal yore watch. I don't know nothin' 'bout it." He bolted out the door, ran to the hackberry tree and saddling his horse, spurred the animal toward the Filaree Ranch.

At home he ran to his mother, who was nursing the baby. Between sobs, he explained what had happened. "Ma, I ain't no thief. Papa always said a Baker's word was good, and I tol' the teacher the truth."

Melissa patted his head and handed him the edge of her apron to dry the tears. Her voice was calm. "I believe you, son. We'll explain to your papa when he comes home."

Carter did not return to school. He could not eat for days and screamed out nightmares in his sleep. Ben Baker said nothing, but he went around the house with a grim face. Melissa was relieved when he permitted the boy to stay home.

The following week at school, the topic of the missing watch was still whispered about by the children. One day at noon some of them were in the flat playing at their pastime of tearing up pack rats' nests. Mary Belle said, "Missus Brownell said a pack rat toted off one of her silver spoons."

Spider picked up a big stick. "Them rats is called trade rats 'cause they leave somethin', even if it's only a horse turd." He poked at the cholla burrs in a new nest under a mesquite tree. The sunlight caught a silver glitter, and he found himself staring at a watch with a puffing locomotive on the cover. He called the other children. Spider ran with the watch in his hand, and handed his discovery to the teacher.

Spider reported at home. "Ol' Stoneface didn't say nothin'," he told his parents that night. "He snorted and swallered like a calf drinkin' sour milk. He turned the watch over and over, blowin' on it, rubbin' it on his sleeve, shinin' it on his vest. He didn't even tell me 'Thank ye.' "

The next morning Carter came back to school. He said nothing.

Mr. Blackmere acted as if he had been there all the time. But Carter did not resume his fire building, and the teacher had to take over the chore.

One afternoon, a barely audible sibilant sound broke the usual quietness of the schoolroom. The children held their breathing in abeyance. Eustace Blackmere had many intense hatreds, and the foremost was noise of any kind. He looked up from his desk and his eyes focused accusingly on Benjy Baker.

Benjy sat in a double seat with Hannah where she watched over him. His legs did not reach the floor, and after an hour or so his muscles ached and he fidgeted. Then Hannah would quietly rub his legs. Recently a saddle stirrup had hit him on the head, leaving an ugly scab. Hannah had doctored the gash, and now took care that Benjy wore a hat to protect his head and that he engaged in no rough play.

The youngest Baker boy was confronting his first reader, and today he was lost in concentrated effort. Unaware of the teacher's baleful glance, he formed the letters with his mouth, and a whispered syllable escaped from his lips. Hannah, looking at the dictionary at the other end of the room, was so engrossed she did not know of Benjy's transgression.

But Benjy's words reached to the front of the room.

The Professor cocked his head to one side like a rooster looking for a fight. He rose from his desk and marched heavily from the platform. Hannah turned at the noise. As the teacher strode down the aisle, fury distorted his face. With a vicious grab, he yanked Benjy by the hair, lifted him from the seat and held him in midair before dropping him. Benjy doubled over, tears gushing, sobs shaking his body. The teacher opened his hand and a fistful of blood-matted hair and a scab fell to the floor. Then the Professor stomped back to his desk.

For a moment, no pupil moved. Then Hannah heightened her thin shoulders, stood up, and walked to Benjy. Bending over his quivering body, she enveloped him in her arms and wiped away the blood that trickled on his face from the wound in his head: Her face was so white that the freckles stood out. She took Benjy by the hand and slowly led him from the room. The teacher gripped the edge of the desk, the purple vein on his temple pulsating and his Adam's apple moving up and down.

The quiet that enveloped the room was smothering. The children took surreptitious glances out the window. They saw Hannah untie and saddle her horse, and lift Benjy into the saddle. She climbed on behind her brother and headed the horse toward home.

When the Professor took one final glance at the Roman numerals of his watch and announced "dismissed," the children removed themselves quietly, almost decorously, from the room. Once outside, however, they erupted into a pandemonium of shouting and activity as they ran for their horses.

Mary Belle, Carter, Annie, and Spider Baker did not enter into the confusion on the schoolground. They were frightened. Hannah had defied the teacher. She had committed the unpardonable. What would their father say? The children shuddered when they considered the consequences. They conjured up visions of horrifying repercussions. They saddled their horses slowly, as if in dread to face the answer at home. Today they did not run their ponies in Lope Valley, nor bicker, nor sing, nor even talk as usual.

The children approached the house with apprehension. The place was surprisingly quiet. No one spoke about school. Their mother was balancing Baby on her hips as she prepared supper, poking chips in the fire and stirring the beans on the stove, adding water to the coffee pot. Benjy had his head bandaged. Hannah was with their father in the corral.

Suppertime was silent. After eating, their father saddled a horse and rode down the trail toward where the Professor boarded. The next morning there was no teacher at school. Their father left for Globe City, the county seat, to find a replacement. Ben Baker put much store by learning.

Three days later he returned, his mission accomplished. In bed that night his wife moved toward him, putting her arm across his chest. For the first time in many years, Melissa Baker felt a tenderness toward her husband. But it was a feeling that soon vanished.

4.

Melissa and her sister Shug sat on the porch, bent over the quilting frame, their voices mingling. Braving Ben Baker's disapproval, Shug had made one of her rare visits to the Filaree Ranch.

Melissa laughed. "Shug, you do beat all. It's plumb comical the way you tell of chasin' yore old man with the garden hoe."

Shug looked at Melissa. "You oughta laugh more, it's becomin'." Then she grinned. "Oh, I wouldn't-a hit him. I jist don't take no backtalk off no man. Never did off none o' my husbands, and they was all good men—far as men go. You'd be a heap better off if you got yore dander up at Ben Baker." For emphasis she bit off the knotted end of thread and spat it on the porch.

Melissa was still smiling. "It does a person good to visit with you. Makes you feel happy and young inside."

Her sister became serious. "Ike Talbott come by the house last week. Watered his pony. I asked 'bout the trouble I heerd he had with Ted Neeson. He said, 'It weren't nothin.' "

"Words, just like always with Neeson," Melissa said. She

remembered the uneasy encounter with him that day on the road to the Roosevelt Dam settlement.

Shug tapped Melissa on the hand, and a hint of mischief came into her voice. "Ike asked about you."

"How is he?"

"Just as good-lookin' as always, a-ridin' that bay pony of his."

Melissa swallowed. "Shug, I'm plumb shamed to say so, but I get flustered when he looks at me and talks so polite-like. I only run across him once in a while, like when he comes by our place huntin' El Bar stock. But I can't get outa my head the way he looks at me."

"It's all right, Melissa, have yore dreams—that's about all you got. And you, such a pretty little thing. And you ain't got nary a white hair like what's creepin' into mine." She laughed. "They don't bother me none though." Shug looked skyward. "Sun's fadin'. I best be going. I wanta ride by Ma's and Pa's."

Melissa walked Shug to the gate. "It's just revivin' to visit with you. You bring fun. You do enjoy life. I can see why yore husbands put up with yore sassiness. I wish I was more like you."

"Ain't sassiness. Just plain gumption. Stick to yore rights." She picked up her bonnet. "Life is for living." She batted her eyes. "And men is for loving." She laughed.

Melissa shook her head and laughed. "Shug, Shug." She watched her sister start toward the Holman place and then she went into the house.

5. Tying the strings under her chin, Melissa pulled her sunbonnet forward and walked out into the unused air of spring. She filled a bucket of water from the pond, inhaling the pungency of the weeds that grew in the water. The past winter had been generous with rain. The surrounding miles that a few weeks previously had been dry and brown were now bedded with grasses and abundant filaree. Small leaves were appearing on the rough mesquite limbs. The birds had returned to the trees by the pond to build new nests or refurbish abandoned ones. She watched a hovering dragonfly dart and light on a cattail blade.

It was on such spring days that Melissa felt a rebirth of life and confidence. Like the plants that pushed through the crust of The Mesa earth after the winter rains, she burst with vitality. She reached down to help a drowning bug out of the water weeds.

Hearing the thud of horse's hoofs beating the earth, she looked up. A black buggy was coming at a fast pace toward her house. She walked through the yard and spoke to Carter, "Who's that a-comin'? So far I cain't see."

Carter was peeling pine poles with a drawknife. Laying the knife on the pole, he shaded his eyes with his hand. "Looks like the Brownell rig."

"John Brownell's gone up on the mountain. It ain't like Martha to come alone in the buggy."

"Yep, Mama, that's the Brownell brown mare. I kin see two heads in the buggy. Big one drivin' and a smaller by the side."

Melissa put down her bucket of water. "That shore 'nough looks like Martha. I know her flowered bonnet. Land o' livin', she's shore usin' that buggy whip."

"Looks like she's in a powerful hurry."

"John Brownell'd be mighty provoked if he seen her whippin' that mare. He's cranky 'bout runnin' his stock—horse or cow."

Melissa was at the road when the buggy with the sweating mare stopped. Carter had left his pole-peeling and followed his mother. From the front porch Annie and Benjy put down their soap-bubble pan and blowers. Mary Belle's red head peeked from behind a curtain in the bedroom.

Melissa held out both hands toward the buggy, her face

lighting with a smile. She was heartened by the rare sight of company.

But she could see immediately that something was troubling the woman in the buggy. Her face was tense; hair escaped from under her sunbonnet as if lashed by a distressed wind. Martha Brownell lifted the child on the seat into Melissa's arms.

"I do declare, Abbie," she said to the child, "you are growing faster than the weeds in my garden. You must be goin' on four years old now—and a big one fer four." Melissa turned to Carter. "You-uns take care of the buggy fer Miz Brownell. Don't water that horse too fast. She's hot." She led the visitors to the house.

In the kitchen Melissa proffered a chair near the table. Pouring a cup of coffee, she handed it to her guest. "Martha, take off yore bonnet and set down. How can I help?"

The children, sensing something important in the visit, stood in the kitchen expectantly. Melissa waved them away. "You-all scat. Git. Annie, you take Abbie outside. Show her how to blow soap bubbles with you and Benjy."

Melissa waited for her neighbor to speak. Martha's emotion kept the words choked in her throat. "Oh, my God, Melissa. I jist had to come see you. I got a hurtin' inside me that prayer ain't helped to soothe. I ain't never goin' git over this. My poor Willie, my boy—" She put her face in her hands.

In the silence Melissa heard a faint squeak. She glanced toward the bedroom door, which was slightly ajar. Mary Belle's eye was visible through the crack. "Mary Belle, this ain't no business of yourn. I'll give you the whippin' o' yore life effen you don't git back in that room and finish cleanin'." She heard the door close.

Melissa tried to reassure her guest. "It's all right. Speak free. We're alone. Mary Belle cain't hear from that room."

Martha mechanically took a sip of coffee. She sobbed quietly. "It's jist hard to git it out."

"You sit there till you feel like tellin' all about it." Melissa got up, and taking a basket of clothes from the corner, picked up a pair of overalls with a tear in the knee. Threading a needle, she began to baste a patch over the torn fabric. Melissa pushed the needle through the material, covertly glancing at her neighbor. She saw her friend's florid, kind face, parched by the wind and slashed by the sun. Although Martha was not much older than Melissa, she seemed used up even by the standards of The Mesa women. Her body had flattened breasts that sagged, a wide and thickened waist, spindly legs supporting a fallen stomach of flabby muscles stretched by neglected care in childbearing. Her hands were calloused in the palms, with fingers bony and clawlike. The hands described the woman's life. They had done labor of digging wet earth for irrigating, shoveling manure from the corral, pulling, twisting, fighting barbed wire. Melissa saw the fingers still clenched over Martha's face, the fingernails jagged, ridged, soiled. Only recently had William, her son, grown big enough to take her place in some of the heavy work.

Martha controlled her voice. Tossing back her head and flinging away the gray strands of hair, she said, "Melissa, Willie's only sixteen, but he's been workin' like a growed-up man, and he's not. He's still my baby to me."

"Martha, we always wanta keep 'em as our babies. Sometimes hurts us to see 'em grow up."

"My Willie went with the men when they drove the cattle to Roosevelt."

"Yes, I know—Ben and Jed Carruthers and Dudley Schmelz went with yore man and Willie."

"The butcher in Roosevelt told John he'd take as many yearlings as he could bring him on this trip. When they reach town, John gits paid fer the stock and they all go to the saloon."

"Did they let Willie go with 'em?"

"John says if he's man enough to drive the herd, he's man enough to drink from the sale o' them. My man don't never drink, and I don't know why he did this time—or why he let Willie go with them."

"Oh, the others probably talked John into it. Men don't like to be made fun of 'fore other men. It galls 'em."

Martha started to cry again. "They said, 'How much of a man is Willie?' They say it's time. It's time he was learnin' his manhood. They say they're gonna turn my boy into a man. They's all drinkin' and they take my baby, my Willie, to the . . . to the . . . whorehouse."

Melissa seethed. "It was an ignorant thing to do. A bawdy house!"

With her weathered fingers Martha wiped away the tears and blew her nose on the hem of her dress. "And him—Willie —only sixteen years old. When the menfolk gits back from town, Willie is peaked as could be. He don't speak. Jist goes in and lays down on the bed. When I asks John what be the cause, he says Willie's gettin' over a drunk, but I'll say John acted mighty sheepish like."

"Martha, I could kill 'em, those men. I do know how you feel."

"But John does laugh and sez they'd give Willie his manhood. Paid for him to be with . . . a woman. A whore, Melissa. I wanted to kill my man. I jist had to tell someone. I been keepin' it inside me till I thought I'd bust. When John rode off with Jed Carruthers, I harnessed up Nellie and come to see you. My Willie. Why, oh God in Heaven, why? They've ruint him."

Melissa felt her head throb, the old familiar ache. She wanted to destroy, to destroy the men who had left this woman suffering. Melissa knew she must restrain her own rage and seek to bring comfort to her friend. "Martha, what's done cain't be undone. It was a coyote thing to do. Menfolks is plain cussed mean polecats. They have a way of lookin' at things that's wrong with us wimmenfolk. It riles us when they do. We cain't never change 'em."

"John says that was the way he was brung up to reach his

manhood—with a woman in one of those places, when he weren't more'n thirteen."

"Ben don't never talk about them things. But I have heerd tell before that's what menfolks do."

Melissa glanced at Martha. She still sat in a stupor. "We wimmen likes to keep our children, but men wants 'em growed up so's they kin work. Ben expects our younguns to work like men. He has Hannah doin' man's work. He gits plumb agger-vated with Carter 'cause he ain't no bigger and no stronger than he is. He tells the younguns what he done when he was their age. Once he trailed some Indians three days to git back stolen horses."

Martha looked up and asked, "That was back in Texas?"

"Yes, I 'spect Ben did have a hard time growin' up. He was ten. His father was dead. One evening when he came in from school, his mother was alone with his younger brother and sister. She told Ben that four Comanche Indians had come by the ranch and stole three horses, knowin' there was no man at the ranch. Stole 'em, the thievin' skunks. Ben said he'd go after the horses. Ben's ma cried and said no, but Ben started out after the Indians anyway.

"The Indians traveled slow, feelin' they wuz safe. Ben slept out at night with only his saddle blanket, and ate his grub in the saddle. After three days he rode into their camp. They wuz surprised, never thinkin' a-body would be after them. They weren't on the warpath. They were just thieves. Them Coman-ches was mean, and you jist never knowed when they might break loose. Mebbe they jist respected Ben, for a boy, to come trailin' 'em—but more likely they's fearful of that army fort of soldiers not far away. Ben got the horses and brings 'em back to the ranch."

"That was a fearsome job fer a little one."

"Ben tells our younguns that he's done a man's work since he was knee high to a grasshopper—and he expects the same outa them. I'm plumb ashamed of the part Ben had in doin' that to yore boy. He didn't say nothin' to me 'bout it. I 'spect inside Ben's a bit ashamed, too. But that don't help matters none now."

Martha felt wrung dry of tears. "It's mighty neighborly of you to listen to my pain. I jist had to tell someone. Yore my friend. Yore right. I cain't do nothin' 'bout it. I am much obliged fer yore listening. I do believe I better git home. I got chores and my garden waitin'. John'd be powerful huffy if supper ain't ready when he comes in. It'd gall him effen he knowed I come here to talk to you about Willie."

"Pshaw. You jist wait a bit. You ain't fit to go home now. You gotta collect yoreself. You got time fer a bite to eat. Bet you ain't had nothin' this whole day." Melissa placed a crockery plate on the table and put out fried salt pork, cold corn bread, cucumber pickles, a glass of buttermilk, and stewed apples. Martha picked at the food, forcing a few bites into her mouth. When she had half cleared the plate, she said, "I'm gonna wash up these dishes and then git to gittin' home."

"Leave them dishes be. I'll clear 'em up when yore gone." She opened the door. "Carter, go git the mare and harness up for Miz Brownell."

Martha Brownell picked up her sunbonnet. "It done me a heap o' good to talk to you. I gotta bear it. My poor Willie. Wish you'd come see me. I got sorghum molassus I'd like to give you. Next week Willie and John go to Dead Man's Draw to look fer cattle. It's rough country. They'll be gone fer two or three days. Wish you'd come over and spend some time with me after you git the younguns off to school."

The guest walked to the porch and took Abbie by the hand. She reached down to whisper in the child's ear. "Abbie, we're gonna go home now. You better go peepee 'fore we leave."

"No, Mama. No, no." The child shook her head.

"Melissa, I do guess I'll haveta stop calling him Willie now. His pa says he orta go by the man's name of Bill now he's got his manhood." As she walked with Abbie to the buggy, she began to sob again.

Melissa watched the departing buggy, the wheels following the narrow dirt ruts that had worn down the sprigs of filaree. Dusky shadows darkened the canyons that gashed the sides of the Sierra Anchas. The silver of the sky was gone, and approaching twilight dimmed the horizon. Melissa thought of Martha, and bitterness welled inside her. She muttered, "Damned menfolks. Damn 'em to hell." She heard the sound of Baby crying, and turned back to the house.

6.

Ben Baker walked to the wagon where the tarpaulin covered the produce from Melissa's garden—the leaf lettuce, red radishes, green onions, and cucumbers. Eggs were embedded in a tub of straw. The man secured the edges of the canvas and turned to his wife. "Eldridge and I'll be gone three, four days. Them workers in Roosevelt'll pay heap for yore garden truck. You want I should bring back flour, lard, dried peaches, and them doodads?"

The morning light was faint, the sun's rays too weak to have much burning power, but even so, the woman had pulled a sunbonnet over her hair. She had been firm about the vegetables, insisting that he take the produce she had raised.

She had the children up at dawn, picking, cleaning, packing the vegetables for the trip. The fast-growing town of Roosevelt was isolated from farming area. The high-paid construction workers had no hesitancy in parting with cash for fresh vegetables. Melissa expected her husband to use the money for food supplies. She also hoped he would buy ribbons for the girls' hair, and marbles for the boys. But she doubted that he would bring her a newspaper or a magazine, or the oilcloth he hadn't brought the last time.

Ben Baker was dressed in his new chambray shirt, his good dark trousers, and his dress boots. His face was freshly shaven, the mustache cut short, and the yellow tobacco-juice stains trimmed off. But the woman saw nothing appealing about him, and she only wished that he would head the horses toward Roosevelt Dam and be on his way.

He left orders. "You see to it that Carter doctors that wire cut on the colt. Have him fix the pasture fence. He kin take a load o' salt to the Gap. Be damned sure that gate's closed to Hell's Canyon." The man tolerated no slackness, especially with his children.

"Eldridge, you-all ready?" He called to a figure coming out the front door. Ben pulled a heavy gold watch from his pocket. The thick railroad-type timepiece had cost him "a goodly sum," as he was fond of telling his children. He had bought it after a profitable cattle sale in Texas years before. He liked to look at the watch and did so often, even when there was no reason for him to know the hour. Then he would look up at the sky and remark that he was checking to see if the sun was in the right position. "Eldridge and I wanta reach town before dark," Ben Baker said.

"Ol' Man Eldridge" was an acquaintance who had ridden by the Filaree to "set a spell" one day soon after the Bakers returned from Roosevelt with the new baby. That was months ago, and he still remained at the ranch. He drifted around the country with his visiting. The women of the ranches were irked with "Ol' El's visitin'," which always meant a burden of additional work for them. The guest did not help Ben Baker with the ranch work. "I never were no hand at cowpunchin'," Pete Eldridge would excuse himself.

But the owner of the Filaree Ranch found satisfaction in listening to "Ol' El's talkin'." The guest was of easy nature, a man who had spent a lifetime wandering, and had tales to match his travels. Melissa had once told her sister Shug that they were nothing but exaggeration. "Plain out-and-out lies."

But they made good listening for Ben Baker. Ol' El made his hours less empty, and on the Roosevelt trip he was to help with "them cussed vegetables."

Baker declared he was no farmer and that a cowman didn't garden. That was woman's work. He even continued to get a neighbor to plant his alfalfa, and left the irrigating to Hannah and Carter. It embarrassed him to be seen as a vegetable peddler. When the wagon reached Roosevelt, he planned to stop at the Tonto Saloon and let Ol' El dispose of the vegetables. Eldridge had no feeling against farming and basked in the importance of selling the vegetables, as it made for social contacts. Now Baker jerked the horses' reins, and the wagon grumbled out into the rutted road.

Melissa mounted the wooden porch steps, avoiding the broken plank. The children were at school, and she planned to do the washing. She abhorred the dingy, yellowed clothes that some neighbors put out. She had told Shug, "I'd be plumb shamed to have my baby wearin' them gray didies. Crawlin' 'round the fireplace, moppin' up the dirt. Draggin' its hind end in them wet didies is filth." Even Ben Baker said, "All them Holmans is a scrubbin' outfit. That Ol' Lady Holman is a heller, but you cain't find nary a speck of dust in her outfit."

Usually Melissa waited until the children were home from school so they could help her, but her parents had invited her to go with them to the schoolhouse dance the following night while her husband was in Roosevelt. She had need to prepare early.

She carried sloshing pails of water and filled the black washpot to boil the clothes. The wood resisted burning. Squatting on her haunches, she blew on the embers until she felt her lungs were near to bursting. With her sunbonnet she fanned the flame. Smoke choked her and perspiration covered her face. She put a can of lye in the boiling water, and when the scum formed, removed it. With a butcher knife she shaved a bar of homemade soap into slivers, dropping the fragments into the water. Then she settled her washboard into a tub of warm water and scrubbed the clothes against the ripples of brass. The harshness of the soap irritated her hands.

Going inside to change Baby's diapers, she placed the urine-soaked cloths on her arms and tied them. The Mesa women knew that this bleached the skin, and Melissa wanted a "lady's" fair skin. She caught a glimpse of herself in the mirror. Her eyes looked dull, but maybe she was just weary of her existence. Were they holes of despair, those tired eyes? Years ago in Texas people had told her that her eyes "spit fire when she was riled." Now, she thought, only cold ashes remained.

The weight of her heavy hair irritated her. She pulled out the hairpins and shook her head, as the curling mass tumbled down.

She went on about her work, taking the beef jerky from the flour sacks that hung suspended from the rafters on the porch where it was cooler, and out of the reach of the rats. Then she took the water bucket from the bench and went outside to fill it. She paused, lost in her worries. Her youth was slipping, and her future seemed even more dreary. Would time pass her by? Was this barren life her only destiny?

The distant thud of hoofbeats interrupted her musing. She saw a figure on horseback riding toward the ranch. She dropped the bucket and rushed inside to brush her loose hair and to pull off her apron.

She heard, "Hello. Anyone to home?" She walked to the porch. Astride his bay horse was Ike Talbott. He lolled in the saddle. He had been at the Filaree Ranch before but always with other ranchers gathering cattle.

Melissa recalled what Martha Brownell had told her. Ike Talbott had lived on a small place with his mother until she died. Then he went to the El Bar Ranch as foreman. Martha had said, "Every female from the Mazatzal Mountains to the Sierra Anchas has set their cap for that man. He's a cagey one, won't have no truck with none of them gals. Handsome as a jaybird he is, and just as hard to catch. Guess he won't ever be lassoed by no woman, now he's getting past thirty-five."

Even her husband was admiring. "I hear there ain't no better cowman this side o' the Four Peaks than Talbott." In the corral at roundup time, the men assigned him to cut out the calves for branding, dehorning, and castrating. "Ike's tougher'n a mesquite root. He can flank a calf easier than most men can throw a cat out the kitchen window. And he's one man won't back up for Ted Neeson."

Melissa was lost with these remembrances when she heard the cowboy's voice. "Howdy, Miz Baker, could I water my old pony?" His words were slow.

Dismounting, Ike Talbott took off his hat and hit it against his thigh, releasing a cloud of dust. He looked at the woman on the porch and grinned. His sound teeth, even and white, contrasted with the bronze of his skin.

"Help yourself, Mr. Talbott."

The cowboy led his horse to the trough. She watched him take off the bridle and loosen the cinch. When the animal had finished drinking, Talbott led the horse to the mesquite pole and bar which served as a hitching post, and with a short rope he tied the horse to the bar.

"The mister home?" he asked.

"He went to Roosevelt. Won't be back for three, four days."

"I came by to tell him there's a spotted two-year-old heifer of his in the draw at Squaw Flat. Dead. Worms in the hip. Thought he'd like to take a look at it. Blowflies got to it— maggots."

"Thank you. I'll send Carter up there when he gits home from school."

Ike Talbott twirled his hat on his forefinger as if waiting for the woman to speak. "I . . . I was just bringing in a pail of water," she said, walking toward the pail.

Ike Talbott grinned. "I'll just tote that water for you. You're a mite light to be luggin' such a heavy weight."

His hand was on the handle of the bucket when she felt the brush of calloused fingers. She jerked her hand away. Her face was hot, and she hoped he didn't notice the flush.

Talbott carried the water into the kitchen. He looked at her, and even in the soft light of the room, she saw the wrinkles around his eyes as he grinned. "I'll just set this bucket here while you give me that coffee you invited me to have."

"I'm sorry." Melissa was embarrassed. She had passed up the first rule of The Mesa, the hospitality of food and drink. Moving to the stove, she took off the lid and stirred the embers. "Coffee'll be hot soon," she said. "Have a seat, Mr. Talbott." She took two cups from the cupboard.

Ike Talbott turned a chair around and sat down, resting his arms on the chair's back. He seemed too big for the spindly-legged chair, too big for the room, but there was something comfortable about the way he seemed to fill the kitchen. She handed him a cup, "Mr. Talbott—"

"The name's Ike, ma'am." He tossed back his head and laughed.

As she reached for the coffee pot to fill her own cup, her long hair fell across her face, autumn-brown and catching the sunlight.

The cowboy from the El Bar stopped laughing. He looked at Melissa. "You got the prettiest hair," he said.

Talbott stood up and came toward Melissa. Taking the cup from her hand, he set it on the table.

"Here's your coffee—Melissa."

The foreman from the El Bar looked down on her. He put his hands on each side of her hair. "You look just like a . . . a little doe with those big eyes—all scairt."

His hands were two hot branding irons against her head. Melissa felt suddenly that she wanted to pull them down and hold them against her breast; she could tell that she was blushing.

Ike Talbott removed his hands and took her small fists in his.

He looked at the scarred brown fingers that lay in his big palms. "My mother had hands like yours."

Melissa could not take her eyes off his mouth. She noted his chapped lips, a crack splitting the center, one that wouldn't heal in the sun and wind and aridity. She wanted to reach up and run her finger gently—so gently—over the fissure. *Married women oughtn't to have such feelin's,* she told herself, and moved her body away.

But he stepped close to her, still looking down. She hoped now that he would press those burned lips of his against her. Then guilt overcame her and she ran to the window and pretended to look out.

He did not follow her. "Are you coming to the schoolhouse dance tomorrow night?" he asked.

Melissa waited before she answered. "I don't rightly know. Ma and Pa said they'd come by and pick the younguns and me up." But she knew that she would go.

Ike Talbott picked up his hat. With a smile he said, "Save me the first dance." Then he was out the door, down the steps, and across the yard to his horse.

Melissa watched as he checked his saddle, lifting it higher and hefting it forward on the horse's withers. He tightened the cinch and ran his fingers under the horse's belly between the hide and cinch. He untied the rope from the hitching post. Throwing the reins over the horse's head, he held them with his left hand on the saddle horn. Putting his boot toe in the stirrup, he made a small bounce and swung his sinewy body up, his leg over the saddle, and settled himself firmly. *Lithe as a cat,* Melissa thought.

He waved and nudged the animal. She heard him laugh, and the laughter seemed to sing out over the stillness. And then he was gone. The woman stood on the porch a long time, and she hated herself. She knew she wanted Ike Talbott.

7.

Melissa lifted a pan of biscuits from the oven and carried it to the table where the children were having breakfast. Spider dislodged a biscuit and reached for the butter. Without raising his head, he said, "Pass the lick."

"Say 'please.' " Mary Belle held tightly to the stoneware pitcher filled with molasses.

"Gimme." The boy snatched the pitcher. "Mama, kin we go to the dance tonight? Grandpa come to school yesterday. We told him Pa was away. He said he and Grandma would stop by then, long 'fore dark today, and git us fer the dance at the schoolhouse."

Melissa pushed the biscuit pan back into the oven. The image of Ike Talbott flashed before her. She thought of her husband and felt the familiar dull ache beginning in her head. "I don't know. Your papa wouldn't take kindly to our gallivantin' off."

Annie pleaded. "Grandma is goin' to take food for us."

"We could take our own vittles. Fried chicken. But I ain't saying—"

"I'd kill the chickens," Carter said.

Hannah, feeding the baby spoonfuls of oatmeal, looked up. "Mama, we sure would like to go. It's Saturday and we're free from school."

Melissa looked at Hannah's face. *'Tain't fair to a young girl like Hannah. That child don't git to go nowheres. No chance for frolickin'. Does a man's work. Her papa ought not to deny her a bit o' growin' up. Lord knows she'll have her dreariness soon enough.* Melissa pressed her fingers tighter against her temples. *Men shouldn't dominate wimmenfolks that way.*

But it was Ike Talbott she mainly thought about. *He toted*

water fer me. Been a long time since a man showed me I was
a lady.

"We might be able to go," she said, finally. "I ain't exactly
sayin' we can go. We got ranch work to do. We gotta git ready.
Hair washin'. Bathin'. Vittles to take."

Mary Belle jumped up from her chair and grabbed Annie.
The girls clasped hands and skipped around the kitchen. Spider
exploded into hopping on one foot and then the other. Melissa
said, "Spider, you-all is actin' like a wild Comanche Indian."

Carter clapped his hands. "Hallelujah! Praise the Lord!
We's goin' to the dance."

"Carter, I jist said that mebbe we could plan on it."

The baby, alarmed by the commotion, began to cry. Mary
Belle took the child and cuddled it. "Hush yore cryin', Velma
Marjorie. We's goin' take you to the dance, too."

The children gulped the remains of their breakfast and left
the table to run outside to feed and water the chickens and
search for eggs, hay and grain the horses, turn the irrigation
water into the alfalfa, cut the firewood, bring water into the
house, doctor the sick calf, and pick vegetables that were ripe.
Rarely had a day seemed to pass so quickly.

Inside the kitchen, Melissa encouraged herself in her defiance. She stoked the stove, jamming in pieces of wood with
an uncharacteristic vehemence. She called to Carter, "Bring
that there rain water from the barrel under the eaves. We all
gotta wash our hair and bathe."

Carter hollered. "That loco Spider done put horsehair in the
rain barrel!"

Spider's voice reached Melissa. "Carter, blast you! Don't
you touch them. Leave 'em be. They's gonna turn into snakes.
Them's hair from the horses' tails!"

Carter carried a water bucket in each hand into the kitchen.
"Mama, Spider orta be helpin'. He ain't worth the salt it'd take
to blow him to hell. Dodgin' work by chasin' bugs. He cain't
change a horsehair into a snake. He don't know nothin'. Crazy

as a bedbug and no more sense than a damned oi' hoot owl."

"Watch yore language, son." Melissa poured water from the pails into the washtub on top of the stove. "Leave Spider be. He'll grow up, mebbe to be a science man that knows about them things."

The water heated on the stove and the woman swept the kitchen. She took a dishcloth and swished it through the air toward the screen door, where a half-dozen flies had lighted, and still flailing, she opened the door to let them out. Melissa heated the irons on the stove and pressed the embroidered blouse she kept for special occasions. When she was finished, she called the girls in for their baths. "Mary Belle, you and Annie git yore baths 'fore the boys." She set the metal washtub on the kitchen floor and filled it with warm water from the stove.

When the girls finished, Melissa called to Spider. "You come in and git yore bath."

Spider stood in the doorway. "I ain't a-gonna bathe after them girls. That water's dirty."

"You gotta use the same water. We cain't heat no more. Lawsy, as dirty as you are—"

"Mama, I ain't a-gonna bathe in them girls' water. They pee in that water." His voice rose higher. "They piss in their bath water!"

In the bedroom Annie and Mary Belle held back their snickers. Mary Belle put her head through the door. "Mr. Spider, we did not. Don't judge other people by yourself." She shut the door and held her hand over her mouth.

The sun had lengthened the mesquite-tree shadows until they reached the house. Inside, the girls pulled on their long black stockings and buttoned their dresses in the back. Melissa took off the rags which she had used to make curls on Hannah's hair. She brushed the curls around the broom handle. "Hannah, you look like a young lady," she said.

Melissa passed a hand over her own smooth hair and flushed

as she wondered if Ike Talbott liked curls. Lighting the coal oil lamp, she put the crimped end of the metal curling irons into the glass chimney. Removing them in a few seconds, she wiped off the soot and tested the heat by touching them with a moistened forefinger. Then she closed the tongs over a layer of her own hair.

The children were ready. They waited in the kitchen while their mother finished dressing. Melissa picked up a metal box on her dresser. Opening it, she took out a red silk rose. She placed it above one ear, frowned, and removed it. Then she tried it on the other side. Looking in the mirror, she shook her head and put the flower back into the box.

Melissa breathed in, lacing up her corset with effort. She put on the embroidered blouse and stepped into a gored black silk skirt that reached her ankles.

As she dressed, she felt trepidation. Would Ike Talbott be at the dance? She envisioned his long legs striding across the schoolhouse floor, bowing and asking, "May I have this first dance?" She felt his strong hands and the calloused palm as he put her hand in his, as gently, she imagined, as a calf nosing its mother for her teat. Melissa flushed. She remembered that strong outdoor smell about him. Outside she heard the sound of wagon wheels crunching to a halt.

She turned quickly and again opened the tarnished metal box on the dresser. She took out the red silk rose, bent a hairpin, and fastened it in her hair. She took a hurried look in the mirror. She heard Spider's voice from outside. "Mama, they're here. Let's git goin' to the dance."

8.
As Melissa and the children climbed into the wagon, her mother said, "We got quilts in the back for the younguns to sleep on comin' home from the dance. Give me the baby."

She touched the child under the chin with a forefinger that looked like a dried chicken bone. "Granny's little darlin'." She smiled at the child, and the baby opened its mouth, its gums as smooth as the old woman's.

The children settled themselves in the wagon bed. The sun was lowering, and the land was clothed in a green softness of brush and filaree melding. Melissa felt excited and yet peaceful. Her thoughts were light, and the throbbing in her head was gone. Melissa's thoughts were all of Ike Talbott.

The schoolhouse was already brightly lit with kerosene lanterns when they arrived. Benjy ran to the single swing—a worn splintered board that hung on a rope from an elderberry tree. Carter and Spider carried the food baskets inside. Then they raced out to the far end of the yard, where boys were standing in stiff groups in dress clothes that made them ill-at-ease. The Baker girls walked with their mother into the schoolroom, where they found their schoolmates sitting primly on one side of the room. The girls looked one another over critically, noting the ribbons in the hair, the laces, and the polished shoes.

The air was slightly smoky from the fire in the potbellied stove. Seats had been pushed against the walls, arranged to serve as makeshift beds for children later on. Already two babies were asleep under a covering of shawls. The middle of the room was clear, the floor strewn with cornmeal to slicken the boards. The blackboard had been washed clean and, in the teacher's precise script, the word WELCOME had been chalked in.

Melissa joined the women who had placed long boards over the teacher's desk to serve as a dining table. Martha Brownell, her florid face shining with perspiration, looked at the red rose in Melissa's hair. Melissa wished she had not worn it. Ben would not have approved.

She carried the baby to a far corner to lay her down. But the child was not sleepy, and she voiced her protests with crying. Annie came over. "Mama, let me give Baby a sugar tit. I'll quiet her."

Melissa handed Annie a small rag folded over a bit of sugar and tied into a tight ball. The girl put the sugared cloth into the infant's puckering mouth. The cries subsided as the baby sucked and soon lowered its eyelids. Melissa glanced toward the doorway, but did not see the person she was looking for.

Mary Belle walked around the food baskets, pulling aside the white dishcloths and peeking underneath. Her mother slapped her away. "Mary Belle, you are circling that food like a hawk sailing above a yard of chickens. Git goin'. Ain't you got no manners?"

The men began to gather in the room. Jeff Hooper came in, his violin case cramped under his arm. "Thank the Lord, yore here, Jeff," someone said. "We'd begun to think the creek had swallered you up. You lose your bottle?" The men all laughed.

Jeff opened his case, and taking out the smooth brown fiddle, clinched it against his shoulder, drawing the bow across experimentally. He called out, "Git ready fer the grand march. Dudley, take yore lady and lead out. You young fellers pick a purty gal and swing her."

Wrinkling his head in concentration, the fiddler continued to pull the bow across the strings, evaluating the notes. "Goodness me, I wish he'd git done tunin' that there fiddle." Martha Brownell complained. "He's drinkin', so he don't hardly know 'Sally Goodin' from 'Turkey in the Straw.' I'd like to dance a set. Wonder where my old man is? Guess he's still outside a-swappin' lies and cussin' the Forest Service. That young forest ranger came snoopin' around checkin' on our cattle. Told John we wuz running too many head—overgrazing the land. Now, why in tarnation don't that man of mine come on in and dance?"

"Don't be so fidgety," said Old Lady Holman. "When yore as old as I am, you'll reconcile yourself to yore ol' man's cussedness. They gits worse as they git older."

"Git yore partners. The Virginny Reel," the fiddler's voice announced. Women looked for their menfolk. Melissa kept her eyes on the door. Dancers began to crowd the floor. The room grew warmer with all the activity. The dancers felt and understood the music that they had heard all their lives. They clicked heels, stamped feet, concentrating on unfamiliar steps, their eyes on their feet.

Melissa stood aside, her enthusiasm draining. Ike Talbott would not come. The dance was finished, and the next set started. Through the crowd, Melissa saw the door open, and the El Bar foreman's long frame blotted out the darkness at his back. Melissa watched as he joined the men talking at the stove. His eyes met hers. She turned her head away.

Jeff put down his fiddle and went to the drinking bucket. Dudley Schmelz pulled his harmonica from his shirt pocket and began to blow. Someone hummed and then began to sing the words, "Young Charlotte lived on a mountainside in a wild and lonely spot . . ."

"Dudley can sure handle that mouth organ, but he does pick the sad tunes. Makes my heart ache." Martha Brownell said. "Guess he gits that from his preachin'. He's seen the sadness at his burying services."

Jeff announced a waltz. Melissa walked to Baby and pulled a cover over the sleeping child. As dancers began gliding across the floor, she heard his voice. "Ma'am, please may I have the honor of this dance?" She did not, could not, speak.

Talbott took her arm, guiding her onto the crowded floor. Pulling a white handkerchief from his pocket, he wrapped it around his right hand and placed his hand in the middle of her back. Underneath his breath he counted steps, one-two-three.

Melissa felt awkward. It had been a long time since she had danced. Ike tightened his hold, pressing his hand closer against her back. She saw the brown sleeve holders keeping the excess length from his wrists. He pumped his hand holding hers up and down in rhythm to the music.

She was excited by his closeness, his smell, his bigness. Lowering his voice, he asked, "Might I see you alone—outside by the wellhouse?" They danced silently. Melissa did not speak, but she answered with her eyes. The music was still playing when he left her by the row of desks and walked out the door. When the music started again and the floor was crowded, Melissa edged her way to the door. She had not bothered to get a shawl, and she shivered as she stepped outside. Her eyes adjusted to the dimness. She saw the bay horse tied at the fence, and then, discerning the wellhouse, walked toward it. The schoolyard was empty, but she sensed he would be there.

As she reached the edge of the building, a firm arm reached out and pulled her into the shadows. He clutched her. She felt his breath. "I have waited so long—for this. Seems years I been watchin' you and wantin' you." His breathing grew heavier. Putting his lips against hers, he crushed her body close to his own. Melissa did not try to move away.

Talbott pursued her face in a race of kisses, covering her lips, her forehead, her neck. She felt the harshness of his sunburned lips, and it hurt her with a pain she enjoyed. He pressed his hands down her back, and under her arms, toward the front of her blouse. She began to shake. He gulped, "I want . . ."

Footsteps sounded on the gravel—lumbering, broken, stumbling footsteps. Ike drew her deeper into the darkness. She could make out two weaving figures in the yard. "You want a snort of this cougar piss?" One figure pulled a bottle from the top of his boot and extended it to the other one.

The drinking man gurgled. "Damn rotgut you got here. Burns my intestines."

"Don't cuss a free drink, you horse thief. Yore a lousy bastard to insult my likker. You don't show no 'preciation. No respect. No friendship. Hold this bottle. I gotta take a leak. I could flood out Tonto Creek with what I'm a-holdin'." The figure faced the wellhouse and fumbled at the front of his pants.

Melissa was glad the darkness hid her embarrassment. She lowered her head, but heard the sound of liquid splattering on the gravel stones. A thick voice announced, "Let's take another snort and empty the damned thing." There was the sound of glass breaking. The figures lurched and moved away. All was quiet.

Ike Talbott put his arms around her and tried to resume his attentions. But for Melissa the spell was shattered. She jerked away. "I haveta go. Don't wanta be missed."

"I must see you again," he pleaded with her. But she pulled away. The yard was clear. Then she walked quickly toward the schoolhouse door and stood outside until she heard the music begin and the noise of the dancers. She stepped inside and lost herself in the crowd.

Martha Brownell was putting out plates. "It's past midnight. We oughta eat. Younguns is all asleep and we gotta git home." The women set out home-baked bread cut in thick slices, chunks of roast beef, fried chicken, pots of brown beans, potato salad, pies, and cakes. Old Lady Holman arranged her watermelon preserves, tomato pickles, and spiced peaches. When the supper was eaten and the remains cleared, the women awakened the sleeping children, carrying them or leading the older ones to the wagons and buggies where the men waited. Melissa followed her family outside. She looked at the fence. The bay horse was gone.

9.

It was the Sunday morning after the schoolhouse dance. Melissa lifted the kitchen's hinged window, hooking it to the wall with a leather thong. She looked outside and breathed deeply, feeling an unaccustomed lightness. She swept the pine floor of the room, picking up the broken straws that fell from the broom. Suddenly she knew she had to get away, if even for a few hours. "Sister," she said to Hannah, "yore papa and Ol' Man Eldridge won't be back from Roosevelt until later today or tomorrow. While they're gone, I'm goin' to ride over to Aunt Shug's. Think you could watch over the younguns?"

The thin-faced girl nodded. "I'll saddle up Brownie for you."

Taking off her wash dress, Melissa put on a heavy brown divided skirt which reached nearly to her ankles. Only her abdomen resisted when she strained to button the waist. *Belly so stretched since Baby was born that I still can't cinch this thing.* Sucking in her breath, she finally fastened the button.

From the washtub on the porch, Melissa cut hunks of comb honey, filled a lard bucket with them and clamped on the metal lid, putting the pail in a clean-washed flour sack. She suckled the baby, changed the wet diapers, and tied a cap on the child's head. Meanwhile Hannah secured the flour sack with the honey onto the saddle, tying the leather strings at the rear. Melissa mounted and reached for the small pillow Hannah handed her, wedging it in the space between her body and the saddle horn. Hannah lifted the baby to the saddle, and Melissa placed the child on the pillow. She laid the reins in her left hand, looping them between her second finger and the one encircled with the wide gold band.

Melissa walked the horse easy and gave herself time to look at the countryside. Filaree had greened the earth, and by the road where the rain had settled in a depression, the plants grew a foot tall and fell over with their purple blossoms entangled.

The warmth of the day reminded Melissa that she must again caution the children about rattlesnakes. The previous year Ben had shot one in the house, coiled under the bed where Annie was sleeping. The year had been a bad one for rattlers. His best cow dog had died of a rattler's venom. While hunting for stray cattle, her husband had discovered the entrance to a snake den. Returning with dynamite, he had blasted the area, spewing rocks and rattlesnakes for yards. He had killed the ones that escaped with a shotgun.

Melissa had time, too, for thoughts of Ike Talbott. The memory of the meeting in the wellhouse shadows brought color to her cheeks. Today was a good day for her. Even the heaviness of her hair didn't bother her. It didn't surprise her that the headaches disappeared whenever her husband was gone from the ranch. She enjoyed letting the horse loiter at a tortoise-like pace, stopping to nip at bunch grass. And she continued to daydream about Ike Talbott.

She reached the trail by Tonto Creek that turned off to Shug's house. Shug's baptized name was Eunace May, but she had acquired the nickname Shugah. As the years wore on, the name became Aunt Shug, though menfolks agreed, "She ain't sweet as sugar by a damn shot." At the present time Shug lived alone in a two-room frame-and-tin house. She had told Melissa, "I've run off my old man. He got ornery as a billy goat." Aunt Shug had "run off," or "deserted," or "abandoned" six husbands. Her temperament didn't take to marriage. As Ben Baker once put it, "Shug's too contrary to pull in double harness. If she ain't the lead horse, all hell breaks loose."

"She got her independence," Melissa had answered. "Won't take no meanness off no man. With no younguns, she kin go her own way."

Shug was a favorite with the women on The Mesa. Her trouble with men did not lessen her liking for them, and she always seemed to get a new husband as soon as she was rid of the old one. In between husbands, she made a living for herself. At times, "the pickin' was pore," she said, "but I won't accept charity long as I got hands to work with." And work she did.

With Shug around, there was always fun-making, the talk full of spice and gossip. Shug loved singing. Her rich voice poured out with effortless vibrance. When she washed dishes, she accompanied herself with a refrain she had brought from Texas: "Old sow woke up one mornin'/Found two little pigs in bed./She whispered low in her boar's ear/Pal, let's move our bed."

Shug's house came into view. She had the reputation of being "the cleaningest woman this side of the Four Peaks."

The cupboards were lined with newspapers, the marred knives and forks in rows, the chipped dishes stacked neatly, the cookstove polished, and the yard swept.

Melissa pulled up her horse under the shade of a tree. Before she could alight, her sister flung open the screen door, drying her hands on her apron and crying out a welcome. "Melissa, yore a sight for sore eyes. Hand me the baby. Turn yore pony in the corral."

Inside the scrubbed kitchen, Melissa gave Shug the pail of honey and sat down at a round table covered with a red-checked tablecloth. Shug held the baby over her shoulder. "Pore little thing—you got gas in yore belly?" She patted the child on the back. The baby expelled a burp, and curdled milk trickled from its mouth. Shug handed the baby to Melissa. "Give the youngun some titty." Melissa, opening her waist, absently guided the child's mouth to a nipple.

Shug bustled around the kitchen. "Bet yore plumb starved. I'll set you out a bite. Corn bread and clabber milk."

"Don't bother gittin' me anything. I'll just sup some coffee."

"It's not often you come visitin'. I intend to lay out some grub. Sucklin' that youngun has took the flesh offen you, Melissa."

"I never was one to put on fat."

"Here's a mess o' greens with salt pork. These beans'll put something in yore gut, mebbe enough to stand up to that man of yours, so's you can demand yore rights. Oh, I know it. I'm too outspoken. Gits me into trouble. Even loses me husbands." She laughed.

Shug jerked a flour sack off the table, exposing salt and pepper shakers, a sugar bowl, a broken-handled cup with teaspoons, and a jar of red and green chili peppers. "Beans need chili," she said. "Dig in."

Melissa extracted a piece of salt pork from the collard greens, chewed on it for a few minutes, and then placed the pork between the baby's lips. The infant sucked on it contentedly.

Shug said, "I'm gittin' you some of my piccalilli to take home. It's in the cellar." She kicked off her shoes. She wore no stockings. "These here shoes is a-killin' me. They's too small but they was give to me."

Shug walked to the rear of the room where a door opened into a dugout area in the adjoining hillside. Wooden shelves lined the earthen walls and held jars of fruits and vegetables. "Melissa, kin you eat some canned termaters?"

As Shug stepped into the dark cellar, Melissa called after her, "Shug, that's a good place to git stung. You watch out fer scorpions."

Laughter echoed from the dugout. "Them scorpions better watch out fer me. My old man used to say I was more pizen than them, that they'd die effen they stung my old hide."

"Shug, put yore shoes on."

"Scorpions! I've had husbands with stingers more powerful than them insectipedes."

The women moved outside under a covering, supported by four cottonwood poles and thatched with burrobrush roofing that kept out the rain and the harsh rays of the sun. On hot summer nights Shug slept here on a canvas cot.

Shug dipped a teaspoon into a can of snuff and pushed the brown powder into her mouth, placing it under her tongue. She busied herself with crocheting some long strips of colored rags.

Melissa settled herself. "I get plumb starved for good talk. Never see nobody, nor palaver at all. Nobody comes to the ranch."

"How was the dance?" Shug asked.

"Oh, the dance was . . . wonderful!" Melissa was relieved that her sister appeared not to notice her blush.

Shug put down her crochet needle. "Did you hear about Ted Neeson?"

"No. What happened? He's a mean one, that Neeson."

"He threatened to kill the Fulton boy, the youngest one, the one they call Tommie. Jist because Ted is a deputy sheriff, he hides behind that badge. Someday his big mouth is goin' to meet a body what'll close it fer him."

"Does skullduggery, I hear tell."

Isolated as she was at the Filaree Ranch, Melissa knew of Ted Neeson and his threat to "shoot out yore goddamned eye" to anyone who crossed him. As deputy sheriff of the area for many years, he had intimidated most of The Mesa folk. The man also owned a small cow outfit, and his cattle had increased suspiciously fast. As Mesa folk said, "Neeson's cows calve twice a year." No ranchers confronted the deputy when they missed stock, but behind his back they told one another that "Neeson throws a long loop." Most men of The Mesa were family heads who hesitated to begin an argument with the violent Ted Neeson, yet the feeling was that a blowup would come one day when a rancher was pushed too far.

"It seems that in the Tonto Saloon the other day Neeson was blowin' off his mouth 'bout someone stealin' a calf—same as he always done." Shug spit some snuff juice into the can by her chair. "Dudley Schmelz says he heard Neeson sayin' the Fultons mighta took that calf. 'Tweren't no Fulton there 'cept that young Tommie, who's barely grown. Tommie went to the privy back of the saloon. Neeson's drinkin' bad. He followed the boy, put his six-shooter against his back, and said, 'If you Fultons have took my calf, I'm gonna shoot yore goddamned eye out and then throw yore stinkin' carcass in this privy hole.' The boy didn't say nothin'. They was alone."

"Why, that little Tommie Fulton couldn't stand up to that mean skunk."

"Tommie says they hears footsteps and in walks Ike Talbott."

"Oh," Melissa heard herself gasp. "Ike Talbott?"

"Neeson puts his gun away nice as elderberry pie. Ike Talbott's one man what ain't scairt o' Neeson. Dudley says that Neeson come back to the saloon a-cussin' Ike and says that one of these days he'll settle a score with Talbott. But he don't say so around Ike. I fear he's layin' fer Ike."

"Ben don't never bring home no talk from town," Melissa said. "Ol' Eldridge says there was some talk 'bout filing charges against Neeson fer stealin', but nobody wants to take the lead."

"Melissa, have you still got that Ol' Eldridge hangin' around? He'll sit twenty years behind yore stove, let you wait on him, cookin' his grub, washin' his clothes. He orta be run off."

"I've told Ben but he says—"

Crying came from inside the house. Melissa jumped up. "Law alive, I was so enjoyin' myself until the youngun bellered. I'll move on to home. Wish you'd come see me, Shug."

"Ben Baker don't cotton to me. Someday when he's gone, you send Carter a-gallopin' over here, and I'll come set a spell with you."

Melissa turned her horse toward the Filaree. Staring out across the silent land, she thought of Neeson's threat and shuddered.

10.

It was Monday afternoon when Ben Baker and Old Man Eldridge pulled up the wagon at the Filaree Ranch. Baker got down and called for the children to come unload the wagon. "Hannah, I'm gonna need a hand."

Melissa walked from the house. "Hannah ain't here. She and the younguns went with Ma and Pa to clean the weeds outa the graveyard. Only Carter's here. He's irrigating the alfalfa. I'll call him."

"Hell's fire and damnation. I don't approve of those younguns goin' off with your kin."

Ben Baker's skin was blotched with dust, and the dust whitened his eyebrows and mustache. He nudged back his grimy hat, exposing the upper part of his brow, pale where the sun had not reached it. His lower forehead was burned as brown as the harness reins he held in his hands. Circles of sweat darkened the armpits and the back of his blue shirt. The edges of his eyes were rimmed red, small blood vessels streaked from the corners marring the white. His nose displayed purple vein marks. He swore at Carter, "Damn you, ain't worth powder and lead it'd take to blow you to kingdom come. That ain't where you unload the flour. Take it to the house." Melissa smelled whiskey on his breath.

Eldridge walked toward the house, leaving the unloading to the children and Ben Baker. In the kitchen, he refreshed himself at the galvanized bucket of water. Taking the tin dipper, he slurped the water, swallowing in great gulps. He meandered to his favorite stakeout to reestablish his claim, the chair behind the cookstove. As he went, he reached for a cup and saucer and poured himself a cup from the pot of coffee boiling on the stove. Settling himself in "his" chair, he "saucered" the coffee. When he lifted the cup to his mouth, the steam warned him. Pouring a bit of the hot liquid into the saucer, he blew on it, and then lifted the saucer to his lips.

Melissa looked up from the board where she was cutting salt pork into thick slices. "Howdy, Eldridge. How's yore trip to Roosevelt?" She tried not to sound uncivil.

Eldridge related his version of the run-in with Neeson, Tommie Fulton and Ike Talbott, which had taken place the night before the dance. "Neeson left the saloon, said he was headin' this way and might get him a varmint on the way. Some thought he was headin' for the El Bar Ranch."

Melissa put her hand to her breast as if to hide the pounding inside. As casually as she could, she asked, "Why would he be headin' toward the El Bar?"

"Oh, he's been talkin' big about having a set-to with Talbott."

Melissa felt a chill go through her. She did not wish Eldridge to see her. She busied herself by going outside and driving the flies away from the screen door where they hovered; the odor of the yeast bread rising had brought them to the door.

That night after the family had gone to bed, Melissa stood in the room she shared with her husband. She brushed the hair she called "hateful" and spoke to the unpleasing hump under the patchwork quilt. "Eldridge says that Ted Neeson's a-comin' up here with idee about gunnin' fer Ike Talbott. I am afeerd—"

The bulge under the covers grunted. "Naw. That's drunk talk. He's really yeller. Thinks he kin scare Ike."

"Eldridge said—"

"Neeson ain't a-gonna push Ike too far."

Her husband's voice softened and he said, "Did you-uns git along all right while I was gone? I tried to git what you wanted —the ribbons an' the gimcracks." His unaccustomed mellifluousness dismayed her. Melissa hoped it didn't mean what she thought. She felt her flesh tighten. She dreaded the closeness of his body—and she wanted no more children. To delay going to bed she busied herself, putting away clothing and rearranging articles on the bureau. She moved the porcelain chamber pot from the corner to a place under the bed at the foot, and waited. She listened for his regular breathing.

Ben Baker raised his hulking shoulders on one elbow. "Ain't you comin' to bed?" His voice was commanding. "Fiddle-faddlin' around." Melissa walked slowly to the coal oil lamp on the bureau. Holding her hand cupped above the chimney, she extinguished the glow. In the darkness she found the bed and pushed her body between the sheets. She felt the roughness of the unbleached muslin. Her husband's bulging stomach moved toward her frail body. She stiffened, turning her face from the tobacco breath and the stale sweat odor, and closed her eyes.

11.

The next afternoon Ben and Hannah went to the pasture to change the irrigation water. Mary Belle and Annie walked to their secret playhouse behind the orchard, where they moved their furniture of rocks and moss rugs. Spider, with cheesecloth tied around a hoop of baling wire, swept the bushes for errant bugs. Carter sat spraddle-legged on the floor of the porch, braiding leather strips to repair a bridle rein. Baby crawled on a quilt spread on the floor near Melissa, who was cutting Benjy Boy's hair.

Inside the house, Eldridge lolled in his chair behind the stove, picking his teeth with a broomstraw and turning the pages of The Sears, Roebuck Catalogue. He mused over the harness department, tracing the words with his forefinger. A midafternoon stillness lay over the ranch. Even the chickens and stock settled in the shade to rest.

"Ouch, Mama—that hurt." Benjy hunched his shoulders. "Them scissors is dull. They pull."

Melissa lifted the shears. "Sorry. I didn't go to hurt you. Sit still. Turn around." She pulled Benjy's head toward her and snipped at the brown hair streaked and sunbleached to the color and dryness of straw. "Yore hair's like a thatch of dried foxtail weed, and that sun's blistered your nose. That's what you git fer not wearin' a hat in this godawful country."

Except for the flies that buzzed about the porch, hovering at the screen door, nothing disrupted the quiet. Melissa spoke to Carter. "Son, do you feel somethin' funny in the air?"

"Naw, Ma. It's jist like enny other day."

"Seems particular still. Like somethin' brewin'. I'd say a storm was comin' but there ain't a cloud in sight. No wind, but jist that fearsome hush. I got a feelin' . . . ." She cut a tag end of Benjy's hair.

"Look, Mama, down the road. Somebody's a-comin'. I kin hear the horse beatin' the dirt." Carter extended a hand toward the road.

Melissa looked where Carter pointed. She saw a blur of movement amid a haze of dust, coming closer to the ranch. She kept her eyes on the dust cloud until the blur materialized into a rider on horseback.

Carter stood up, stretching his neck for a better view. "Hit's a sorrel horse. Looks like Uncle Jimso's mare. He's whippin' that horse somethin' terrible." He watched the man on horseback loom nearer. "Yep, that's Uncle Jimso."

The man and animal reached the front gate. The rider pulled hard on the reins, causing the mare's hind feet to slide in the dirt, and her front hoofs to pull off the ground; froth dripped from the animal's mouth. Jimso Holman was off the horse in a leap. Throwing the reins over the animal's head, he let them drag the ground. He ran toward the house and bounded onto the porch.

"Where's Ben? Where is he?" Before Melissa could answer, he screamed, "Dammit to hell, where is he?"

Melissa said, "Jimso, whatever ails ye? Set down and get yore breath." She called to Benjy, "Run git yore pa. He's in the alfalfa." She was concerned. It was seldom that her brother showed at the Filaree Ranch, knowing Ben Baker's feelings as he did.

Melissa went inside and brought her brother a dipper of water. Old Man Eldridge came out, scratching his head of thin, graying hair. "What's the ruckus about?" He looked at the heaving horse at the front gate. "Yore powerful fussed. You best cool out that horse."

Jimso swigged down the water and flopped on the porch floor, his legs hanging off the edge. "Sis, I'm sorry 'bout cussin' and gittin' riled up." He motioned to Carter. "I'd be obliged if you'd walk that old pony. He's hot. Loosen the cinch."

"Jimso, what is it?" Melissa asked.

"Sis, there's bin a killin'. I found Ted Neeson's body. Down the road. I guess he was killed. I didn't stop to look. He shore didn't git bucked off his horse—"

Ben Baker hurried onto the porch, the fast pace out of keeping with his usual stolid movements, with Benjy running ahead. His glance was hostile as he looked at his brother-in-law. "What the hell? Sendin' Benjy yellin' fer me to run?"

Jimso's words tumbled one over the other. "Ted Neeson's dead. I found him. In the road. Was cuttin' across startin' for home."

"Where was he?"

"On that road turning off toward the El Bar."

"That's not far from here."

"That's why I come here. Yore ranch was the closest place. I didn't stop to look him over. I knowed I'd best git help. Gotta report this to the sheriff. They'll wanta investigate. We'll need a wagon."

Ben Baker spat on the ground. "So the sonofabitch is dead. He had it comin'. Wonder who done it?"

"I don't know. I didn't touch him—just saw the blood and the flies buzzin', and I lit a shuck over here."

Baker waited to see if Jimso had finished. "We'll harness Roanie and Baldy and git the wagon to carry the body." He turned to Carter, who was tugging his sleeve. "Go git that big tarp and throw it in the wagon. No, take that old torn wagon sheet in the barn. Neeson ain't worth ruining a good canvas."

"Papa, kin I go with you? I could help." There was a tremor in Carter's voice.

"No. Ain't no place fer younguns. Don't know what we'll run into. Eldridge and Jimso and I'll have our hands full without havin' you to worry about."

Carter took flying jumps as he ran to the barn and carried the torn tarp to the wagon. After the men had left in the wagon, he went to the barn and took a rope off the nail. Running to the pasture, he caught Brownie, fastened a hackamore around the horse's head and muzzle and led him through the back pasture gate. Jumping on bareback, he took a shortcut which avoided the road, and headed his horse toward the river that went by the turnoff to the El Bar Ranch.

There, he hid his horse back among the willows that grew thick along the banks. Rolling up his britches' legs and carrying his shoes, he walked downstream. When he approached the El Bar crossing, he waited, looking in the sky for the telltale buzzards. Last week he and his father had found a dead cow by following their circling.

He listened for the sound of the wagon but heard nothing yet. He entertained himself by taking a reed, breaking it, and pushing out the pithy center; then he blew a low whistle from the hollowed weed. He heard the far-off rumble of wagon wheels. Throwing away the reed, he crept out of the water. Drying his feet in the soft sand, he put on his shoes. He heard the wagon come closer and then stop.

Carter positioned himself behind a thicket of heavy brush on the bank, and cautiously peeked through the cover. He saw his father, his uncle Jimso Holman, and Old Man Eldridge staring at a crumpled heap of clothing in the road. When the men walked back to the wagon, the boy eased his body closer and erected a blind of reeds in front of him. Motionless, his body flat, he waited.

Ben Baker pushed the body over with the toe of his boot. "The bastard is sure dead. Shot in the chest. Whoever it was, the killer done us all a favor."

Jimso spoke. "Look. His head. Turn his head. They shot his eye out." A second shot had forced out the eye, leaving a gaping hole in the skull.

Ben Baker's gaze settled on a small object near the head. Insects were already clustering on it. "My God! Here it is. His goddamned eye!"

Eldridge edged closer. "You suppose the law would want that—as evidence?"

Jimso took a Bull Durham tobacco sack from his shirt pocket, and emptied the contents on the ground. With two sticks he lifted the eye and dropped it into the sack. Then stooping, he dropped the packet into the man's shirt pocket. "Here, Neeson, is yore goddamned eye."

"We've done all we can," Ben Baker said. "Where d'ya suppose Neeson's horse took off to? 'Spect he'll turn up. We'll start to Roosevelt with the body."

Carter pushed a wider peephole in the reeds and found himself looking at the first dead person he had ever seen. The man's upturned face, even at this distance, looked pale in the hot sun—or was it just the dust that made it look that way? Carter could see green flies weaving above the spot where the eye was missing. The flies buzzed and fought for position. The odor of death reached the boy. He held his mouth with his hand. He thought he was going to be sick.

But he remained where he was as if magnetized by the sight of death. The boy watched the men pick up the body by the legs and arms and throw it into the bed of the wagon. Then his father flopped the canvas over the body, and got into the wagon with Eldridge. Jimso followed on his horse. The boy waited until he could no longer hear the wagon. He slid his body down the bank and started back across the creek. But long before he reached the horse hidden in the willows, he had to lean over and vomit.

12. Melissa was in the kitchen making bread when she heard the knock at the back door. Someone whispered her name, and the knock sounded again.

She opened the back door. Ike Talbott stood there. "Yore alone, ain't you, Melissa? I been watchin' the house. Saw Carter ride off." She sensed an urgency in his voice. "I got to talk to you. My horse is tied in the elderberry trees. Follow me." With his great strides he was off the porch and away.

With a growing feeling of apprehension, she poked wood in the stove, took her sunbonnet off the wall, and hurried after him. She found him standing behind a big tree.

"Melissa, I don't have much time. I got to leave The Mesa. Had a run-in with Ted Neeson. He come up here gunnin' for me. We met on the road yesterday. He cussed me and pulled out his gun, but he missed. I shot back. I hit him twice. He fell off his horse. I didn't wait to see anything else. But I know I killed him."

Melissa reached up and pulled Ike's head toward her. "He had it comin'."

Ike put his hands on her shoulders. "I been hidin' out all night. Sure, if I hadn't shot him, he'd have killed me. But Ted's got relatives with lots of power in Globe City. They're a mean outfit. And the sheriff is wantin' reelection. He'd do anything to cinch that job. He'd have all the Neesons behind him if he nabbed me. I can't wait for no trial, and 'twouldn't be a fair trial nohow. It'll be prison for me if I stay."

The woman bit her lip. "He needed killin'. He's done more thievin' and scarin' good people."

"I know. I know. But that won't save me. I got to make a run for it. I'm gonna hide out at Big Mesquite Thicket for a week or so, and then stay in a hideout I know in the Sierra Anchas. I'll hang around there until this cools down. Then I'll make for New Mexico. I got friends in Silver City."

Melissa wiped away tears. "I'm goin' to the house and pack you some food."

"Melissa, I want to leave you my six-shooter. Hide it. I don't wanta be found carryin' a gun if the sheriff catches up with me." He laid the gun in her palm. It was a Colt .45. "I ain't never gonna carry a gun no more," he said.

She ran her fingers over the gun stock. "I'll keep it where nobody'll find it. Don't worry. I'm goin' to the house and pack you some grub," Melissa said. "You wait. I'll make haste." She sprinted toward the ranch.

At the house she secreted the gun high on a ledge on the back porch. She went inside and packed a flour sack with food. Leftover fried meat. Biscuits. Jerky. Apples. Canned corn. Coffee. She looked down the road to make sure no one was coming and raced back down to the elderberry trees.

He put his arms around her until she hurt for breath. "My sweet girl. For years I've wanted you." Then he picked up the sack and walked to his horse.

Melissa did not watch him go. She held her head down until she heard the sound of the horse's hoofs diminishing.

At the house she sought a place to hide the gun. She had to do it quickly before someone came back. The trunk? The bottom dresser drawer? The chest with the quilts? None of them seemed right. She stumbled on the loose floorboard on the porch. The answer came to her. She pried at the nails with the claw hammer until the board was free. Wrapping the gun in a ragged piece of sheet, she reached far under the porch, placing the pistol on a joist against the house. Carefully she replaced the plank and nailed it securely.

She had put the light bread loaves into the oven when Old Eldridge came into the kitchen. "Ben let me out at the bend," he said. "Him and Jimso went on to take the body to Roosevelt. That Neeson was a horrible sight. Two shots. Blood. Flies. And his eye was shot out. What d' ya think of that?"

Melissa forced her voice to sound casual. "Who do you think shot him? Any idea?"

"Anybody could've done it. He had more enemies than that old shepherd pup has fleas. But whoever it was, the sheriff'll be lookin' mighty good fer him."

Melissa's mind was on Big Mesquite Thicket. "When d'ya think the sheriff might get here?"

"Could be sometime tomorrow. Ben and Jimso was gonna drive right on. Oh, Ben told me to tell you. Wanted you to get word to Brownell that he couldn't go lion huntin' with him now. John found a calf, part eat up, covered with twigs. Cougar work. John was takin' his dogs, and he and Ben were goin' after the cat."

"Carter ain't here. When he comes in, I'll send him." *Lion hunting?* She thought of the man, tawny as a cougar, who was riding toward Big Mesquite Thicket.

13. Melissa was surprised to see her husband ride into the ranch on horseback the next afternoon. "I let Jimso take the body to Roosevelt," Ben Baker explained as he unsaddled. "I borrowed a horse at Oatfield to come back here so I could go with Brownell after that lion. At the Dam, Jimso was goin' telephone Globe City about the killin'. I expect the sheriff'll be out here any time now. But he'll find lean pickin' when he comes up here tryin' to git talk outa The Mesa folks."

That night the children were already in bed when the sheriff and his deputy knocked on the door at the Filaree. The men looked wearied. The sheriff obviously wanted to waste little time on questioning. "Baker, when you picked up the body did you see anything that'd give us a lead on the killer?"

"No. We just picked up his body and left. We saw tracks but we didn't pay 'em much heed."

"We're goin' go back and see those tracks. We been ridin' all this day across The Mesa. Seems strange nobody knows anything. They won't talk. That youngest Fulton boy said he saw Ike Talbott riding over the ridge the day Neeson was shot."

"Sheriff, don't pay no mind to that Fulton boy. He ain't right bright. He coulda seen anybody ridin' and not knowed who it was."

"We're goin' go to the El Bar and see. Then we'll circle this whole country and stop at every water hole. We're gonna stay here till we find the killer. He's still here." The sheriff showed his irritability. "Funny no one saw or heard nothing. Tonight we stay at the Brownells', and at daylight we're striking out hunting. We'll come across him." The officers rode away.

Baker turned to Melissa. "That sheriff is around here sniffin' like a hound dog pickin' up a lion's scent. He'll be off in the mornin' like he's on a hot trail, a-runnin' and a-bayin', tryin' to tree that lion."

Baker started toward the bedroom. "I'm goin' to bed. I'm plumb wore out. Been ridin' almost solid for two days. Pertnear asleep right now." He closed the bedroom door.

Melissa waited. She had a plan. She blew out the kerosene lamp and went into the bedroom. In the dimness she saw her husband's form in the bed, his face turned toward the wall. She dawdled, playing for time. She took off her dress and under-clothes, hanging them on the wall. Her shoes she placed by the open door. She removed the bone hairpins from her head, letting her long hair fall to her waist. Slowly she pulled the long gathered nightgown over her head and slid into the bed, letting her slim body rest on the outside rail. She waited.

Her husband's breathing became deep and regular. His heavy snores reverberated through the room. Melissa moved one leg from under the cover and stopped. She pushed out the other and waited again. Then she picked up her shoes and went out into the kitchen, where she took a sweater from a nail. She made her way to the barn by the faint light of the moon, and fumbling against the inside wall, searched out a bridle.

In the corral, the horses were asleep, resting their bodies on secured, locked legs. Melissa recognized her favorite, Brownie, and walked slowly toward the horse, talking as she touched his flank, so as not to startle him. After forcing the bit into his mouth, she pulled the bridle over the horse's ears, and led him silently from the corral to the open trail. She paused to take a deep breath, then leaped on the animal. Straightening the folds of her full nightgown, she kicked Brownie into a gallop.

Her long hair blew back from her face, and she inhaled the wind. She rode two miles down the trail, until she could see the dark outline of Big Mesquite Thicket. She made out a faint glow in the darkness ahead. It was the embers of the fire. She stopped before she entered the enclosure and called softly, "Ike. Ike." A blanket-shrouded form stirred and a head lifted. "Who is it?"

"Melissa." She slid from the horse's back.

"My God, Melissa! What're you doin' here?" Ike Talbott stood up and reached for her.

"I had to come." Quickly she related all she had heard the sheriff say.

Talbott held her tightly. "Don't worry. I won't wait for daylight to leave."

"Ike, you've got to hurry—now."

But she did not resist as he pulled her to the quilt on the ground. Melissa quivered as she lay beside his body. Suddenly her desire for this man consumed her. Ben Baker did not matter. Her children faded into the background. She lay quietly and let him do what he wanted.

"I got to go," she said. "Look at the moon. I'm fearful for you."

"I can travel fine."

As she stood up and adjusted her nightgown, he put his lips against her neck. She reached for the horse's bridle. Ike's voice came behind her. "Here, I'll lift you up." He made a cradle of his hands and hoisted her onto the horse. "You know I'd go with you if I could," she said.

"I know."

She reined the animal out of the thicket. The horse lunged ahead and broke into a gallop. Melissa knew that she must not look back.

14. Outside on the porch Old Man Eldridge sat visiting
with William Brownell. The Brownell boy, since quitting
school, had gone to work on the El Bar outfit. Today he had
stopped by the ranch as he passed, hunting for stock.

Melissa, sewing, heard snatches of their conversation. "Say,
William, has the El Bar heered anything about Ike Talbott?"

She jabbed her finger with the needle as she strained to hear
the answer.

"Nothin'. Sheriff come out again with questions. He's talkin'
about goin' to arrest Ike. The El Bar just wants to forget the
whole business. They're glad Neeson's dead." The boy said
goodbye, and Eldridge came inside.

The old man refreshed himself at the galvanized bucket of
water, helped himself to coffee, and established himself in the
chair behind the stove, saucering his coffee. Hearing the slurping sound, Melissa's head began to throb. She wished that her
husband would listen to her for once and ask Eldridge to leave.
She was coming to hate his uninvited presence.

Hannah, who had been making a new shirtwaist for school,
came into the kitchen. Over her petticoat she wore the unfinished blouse; one sleeve was pinned to the garment, but her
other shoulder was bare. "Mama, can you help me? I cain't get
the sleeve to fit right."

Before Melissa could answer, she heard the baby cry.
"Annie, go give Baby a sugar tit while I help Hannah."

Melissa turned and saw Eldridge still slurping his coffee, his
Adam's apple moving up and down as he swallowed. His eyes
fastened on Hannah's bare shoulder.

Melissa examined the sleeve, taking out the pins and putting
them in her mouth. She mumbled, and Hannah understood
that her mother wanted her to stand in brighter light. Hannah

moved toward the window where the sun's rays fell strong on her white skin. Melissa could see that the girl was maturing into womanhood. She glanced again at Eldridge. The old man's gaze was still fastened on Hannah's bare shoulder. Eldridge flicked out his tongue, slowly drawing it across his wrinkled lips. "Come to the bedroom, Hannah," Melissa said. "I'll finish pinning yore blouse in there."

In the other room Melissa sat down in an attempt to calm herself. Her hand shook with fury. "Just a minute, daughter, I'll git to the pinnin'." She kept the girl in the bedroom a long time, and by the time they returned to the kitchen, Eldridge was gone.

Melissa prepared supper. "We're goin' to eat early. Yore papa's still out ridin'." Eldridge was not around. The children ate and went to bed.

When Ben Baker came in, Melissa filled his plate with food, still warm on the stove. He said, "I wasted a whole day ridin' with the sheriff, lookin' for Talbott. Glad he cain't be found. I'm gittin' up early in the morning, gotta make up for this wasted day." He walked into the bedroom.

Melissa had barely dropped off to sleep when the bedroom door opened and she heard Hannah's voice. "Mama, Annie's cryin' somethin' awful. Maybe she's sick. She won't tell me where she hurts. When I ask her, she cries all the harder."

"You go back to bed. I'll come see what the matter is." Melissa went into the girl's room and patted the child until the sobbing eased. "Do you have a hurtin'? Is it your earache again?" Annie erupted into uncontrolled sobbing.

Melissa was alarmed. "Tell me where the pain is."

Between gulps, the child said, "I . . . M-Mister-Mister Eldridge . . ." she was stuttering worse than usual. "H-he asked me did I want to go huntin' rabbits with him. You were with Hannah fixin' her dress. He told me . . . he n-needed help. T-that you wanted rabbit for supper. I said I would help him." The girl again broke down in tears.

Melissa patted her daughter's head. The girl continued: "He walked me to the big cottonwood tree. There was n-no rabbits. He told me to l-lie down on the ground. He lifted my dress. He said it would feel good. And I wasn't to tell anybody. He put his fingers—Mama!" Weeping convulsed the child.

Melissa's mind went blank. The urge to kill swept over her. She tightened her arms around the child, now exhausted into quietness. She said, "Tell Mama. Did Mister Eldridge do—anything else to you?"

The child's voice was still broken with sobs. "No. When he put his fingers up under my dress, I jumped up and ran home, fast as I could. Then I stayed out by the barn till suppertime."

"It's all right, Annie. Mother understands. Just go to sleep." She kissed the closed eyelids and smoothed the hair of the quivering child. When Melissa was sure that Annie was asleep, she went back into the bedroom and woke her husband. "Ben Baker, I wanta talk to you."

"Christ A-mighty, woman, not tonight. It's late. I'm tired. Talk to you in the morning."

"No. It won't wait."

"Hell's fire and damnation. It's near morning now, and I ain't in no mood fer gabbin'."

The man tried to quiet his wife, but she would have none of it. She had to tell him what had happened to Annie.

"It's nothin' but child's talk," he said in a gruff voice. "Pay it no mind. Eldridge didn't mean no harm. She mighta thought—"

Melissa clenched her hands. "It *ain't* no lie. Eldridge is a coyote, a mangy varmint. Oughta be quartered and hung up. He—" Her voice broke and angry tears smeared her cheeks.

"Dammit, hush. The youngun exaggerated. Eldridge is a friend. Didn't mean nothin'. No harm."

"*No harm?*" Her voice was incisive as a knife. "You run that skunk off this ranch—or so help me, God, I'll kill him. First thing in the morning, you tell him to git."

"I ain't a gonna do nothin' of the sort." Ben Baker lay down again, and soon fell asleep. Melissa thought of Eldridge out there on his cot, and of how men castrated young bulls in the corral at branding time. She pictured herself in that corral, holding a bone-handled knife above his groin . . .

Ben Baker arose at daylight. She heard him saddle his horse and ride away. Her anger surged anew. The house was quiet and the children asleep. Annie was asleep, too, and Melissa bent and put her lips against the tear stains on the child's cheeks, and tasted the salt. Then she opened the screen door and looked on the back porch. In the dim light she saw the bundled form of Old Man Eldridge on the cot.

Still in her nightgown, she went back into the kitchen and took the shotgun down from the rack. With the gun barrel she poked the figure on the cot. The old man raised a gray head above the quilts and grunted. She waited until she knew he was awake.

Her voice was hard. "You yellow-livered bastard. Git up. Git yore bundle of clothes and git off this ranch. I mean, git yore horse and ride—plumb outa this country!"

"What? What?" The old man sat up, clutching the quilts around him.

She prodded him with the barrel, her voice rising in fury. "Don't ask questions. Just git! I don't mean jist off this ranch, I mean outa this country. You skunk. Filthy polecat. They don't come no lower than you. My little girl, Annie—" Tears stopped her words.

The man quivered, "Now, Miz Baker, don't git excited. I—"

She shoved the gun barrel into the man's face. "I'm goin' in the house and git dressed. When I come out here again, I don't want to see you. If you ain't gone, I'm gonna let you have both barrels. You'll be deader'n Ted Neeson. It won't be just yore eye that's shot out. Now, git!" The cold barrel struck the man's nose.

Melissa stumbled back into the kitchen and supported her

trembling form against the door frame. She heard the man moving on the porch.

She poked pine kindling on some paper in the stove and lighted the fire, opening the damper. When the fire took blaze, she added juniper chips and listened to the crackle, and then closed the damper halfway. She did not go into the bedroom to dress, but sat in the kitchen with the shotgun resting across her knees, listening.

Outside a rooster announced the coming of daylight. A hound growled. But Melissa was waiting for another sound. Then she heard the horse's hoofs. Rising, she looked out the doorway. Old Man Eldridge was kicking his horse down the road, a bundle of clothes tied behind the saddle cantle.

Melissa walked outside on the porch, watching the retreating figure. Then she held the gunsight to her eye, aimed, and pulled the trigger. The gun was empty. "SONOFABITCH!" she bellowed at the minuscule man on horseback.

15.

Ben Baker wanted to take Carter with him on the hunt for mountain lions and missing cattle. But Melissa refused to let her son lose even two days of school. "If it has to be, I'll take the baby and ride up with you. I kin keep camp and watch the corral. We kin leave Hannah here. She's took care of the outfit before."

"Suits me. I didn't want him out of school, but since Ol' Man Eldridge is gone, since you run him off—"

Melissa flared. "Mebbe we best leave that old devil out of it. All the good he'd-a done you was palaver. Don't use him as a excuse."

"All right. Sizzle down. We'll leave in the mornin'. The road's good enough to take the wagon to the Old Role Place, where we kin camp. I kin ride the mountain from there."

The next day Ben and Melissa Baker set up camp at Walnut Gulch, named from the gigantic black walnut trees that towered above the creek flowing into a narrow canyon. A quarter of a century earlier a family had settled here. They had long since been "starved out" and had moved on, leaving scattered ruins as a reminder of their striving. The Mesa ranchers referred to Walnut Gulch as "the Old Role Place" after the family which "couldn't last out the drouth." Increasingly these days, Ben Baker talked of selling out the Filaree, and Melissa wondered if it would share the same fate.

Now the man rode the hills; his wife stayed alone in the abandoned homestead. She encountered the presence of the Role woman everywhere, in the loneliness, in the box nailed to the tree for an outside cupboard, in the river rocks lining the pathway, in the gnarled plantings of vines and bushes. In these mournful remnants, Melissa could sense the frustrations she must have endured, the agony of defeat.

Melissa walked to the corral and ran her hand over the cedar posts. She knew that the Role man, too, had tried. Cedar trees grew in higher country, and he must have traveled miles to bring them to the homestead, knowing that they would not rot in the ground like the cottonwoods from the creek. Melissa stepped along the barbed wire fence enclosing the home area, the wire rusted and twisted and broken, parts sagging and imbedded in the earth. Of the house, only the chipped and broken settlings of a fireplace remained. The roof had years ago fallen in. Ranchers, camped for the roundups, had used the planks for firewood and had thrown their trash into the fireplace. Before she could cook there, Melissa had to clean out the debris.

On the open flat of a hillside Melissa came upon a tiny oblong mound of dirt, nearly obscured by weeds and foxtail grass, but unmistakably outlined by granite river rock. She picked up a splintered wooden cross; the crude lettering that had been cut into it was barely visible. She stepped back hastily as if she had trespassed. She was certain that the mound marked the grave of the baby who had been born to the Role woman. Melissa Baker stood, silent and depressed, staring at the mound and remembering her loss of her own first-born, left in a similar ranch grave in Texas. Part of her had died with that first child; a love had been buried in Texas. She thought of the Role woman who must have stood here, crushed by the same grief.

The wind in the sycamore trees made a rustling conversation with the leaves. The breeze blew against the wetness of her cheeks, and it tangled the strands of hair escaping from under her sunbonnet. Melissa strained to control the trembling that threatened to attack her. The loneliness of this place frightened her. She felt small and lost, isolated and unimportant.

Back in camp, she prepared the bed for sleeping. Tugging at the heavy canvas bedroll on the ground where the man had tossed it, she hoisted it onto a sagging bedstead that some previous camper had left. Untying the rope from the bedroll, she pulled and straightened the tarp covering, spread out the comforters, and averted her nose from the sudden rush of mustiness. Unused and unaired since the last camping trip, the bedding was dank with human odors, and she spread the quilts and blankets about on the ground and bushes to freshen them.

She went to the wagon bed where she had left the baby on a quilt to exercise. She changed her diapers and breast-fed her. She put the baby in an Indian cradleboard she had brought, lacing the child's body against the board with her arms free, and handing her a piece of jerky to suck. The child stuck the dried beef in her lips and began to mouth it. Melissa hung the baby in the cradleboard on a tree in the shade. Though it was already late afternoon, the sun was still hot.

Ben Baker rode in, carrying a bundle wrapped in an old tarp piece over his saddle.

"The Brownells butchered a yearling and give us a quarter."

Baker threw the bundle on the ground. The hound and the

shepherd dog sniffed the meat, stirring up the weeds and dust. He threw a rock at them. "Git away, you scoundrels. You'll git yore share." Untying the canvas, he sliced off a piece of meat and gave it to Melissa. "This 'nough fer supper?" Then he tied a rope to the end of the meat, securing it under a bone joint; throwing the end of the rope over a limb, he pulled the meat fifteen feet off the ground. "That orta be high 'nough to keep them damn hounds from reachin' it."

They rose before daybreak. The thin sky had not yet shown light above the Sierra Ancha horizon. The air was biting with chill. The man lowered the meat, which was as cold as if it had been packed in January snow from the Four Peaks. He cut off some for the woman for breakfast and rewrapped it. He insulated the remainder by wrapping it in an extra saddle blanket and placing it in the center of the bedroll, covering the whole in a canvas which he left in the shade.

The woman dressed in the shivering blue of the dawn. Dutifully she gave her breast to the baby and then laced the child onto the cradleboard. Life in the camp was awakening. Baker said, "Them damn quail is makin' a hell of a racket comin' off the roostin' tree." A jackrabbit scurried from the brush to stop and look at the human beings and then to scamper off. The man had made a fire, and Melissa stopped to stare at the weird flame pictures that formed and re-formed to burn anew. Baker sat on a rock to pull off his boot. "What ye moonin' over that fire fer?" He put his hand on his boot heel and slipped off the boot. He shook out a pebble. "Nigh crippled me, that rock." He forced his toe into his boot and stood up. "I'll feed the horses. After breakfast, I'll work the ridge fer a couple of hours. Then we'll break camp and head fer home." He cleared his throat and spat on the ground. The woman turned away.

Before noon Ben Baker returned. They packed up the camp gear, loaded it into the wagon, and rode out of the lonely spot. The spirit of the Role woman and the memory of the isolated grave on the hillside continued to haunt Melissa.

Thunder sounded, and she looked at the mountains to see dark clouds forming among them.

16.

Hannah came into the house. "It shore looks like a storm is comin'. And I jist got the clothes hung up. Mebbe it'll pass us by." The skies grew darker, lightning ripped the Four Peaks, and guttural thunder rumbled the air. The rain began in scattered drops. Hannah went to the door and looked out. "Carter, you boys come in. Put the chickens in the hen house."

The air became electric. Far-off rain scented the land. The atmosphere throbbed. The animals moved irritably and raised their voices. The colt raced up and down the pasture. The milch cow bawled in apprehension. The children stayed together in the kitchen as the spring storm gathered and broke in violent force, pounding the house and making rivulets in the yard. Hannah built up the fire. "I'll make some cocoa," she said.

The children walked outside to the porch and watched the road turn into a small river. They grew restless. Hannah suggested games, and for a while they remained in the house. The storm slipped away as suddenly as it had arrived. The children watched the wind blow the dark clouds westward and the sky show blue again.

Mary Belle and Annie walked outside. "Let's go down and see if the water in that ol' wash has come up," Mary Belle suggested.

"We ain't allowed to play there. Mama says it's dangerous. Water comes down off the mountains."

"It wasn't much of a storm. Sky's blue now." Annie followed Mary Belle to the arroyo. "See. It's dry. Let's go play on Big Rock." She pointed at a large flat boulder, an island of stone in the middle of the creek.

Annie planted her feet on the bank. "No! Mama says we cain't play there when it's been rainin'."

"Mama says, Mama says. Scairty cat. You are Mama's little goody girl. You always try to act so sweet so everybody'll say you're so good." Mary Belle climbed to the flat surface of Big Rock. "I'm on my castle. I can see for miles."

"You come back here, Mary Belle Baker. You come off that rock. I'm gonna tell Hannah."

"Hannah ain't the boss o' me."

"You'll get yore britches tanned when Mama gets back."

The girls, arguing, did not hear the rumble in the creek. The flood seemed to come out of nowhere. Then, with a roar, the water pounded past Big Rock, an angry, swirling, brown, crashing from bank to bank. The flood tore at the earth, spitting up froth, heaving skeletal trees, and rolling boulders; a dead skunk swept by and was sucked under. Mary Belle crouched low on the rock island, her eyes riveted on the rising waters, her face whiter than the crest of the waves that whipped around her.

Annie screamed from the bank, but her voice did not carry above the crunching voice of the flood. "Mary Belle, I'm goin' git Hannah—" She ran toward the ranch house.

Huddled on the rock, Mary Belle watched boulders as big as her mother's washtub crash by. The waters screamed and rose higher. Lifting her eyes toward the bank, the frightened girl saw her mother, waving and yelling; the other children were grouped around her on the bank. A tree limb swept by, catching Mary Belle and knocking her flat. It was all she could do to hold on.

The girl looked at her family on the creek's bank. She saw her father riding the big mule, Jumbo, to the water's edge. He was coiling his rope as he rode. Her father reached the bank and forced the mule into the water's edge, testing. The mule balked.

Ben Baker tried again and was forced back by a sudden wall of water carrying a cottonwood ahead of it. The man and the mule backed out.

The family on the bank and the isolated girl on the rock waited, waving arms and shouting to each other, and watching the water. They waited. Time dragged. Then Mary Belle saw her mother making measuring signs with her hands. She was pointing to the rock's edge, and Mary Belle could see that the water line was lowering.

An hour passed. Ben Baker whipped the big mule into the water again. Jumbo stepped hesitantly and then was out into the muddy flow. Slowly, the rider and animal worked their way across the creek bottom toward Big Rock. Baker guided the mule to the lower end of the rock where the water flow was broken. Reaching out his hand, he pulled the trembling girl onto the back of his saddle. Mary Belle closed her eyes and scrunched her body close against her father, her arms clutching him around his waist.

The big mule pulled itself out of the water and climbed to the muddy bank. Gruffly, Ben Baker told Mary Belle to get off. "You got no more sense than God gave a goose," he said. Then he remounted and rode to the house.

Mary Belle felt her mother's arms around her. "Mary Belle, you-all needs a good thrashin'." The child did not answer; her head was bowed in sobs.

Carter's voice held disgust. "Mary Belle, you're plumb loco. What'd you wanta do that for? You know we've been tol' and tol' not to—"

"Hush, Carter." Melissa stopped the boy. "The child's had enough of a scare."

"Mama, why didn't you let her stay out on that rock till the flood stopped?" Spider asked. "Papa coulda been drowned."

"We couldn't. See that storm in the mountains? Another rain's comin', and it's gettin' on dark. We's lucky it went down enough for your papa to cross. Any more water would've covered Big Rock. And thank God, we got back in time."

The group trudged to the house, Melissa holding Mary Belle's hand. The girl continued to sob uncontrollably. Melissa tightened her grip. "That's all right. You've had a hard lesson."

Ben Baker had unsaddled the mule and was gone. The rain had resumed. Melissa said, "You-all stay in outa that rain. If you want to, you can cook up a batch of taffy. I'm just gonna walk out on the porch."

Melissa Baker wanted to be alone. She suddenly felt let down. At the Brownells', Martha had told her that the sheriff had left The Mesa, getting no information from anyone, only knowing that Ike Talbott was not at the El Bar. "Ike just had took his pony and vamoosed. Nary a person knows what happened. Everybody on The Mesa knowed it was Ike what done ol' Neeson in, but they wouldn't tell the sheriff nothin'. That Fulton boy tried to tell he heard a shot, but his pa shut him up fast."

Melissa watched the rain roll off the tin roof. The breeze brought the odor of wet dung from the corral. She looked at the unpainted porch, the rain making the wood dark and dirty-looking. The old feeling of futility bore down on her. Her love for her children did not sustain her. The drudgery of ranch life stifled her. The loneliness of it crushed her. And now the El Bar cowboy was gone. She looked toward the Sierra Anchas with a feeling of helpless yearning. She recalled the feel of Ike Talbott's harsh lips and treasured the secret memory. Where was he now?

17.

Benjy dragged his feet to the door. "We come home from school early. I feel bad. My throat hurts."

Melissa looked up from the chair where she sat darning Carter's socks. She held a dried desert gourd, her "darnin' egg." Pushing the gourd to the toe of the sock, she fastened her needle in the wool. "You do look tuckered out. Your face is on fire. Come here. Let me feel you-uns."

The boy coughed, and a rumble shook his chest. Melissa put

her hand on his forehead. "Burnin' up with fever, boy. Wipe yore nose. I'll git you a clean rag."

The other children followed Benjy into the kitchen. Hannah pulled off her bonnet and put her school books on the table. "Teacher said Benjy's sick. He coughed all day. Teacher says there's sickness goin' 'round. Lizzy Beth and Jed Gleason are out of school with the fever."

Melissa nodded toward Carter. "Bring that iron cot from the screen porch. I'll make Benjy a bed in the kitchen, where it's warmer." She turned to Benjy. "Git undressed and into bed. I kin keep an eye on you here. Do you want some soup off the beans?" Benjy, shaking his head, stared dully at his mother. "Or some buttermilk? I'm gonna put a poultice on you first thing."

Melissa stoked the stove with heavy mesquite wood chunks and adjusted the damper. "Carter, fill the woodbox. No cedar, no juniper, no manzanita. Mary Belle, bring that chamber pot and put it here for Benjy, by the cot."

She sliced onions and boiled them. The room grew heavy with the fumes. "Mary Belle, bring me that worn-out sheet, the flannel one in the trunk." Tearing the sheet, she covered the boy's chest with it and put the boiled onions on top. "Benjy, I don't wanta burn you, but I gotta make this as hot as you can stand it." There was no reply.

In the stillness of the night, Benjy's repeated coughing echoed through the house. Melissa awakened in alarm. She felt his brow. The boy coughed, his body wracked with the agitated hacking. Lifting Benjy in her arms, Melissa held him while he fought to spew out the phlegm that clotted his nose and throat.

Going to the screen porch, Melissa opened an old storage trunk and took out three worn quilts, which, with a cushion, she spread on the floor. She lay down on the pallet beside Benjy's bed and tried to sleep. Dreaming flashes frightened her. Benjy coughed. She got up and held him in her arms. At daylight she rose, her eyes burning with fatigue, and began the deadly routine that monopolized her days: building the fire, filling the water buckets, preparing breakfast. Drums beat inside her skull.

Her husband had slept throughout the night. Now he came out of the bedroom, pulling his suspenders over his shirt. One end snapped loose. "Damned galluses, ain't worth a hootin' holler in hell." He looked at the boy under the covers in the corner cot without comment. Taking his hat off the wall, he walked out the back door.

Melissa roused Benjy. "How'd you like a biscuit soaked in hot milk with sugar?" The boy drooped his head. "You orta eat somethin'. Could you eat chicken soup if I fixed it?"

The boy seemed unable even to shake his head.

She went outside where the chickens were scratching for insects and seeds. With a handful of corn she enticed them inside the closed chicken house, where she cornered an old black and white barred hen she figured was a nonlayer. Grabbing the fowl by the legs, she carried it squawking and flapping to the yard. With an experienced twist of her hand and wrist, she wrung the hen's neck. The body flopped in the dirt. Melissa scalded, plucked, singed, and cleaned the bird and took it inside to boil. She hoped that the smell of the chicken soup would tantalize the boy, but he refused to eat.

That afternoon when the children returned from school, they reported that the Williams children were out sick with the fever. Annie sneezed. Melissa said, "You look feverish yourself. I'm gonna give you a dose of salts. Won't hurt you nary a bit." In the evening Annie did not eat supper and she did not join the others at the kitchen table to study. She lay alone in the girls' room.

The next morning Melissa examined Annie. The girl coughed, her eyes exuding a discharge that ran down her cheeks.

"Mama, I cain't swaller. It hurts." Melissa looked into Annie's throat and saw swollen, inflamed tissues that nearly closed the passage. "Carter, you and Spider lug them bed-springs from the barn. Gonna make a bed fer Annie here."

Ben Baker came into the kitchen. "There's not enough room fer a cat to holler," he said, and stomped out the door, leaving Melissa alone again with the sick children.

She took dry mustard and mixed it with hot water. Protecting Annie's skin with a flannel cloth, she spread the plaster on her chest. Then she took a spoonful of sugar, which she moistened with kerosene. "See if you can swaller this coal oil and sugar. It'll clear yore throat."

Hannah, Maribel, Carter, and Spider rode off to school. Benjy was better, but Annie continued to cough and could not eat. Melissa tried to comfort them and feed them bits of nourishment. She made trips outside for firewood and to bring in water. She stirred up a batch of corn bread, baked it and set it aside. She put dried beans to soak. As she worked around the room, she caught her reflection in the mirror: Her face was strained, her eyes glazed. She tried to forget the aching in her body.

By the time Melissa made supper that night, she was in a near stupor. If her movements had not long ago become automatic, she would never have gotten through the meal. She was not hungry. She washed the dishes, rinsed the dish towel and hung it outside to dry, then swept the floor. Her husband moved his chair in a manner Melissa described as "fidgety."

"How are the sick younguns comin' along?" he asked.

"Mr. Baker, they's powerful sick. Cain't eat. I'm nigh worried to death. If Annie don't git better, we better take her to Roosevelt to the doctor. I'm afeerd the others will catch whatever she has."

Reaching in his pocket, he extracted some Battle Ax Plug and bit off a chew of tobacco. "Naw. Younguns is allus takin' down sick. They gits over it better'n old folks. Yore imaginin' it worse'n what it is." He got up from his chair as if he had finished negotiations. "I'm gonna mosey over to Brownells' and

stay a day or two. He's gitting his field ready for planting. I'll
give him a hand."

Rage flamed within Melissa. Ben Baker was not one to do
a farming task, saying he was a cowman, not a squatter with
a dirt farm. The orchard and fields of the Filaree Ranch were
the result of the love and knowing care of the man who first
settled there, not her husband. She did not believe him when
he said that he wanted to help with Brownell's planting. She
was feeling too low to question him. He probably just wanted
to get away from all the sickness on the ranch. But she could
have sworn that she detected a guilty look in his face, as if he
were hiding his real intention. As Ben Baker rode off, Melissa
wondered if he was headed for the Tonto Saloon.

The fretful wail of the baby interrupted her angry thoughts.
Picking up the child, she observed the inflamed eyes and the
flushed cheeks. She said to Hannah, "I'm afeerd the baby's
done took the sickness. When one gits it, they all takes it."
Baby's breathing was labored and Melissa saw the mucus clog-
ging her nostrils. "Carter, git me a reed from the pond. I gotta
make a straw."

When Carter returned, Melissa removed the pithy center
from the reed and blew through the hollow tube. She inserted
the reed up the baby's nose and, putting the other end in her
mouth, she sucked, drawing out the mucus which clogged the
child's nose and air passages.

She propped the baby up with a pillow to ease her breathing;
throughout the night she continued to use the reed to clear the
child's nose. With her husband gone, she kept the door of the
bedroom open so she could check on Benjy and Annie in the
kitchen. Several times in the night she rose to replenish the fire.
She was determined not to let herself give in to the illness.

The next morning she held her hand to Benjy's forehead; it
felt cooler. His eyes were clear. But Annie lay in a semicoma.

That night when she was making ready for bed, Melissa
swallowed and felt a tightness in her throat. She swallowed

again and the effort pained her. The tightness began to turn to a gritty rawness, and she developed a dull ache in her head, which clouded her thoughts. She had difficulty breathing, each intake of air grating her throat and bringing a stabbing pain to her heart.

Melissa went to bed and felt her body floating in a dizzy rise and fall. She drifted in and out of unconsciousness. She forced herself up and staggered into the girls' room. In the semidarkness, she held to the doorframe to steady herself. "Hannah, get up." Her voice was choked. "I'm a-comin' down sick. You'll haveta git the breakfast and git the younguns off to school."

"Mama, shouldn't I go to the Brownells' and fetch Papa?"

"Yore papa don't tolerate sickness. You send Carter ridin' to Aunt Shug. Ask her to come over. Carter won't be too late fer school if he starts now. It's comin' day. I jist ain't able—"

Hannah was stricken with fear. When her parents kept a child out of school, the reason had to be serious.

Melissa mumbled. "Tell teacher . . . send Carter's work . . . if he misses his lesson." She tottered back to bed, edged herself between the covers, and let her limp body drift into insensibility. The next thing she knew, someone was bending over her.

"Melissa, it's Shug. I've come to help you. How air you?"

"Look at the baby. Is she . . . dead?"

Shug rushed to the box and picked up the child. It cried faintly, the whimpering interrupted by coughing. She was wet. Shug put on dry diapers, laid the child back in bed and covered her.

She built up the fire in the kitchen, put on a teakettle and a pail of water, and told Melissa, "I'm gonna make you some greasewood tea. I've got a remedy for the hurtin' in your chest. Soon's the water's hot, I'll clean the younguns. They'll feel a heap better." The woman in the bed did not move. Shug forced a cheerfulness she did not feel; she was afraid. "Don't fret none. Everything's goin' be fine."

When she next went to tend Melissa, she heard a babble but could not distinguish words. "Why, Melissa, you've gone plumb outa yore head."

Benjy said, "Is my mama goin' to die?"

"No, yore mama's goin' get well in no time a-tall. Yore Aunt Shug's goin' get food down her." A tight feeling clutched Shug's chest. She hoped her words to Benjy were true.

The figure in the bed looked at Shug, unseeing. "Why did the baby die? I done wrong in not wanting her to be born. God is punishing me." Shug drew her sister's skimpy body to her. "Melissa, the baby's fine. She's a heap better. You ain't done no wrong." She wiped away her own tears.

But Melissa didn't seem to hear. "God, don't take my baby. Don't punish me. It was a sin—me hatin' her birthin'. Dear Lord, give me back my baby."

Shug went to close the door; she didn't want the children in the kitchen to hear. Benjy's voice was shrieking. "Who died? Aunt Shug, who died? Is my mama—?"

"No. Yore mama's powerful sick, but she's gettin' better. Nobody died. Yore ma don't rightly know what she's sayin' 'cause she's outa her head."

When the children came home from school, Hannah asked, "Aunt Shug, should I get Papa at Brownells' house?"

"I don't think yore pa would like me bein' here. Let's wait. If yore ma don't git no better by mornin', we'll send fer him. Benjy's doin' fine, and Annie's fair to middlin' today. It's just yore ma. If that fever breaks, she'll start to git better. By mornin' we'll know."

That night Shug established herself in a rocking chair, which she stationed by Melissa's bed. She dropped off for short stretches, only to be awakened by Melissa's ramblings. "Dear God in Heaven, forgive me for my sin. I killed my baby. I willed her to die 'fore she was born. My sin . . ." Shug quailed in the darkness as she listened to her sister's self-reproaches and her desperate pleas for atonement.

Toward daylight Melissa's ravings ceased, and she slept. Shug rose and walked to the kitchen window, where the rising sun was lighting the Sierra Anchas. She knelt, frightened, by the window sill, clasped her hands, and pleaded: "Dear Lord, I ain't much on prayin' but I need yore help. Don't bring death to Melissa. She ain't had much enjoyments in her life. Growed up without much girlhood. In womanhood she's had few pleasurements. Just work and babies. If you took her, she'd leave a passel of younguns. God, don't take her now—she's had so little livin'."

Shug rose stiffly from her knees and saw that light had spread into the kitchen. She dressed and began the day, starting the fire anew and putting on the coffee pot. She cooked breakfast and sent the quiet children to school. She washed Benjy and Annie, and from her satchel brought them a deck of cards. "Yore pa don't hold to card playin' but you needs to have quiet and rest. I'm pleased to see Annie's up to playin'. Baby looks a little more peart this mornin' too."

She tiptoed to the bedroom. Melissa lifted her head. Her face was wan, but Shug discerned an attempt at a smile on her sister's lips. She put her hand on Melissa's head. "Fever's down."

Melissa's eyes were clear, her voice a whisper. "Shug, I didn't know you was here."

Shug grinned. "I know you didn't. You been sick. Yore fever's broke now. You'll be up in no time—what with a little rest and vittles under yore belt."

Shug walked from the room before Melissa could see the wetness in her eyes.

18. A year passed. It was 1911. Hannah had finished the
last grade in The Mesa school, and rather than have her stay
home, her father permitted her to repeat the eighth grade. He
allowed as it was a shame that they did not live in a place like
Tempe, because then Hannah could go to high school.

Then one day, as Melissa was in the midst of cleaning house,
Ben Baker returned from a trip to Roosevelt and announced,
"I done it. I made a deal to sell the ranch."

Sell the Filaree Ranch? It took a moment for the reality to
settle on her. She put down her broom and faced her husband.
Ben Baker was about to relinquish the most important thing
in his life, the filaree land with the cattle that grazed from the
base of the Sierra Anchas to Tonto Creek.

The sadness in his voice touched her. "There was no other
way," he said. Then he turned to go out the door. "I'm goin'
ride over to Brownells'. John said he saw fresh lion sign again.
We think it's the same one—the one we never got." She knew
he wanted to be alone.

Melissa was in the back, pouring scrub water on the honeysuckle vine when her mother came around the corner. "Ma, I
wasn't expectin' you."

"Thought we'd come over while Ben's in Roosevelt. Yore
pa's in front."

"Ben come back, but jist rode over to Brownells'." She saw
the shepherd dog lift its leg on the honeysuckle vine. "Git!"
She threw the water at the dog. "Come in the house. I need
to talk to you."

The three of them sat in the kitchen, over coffee. "Ben has
sold the ranch," Melissa announced. "We'll go to Tempe,
where there's a high school."

Sarah Holman tapped her fingers on the table. "I know he's

been talkin' about sellin'. For all his cussedness—and the good Lord knows he's got plenty of it—he does put a heap of stock in his younguns' learnin', more than ary man on The Mesa."

"Ben Baker'll be sorry he give up this ranch." Silas Holman was cleaning his fingernails with the point of his pocketknife blade. "Best place there is here—lots of water, good grass."

"Pa, he's givin' up the ranch so the younguns can get more schoolin' in the Valley."

Melissa's mother refilled her coffee cup. "We'll miss you-all. Didn't get to see too much of you, but there's nothin' like yore own kinfolks near."

"We ain't gone yet. Ben says the man is in a hurry to take over, though. It's come so sudden-like, cain't hardly think straight."

"Shug and I'll be over to he'p you pack when the time comes."

Holman ran the point of his knife under his fingernail. "Why all the folderol about schoolin'? What's wrong with your gals gittin' hitched to some fine feller on The Mesa? Now there's young—"

"Hush, Pa." Sarah raised her voice. "There's higher things in mind than marryin' off your girls just 'cause they's growed. If you'd had higher ideas, our Effie wouldn't a gone off with that scalawag she married up with."

"Hannah's old enough to catch a good man. You was four-teen when we was wedded."

"Yes, and I've paid for it every day of my life since."

"Ben don't know nothin' but the cow business. What'll he do in Tempe? He ain't so young no more."

"That's right, Pa. He's up in years. All he knows is stock. He couldn't no way be happy without cattle."

Sarah rose. "We better go 'fore Ben gits back."

"Oh, visit a mite longer, Ma. Mr. Baker won't be back fer a spell. He went to see 'bout goin' lion huntin' with Brownell. He says Carter is to go to Upper Mountain to fix the gate. The

new owner is comin' to look the place over. I'm fearful for
Carter to go to Upper Mountain alone. But Mr. Baker says
when he was Carter's age, he was doin' all the ranch work and
ridin' farther in Comanche Indian country."

"Melissa, don't you let that boy go up there alone." Sarah
Holman motioned to her husband, "Come on, you're gettin'
feisty as a boar hog, and yore rarin' to be gone."

Melissa walked with her parents to their wagon. Her mother
waved her red sunbonnet as they drove away. She remembered
that bonnet waving another time, and she grew bitter.

She returned to her cleaning. It was evening when Ben
Baker rode in and began unsaddling. She heard his singing.
The doleful tune settled on her, and she knew he was sorrowing
inside. His words came to her. "Sam first came out to Texas/A
cowboy for to be/A kinder hearted fellow/You'll seldom ever
see."

He stopped singing when he came into the house. "I'm goin'
with John tomorrow after that lion. I've done told Carter to
go fix that gate in Upper Mountain."

"No." Melissa wrung out her mop. "He ought not to go
alone. It's rough country. Hardly no trail. The gate can wait
till you get back."

"Brownell's ready to start in the morning. That gate
should've been fixed last winter. I want it repaired 'fore the
buyer comes."

Melissa eyes grew fierce. "You go with Carter."

Her husband's voice was a command. "Woman, I told
Carter what tools to carry. You're babying that boy. He can be
up early and back in one day, easy." He walked out. Melissa
heard the door slam.

19.

Melissa walked out in the early morning to the corral. Carter was throwing a faded Navajo saddle blanket on the back of his horse. His mother held out a package. "I'm gonna put these biscuits and meat in yore saddle bag. You have all yore gear? Pliers? Canteen? Don't never start nowheres without water."

"I got everything. Jerky in my pocket. Startin' so early, I'll be back in no time a-tall."

"Wait. What's that rifle doing on yore saddle?"

The boy hefted a gunny sack to the rear of his saddle. "Mama, I'm almost growed. A man needs a gun. I might need to shoot somethin'." He swung himself into the saddle.

His mother put her hand on the horse's neck to delay him. "I don't like you carryin' that gun. Don't you go foolin' around. You fix that fence and skeedaddle home from Upper Mountain. I'll be waitin' for you."

The boy reached the dry lake called Devil's Hole. The shriveled top crust was crisscrossed with cracks, and it seemed even drier than the parched land that surrounded it. He looked for a place to water his horse. Thinking of his mother's admonition, he knew he should save his canteen water. As he was getting thirsty, he remembered what his father had said about drinking from a waterhole. "If you see wiggle tails, the water's safe. They cain't live in poison water. Screen 'em out and drink. They're only hatched eggs of the moskeeters."

The land rose upward into timber, and he came to a small stream. He let his horse drink, and he drank above where the horse muzzled the water. The trail carried him on into juniper and piñon growth, and up into ponderosa pine. He came to a small valley full of flowers, and as his horse's hoofs crushed them, he smelled the fragrance of the mint, geranium, and roses. A long-ago forest fire had left blackened trunks, and the quaking aspen had taken over, their silver leaves shivering in the light breeze. A white-barked aspen held a carved message, the edges dark and curled with the years: "Huntin' horse theeves 1881." He wished he were after horse thieves instead of going to mend a gate. He rode over a bear's track imprinted in the mud.

Carter reached Upper Mountain and saw that the gate could be repaired in a short time. Taking out the biscuits and meat, he sat down to eat. Then he began tightening the loose wire. He hammered and pulled at the gate, wishing his father had let him go lion hunting instead. When the gate was secure, he stepped back to admire his work.

He decided to take a shortcut home on a trail that was seldom used because it was so steep and rough. As he forced his horse down a bluff, the trail became fainter, covered as it was with sharp rocks and grown over with brush. Carter found himself blocked by a low forest of manzanita growth; he could neither go forward nor back. Ahead he saw the trail cleared— if he could only force his way out of the one huge manzanita bush that walled him in. Dismounting, he removed the rifle from the scabbard and stepped away from his horse, sighting the gun on the heavy limb that barred his way. He pulled the trigger; the limb cracked and fell. He pulled the broken bush away from the path and emerged into a cleared trail, the dense manzanita curling each side. He started down the rocky slope singing to himself, "Damanzanita—won't let cow or man through/Yore rough and tough—but I'll get by you."

The horse felt the spurs and he lengthened his gait, jumping over boulders that impeded his passage. The boy stood up in his stirrups and leaned forward. He smelled rain far off and urged his horse to go faster. He liked the feel of the wind washing his face and, opening his mouth, tasted the rain-sweetened breeze. Faster he spurred his horse. The manzanitas by the trailside were impenetrable. Jumping his horse over a boulder, he raced down the graveled mountainside.

20.

After Carter left for Upper Mountain, Melissa busied herself at the sewing machine. Cutting through the center of a worn bed sheet, she stitched the stronger outside edges together. Benjy squatted on the floor behind the machine, moving the wooden shaft of the treadle.

Mary Belle bounced into the room. "Mama, can we go swimmin' in the creek?" She was followed by the other children, adding their entreaties.

Melissa looked up at the peaked face of Hannah. "It might be the last time we'll ever get to go wadin' in Tonto Creek," the child said, and Melissa was bound with a kindred feeling for this girl who loved the land of the filaree.

She stood up and folded the sheet. "We have to wait here for Carter."

"We can get back 'fore he's back." Spider's eyes searched his mother's for a "yes."

Carter alone in the treacherous rugged Upper Mountain. Melissa felt dismay. Perhaps to go to the creek would lessen her anxiety. "Then we'll have to hurry and git back before Carter does. Help me git a bite of food to take, and Spider, git the wagon ready."

The family pulled out toward the creek. But Melissa could not join in the merriment of her children. She looked at the familiar countryside, the scrub plants, the brown-dry earth, the Sierra Anchas and the Mazatzal Mountains; it was as if she were seeing them all for the first time. There were the brilliant red blossoms of the thorn ocotillos, "the devil's candlestick," and the saguaro cactus, and she thought, *We'll never gather their fruit again.*

Hannah, driving the team, pulled the wagon to the river's edge under a cottonwood tree, its branches spotted green with mistletoe. The children settled the quilt at the foot of the tree for the baby and raced to splash in the water. Above them, the crows took umbrage at the intrusion and cawed, raised their wings awkwardly, and flapped their black bodies to a nearby elderberry tree.

Melissa took off her shoes and black stockings and cautiously walked across the sand to the creek. The submerged rocks, their colors heightened by sun, reflected the light in wavy flashes. She waded out several feet, the slime on the rocks making for slick footing. Benjy splashed up. "Got me some frog eggs." The boy ran on to join the others.

She picked her way back to the quilt, dried her feet and replaced her shoes and stockings. When she had spread out the food, she called, "You younguns, come eat. We've not got too long to stay."

"Why do we haveta go now?" Spider said. "Carter will just fool along so's he won't have to do no chores."

Melissa had no desire for food. "I'm worried about Carter. Let's go."

At the ranch Melissa waited the rest of the afternoon. Carter did not come. The sun lowered, the lavender hills deepened to purple and then to black, and as evening approached, her unease increased. Sensing their mother's concern, the children ate quietly and went to bed without complaint.

Melissa, sitting by the lamplight, periodically went to the door to look out and listen for the sound of hooves. She jumped at the brush of a bat flying through the porch. She refilled her coffee cup and waited. She sat in the chair dozing, to be awakened by the hoot of an owl. The lamp had burned away the kerosene. She was alarmed now. Going to the girls' bedroom, she awakened Hannah. "I'm frantic," she said. "Carter ain't come in. You gotta ride to get Jimso. We've got to go hunt him. I got a bad feelin'."

Hannah hurried out of bed, dressed, and scurried to the corral, saddled Baldy and was down the road toward the Holman place.

Melissa stood at the window, time gnawing at her. When she heard the horses' hoofs beating the road, she ran outside holding the lantern high.

Jimso was off his horse, his arms around his sister. "I think yore worried too much about the boy. I feel he had trouble with the gate, and is waiting till daylight to ride home."

"Somethin' has happened to my boy. I want we should start now."

"We cain't make no headway on that trail tonight. Haveta wait till daybreak and then I'll go."

"I'm goin' with you. I couldn't wait here." She turned to Hannah. "You go back to bed. Come day, I'll be gone with Jimso. You watch the little ones. And Jimso, you go lie down on that cot and I'll wake you at day."

21.

It was still dark when Melissa and Jimso headed their horses for Upper Mountain. The predawn was chill and they lowered their shoulders, hunkering over their saddle horns. They reached Devil's Hole at sunup. Following Carter's trail, they came to the white-barked aspen with the carved words of the unknown person hunting horse thieves. They climbed Upper Mountain and found the mended gate. Jimso examined the work. "He done a good job. Looks like his horse tracks go that way, by the shortcut. It's rougher'n hell down that bluff. You best get off and rest a spell 'fore we head down."

"I don't need no rest. Let's get goin'." Though the sun was up by now, Melissa felt cold with apprehension. She and her brother rode down the mountain, not talking, their eyes searching the country. They came to the thicket where the manzanita forest blocked the way, and fought their way through. "That boy had a tough go-round gittin' through here." Jimso got off and pulled away branches to let Melissa pass.

The riders traveled until they came to the place where the boy had shot off the manzanita limb that barred his way, and into the cleared area broken with boulders. "See. His pony tracks showed he was runnin' here."

Suddenly Jimso, in the lead, stopped and pointed. "There's his horse—ahead—between them boulders—lying down."

The animal lay on its side. Even before she rode up and dismounted, Melissa observed the horse turn its head and stare with frightened eyes. One leg, wedged between the boulders, was broken. "Oh, dear God!" Melissa ran her eyes over the area. "Where's Carter?" Her eyes stopped on a clump of manzanita. She stood in mute horror. Submerged under fetters of branches was her son.

She pulled and tore at the shrubs, but they would not give way. The branches that held her son slapped back at her, striking her face and scratching her arms. The manzanita would not relinquish its prey.

Jimso moved Melissa aside. "Sis, let me in." The man broke off small branches, pushing his shoulders into the mass of tangled limbs. He struggled and made a small entry. Melissa tried to claw her way toward the body. Jimso pulled her aside. "Sis, you must let me help. You can't do it alone."

She watched the man break an opening, inch by inch, branch by branch. Trance-like, Melissa stood by as he retrieved the body and stretched it out on the trail. She watched Jimso squat on his boot heels and lay his head against the boy's chest. He put his hand on the boy's cold forehead. Rising, he spoke to the motionless woman. His voice was gentle. "Melissa, it's too late—"

Melissa screamed, her anguish echoing down the mountain trail. The mother knelt by her boy. "It ain't too late. It cain't be. Dear God in Heaven, help me. Give me back my son!" She put her mouth against the boy's lips and began blowing air into the still lungs.

Jimso pulled at her shoulders. "Melissa, you cain't. That don't do no good. He's gone."

The woman did not heed. She blew in and out, again and again. Jimso walked to the injured horse and removed the saddle, bridle, and saddle blanket. He returned to the kneeling woman, and reaching under her arms, pulled her up. "Sis, no."

Now the woman looked down at the white thin skin and the narrow nose, the wide gash and the clotted blood on the forehead. Jimso stood beside her, his arms around her shoulders. "You see, Melissa, the horse was runnin', stepped between them boulders, and as he fell, he musta threw Carter into the thicket."

The woman could not take her eyes off the form on the gravel. Her brother's voice came to her. "I've got to shoot his horse. The gun's still on Carter's saddle. You walk over behind that oak tree while I shoot. It'll be over in a minute."

She moved dazedly behind the tree. As she heard the rifle shot, she remembered Carter's words, "Mama, who knows? I might need to shoot somethin'."

Jimso walked to the tree and softly folded her hands in his. "We best git our horses and go. We'll need help to bring him down off this mountain."

"You go. I will not leave my boy alone."

"Melissa! You cain't stay up here alone by yourself. Might be hours 'fore I get someone to help me, and get a mule and a pack saddle."

"I will stay here with my son. Jimso, do give me the last few hours with my boy. I tell you, I'm goin' to stay." Her voice rose. "You go—now!" She stumbled to the saddle blanket and brought it to the body. Bending down, she kissed the boy's lips and slowly pulled the blanket over his face.

Distraught, the man mounted his horse and spurred him down the trail. The woman sat beside the form covered by the black and red Navajo saddle blanket. Anger welled up. She rose and called out to the emptiness of the mountainside, "Ben Baker, you took the life of my son. You sent him alone . . ."

22.

22. The funeral was held in the morning. Melissa sat in mournful abstraction while Shug pulled her black high-topped shoes on for her and took the long-handled button-hook, forcing the buttons through the resisting holes. Melissa did not recognize the dress Shug forced over her head. She heard her sister explain, "You didn't have nothin' fittin' to wear. I borrowed this and hemmed it shorter." Shug tied a black poke bonnet over Melissa's head and led her to the wagon hitched at the rack in front.

Her husband, standing by the side, took her arm. Automatically she raised her foot and felt Ben Baker help her onto the seat. Ben climbed in on the other side and took the reins. For a moment, like the wispy clouds dissolving in the hard blue sky, reality returned and she thought, *I recollect I sat by this man when I was goin' to the birthin' of a youngun. And now I sit —goin' to give one up.* Numbness came back to her. She could not even bring herself to hate him.

Ben drove slowly. The creak of the wagon wheels was lamentation. When they came to the creek, they found that the water had risen. Other wagons waited. Men on horseback rode into the creek, testing the depth of the water, until the entourage of mourners felt safe enough to cross. The cemetery that served The Mesa folk was a forsaken spot on a hillside. The wagon stopped outside the sagging barbed wire enclosure. The filaree that ordinarily covered the graveyard had turned brown from the heat. A splintered cross listed. Melissa discerned the weathered marking: "Our Mother. 1869–1898." Twenty-nine years old. Women died early here. Work, births, deprivation, loneliness sapped their life; only death relieved them. It seemed the dried grasses were fading back into the earth of The Mesa in just the way that her son was about to. Why was it that already the memory of his face was dimming?

Walking with Shug on one side and her husband on the other, Melissa came to the people waiting in the cemetery. They stood in uncertain groups in the splattered shade of the mesquite trees. The men moved restlessly from one boot heel to the other, awkward in their unfamiliar clothes with the too-tight, too-short sleeves, coats straining at the waists. They gripped the edges of their hats with their calloused fingers, glad that they had hats to twist, to relieve the tension.

The faces nodded at Melissa, but she did not respond. Faces brown and worn like the headstones. She walked on and came to the hole in the earth, gaping like a wound, the fresh red clay piled by the side. Next to it rested the pine coffin, the nails freshly hammered.

She clung tightly to Shug's hand and let herself be led to the open grave. Ben Baker and Shug helped her to her place in the row of chairs facing the coffin. The air stilled, the mourning dove's plaintive call reaching the little group from the cottonwood tree down by the creek. Dudley Schmelz walked to the front, a black book clasped in his hand. "Friends, we will sing." A man stepped forward with a guitar, partially blocking Melissa's view of the open hole, and she was relieved, because she did not want to see it. Uneven voices followed the rough chords of the instrument: "Come to the church in the wildwood . . . O the little brown church . . . dell . . ."

The singing ended. Melissa again heard the dove's echo of sorrow. Dudley Schmelz opened the Bible, his easy voice reaching out over their heads. "Neighbors, we are gathered here today to lay away a loved one. We are here to bring comfort to the ones he left behind. I have knowed this boy, Carter Baker, ever since his family come to The Mesa. He was a good boy, and his folks is good people. He was just comin' into manhood when he was took from us. The good Lord giveth, and the good Lord taketh. We do not question the work of the Lord. We are grateful that the Lord let us have this boy to love for the years he did. We too will someday meet Carter, our loved one, in Heaven. Let us pray." The people bowed their heads.

The preacher's voice rose above the dove's call. "The Lord is my shepherd. I shall not want . . . Amen."

Heads lifted. Melissa watched four men step slowly forward and pull the ropes from under the casket, lifting the box into the grave until Melissa could no longer see the pine boards. The men pulled up the ropes and picked up shovels. As she turned away, she heard the soft thud of earth covering the coffin, and fastened her eyes on a small brown-green filaree plant. She stopped, plucked it, and walked back to the half-filled grave. The men held their spades in midair. She edged herself closer to the hole, and leaning over she dropped the lacy filaree onto the coffin. "Goodbye, son." Her body shook.

The men resumed shoveling. She heard rocks strike against the coffin. She stopped. "Boys," she said, looking at the shovelers, "toss that dirt gently." It was then she heard the stifled sob that escaped her husband's lips. She did not turn toward him, nor did she want to see the tears that dampened his leathery cheeks. Bitterness rose within her: It was not only Carter's death that she blamed him for. Her youth, too, was being buried. Melissa tightened her hold on Shug's hand.

At the wagon, she suffered her husband to help her onto the seat, and they began the empty trip back to the Filaree Ranch.

1.

The next month passed with Melissa busy preparing to move to Tempe. She still sorrowed for Carter, but the demands on her from the household, the children, and the packing forced her to subdue her grief. Shug had come to the Filaree to help her sister with the moving. She took the chewed twig she used as a snuff brush out of her mouth and began scrubbing the pine boards of the kitchen with lye water. "You've scrubbed these boards so much they're danged near white."

"I wanta leave the place decent for the new owners." Melissa tacked strips of cloth on the screen door. "These blamed flies! Last night I burned 'em under the eaves of the porch with newspaper. Killed hundreds." She went on with the packing, folding the patchwork quilt Shug had given her, stacking the washed flour sacks. "Better leave out Mr. Baker's razor strop. He'll wanta shave 'fore we start."

Benjy came in. "This blamed tooth's gittin' looser." Melissa stopped packing to tie a string on the tooth, and with the other end fastened it to the door knob. "Boy, close yore eyes." She slammed the door. The tooth dangled at the end of the string. "Wash out yore mouth good. Now, go on with the movin'." She turned to Shug. "Let's stop for a cup of coffee. I'm about tuckered out."

The women moved their chairs to the end of the porch, where the breeze caught the trumpet vines, the long-throated blossoms welcoming the hummingbirds, whose wings beat in the summer air like iridescent rainbows. Melissa lifted her heavy hair from the back of her neck to let the breeze cool her skin. "Does seem like most everythin' has gone wrong lately. I was choppin' wood. Stick hit me in the eye. Made me sick at my stomach. For a moment I thought I was in the family way again, but I guess not. Just the pain made me sick."

"Them things do come along. My baby turkeys went to eatin' off their toes. I killed a jack rabbit, nailed it to a board, so's they could get some meat. Left me some gimpy turkeys, though."

"Benjy was jumpin' on the bedsprings on the back porch. Bumped against the iron bedpost. Knocked a bump big as a goose egg on his forehead."

From around the side of the house came Spider's voice. "O, that sweet little gal, that purty little gal/The gal I left behind me/She jumped in bed/And covered up her head/And I jumped in behind her."

Shug laughed. Melissa scowled. "Where in creation did that youngun git them words? I'll wash his mouth out with soap."

Shug still smiled. "Yore hard on the youngun. 'Tain't too bad."

Ben Baker walked onto the porch. He did not speak to his sister-in-law. "Miz Baker, we kin pull outa here soon's yore packed. I'll drive one wagon, Hannah can handle one and"— he grimaced—"much as I hate to do it, Jimso'll have to come along to drive another to the Valley."

Shug was reminded she was unwelcome in Ben Baker's eyes. "Guess I'll be trotting home."

As her husband walked away, Melissa said, "Shug, could you stay just long enough for me to ride up to the graveyard? I ain't been there since Carter . . ." She choked.

Melissa felt Shug's strong arms around her and heard her sister's comforting words. "You go right along. I'll stay here irregardless of yore old man. You need to go."

Melissa took the road to the burying ground. Though there had been no rain for weeks, the wagon ruts were already fading back into the earth. She heard the mourning dove—and remembered. She also thought of Ike Talbott, but it was with a remoteness now: The sheriff had never caught up with him. She tied her horse to the post holding the barbed wire fence that kept the cattle from tramping on the graves. Inside she knelt by the newest mound of earth and clasping her hands, bowed her head. *Part of me will forever remain here,* she told herself. Then she mounted her horse and started homeward.

The following morning Ben Baker was up before sunrise. He had always risen before daylight. It had been so in Texas when he was a boy, and had been so with his father and his father's father. He expected that his own children would follow his example. Today he was moving his household off the Filaree, starting the trip to the Valley, to the schools at Tempe.

Putting his feet on the floor, he missed the braided rug. "Damn, she's packed everything."

Fumbling for his trousers on the foot of the bedstead, he yanked them over the long underwear in which he always slept. Melissa, lying quiet in the bed, heard him groan as he stretched. Then she heard the outgo blast of air as he bent his heavy-bellied form to reach for his boots. She shuddered.

Melissa made no movement until she heard him clomp into the kitchen and make a clamor as he built a fire in the cookstove. She heard the rasping of the hinge on the children's door as her husband pushed it open. "Git up. Lyin' abed is foolishness."

Through the thin walls came Spider's muttering. "When I git growed, I ain't never gonna git up 'fore the sun comes up. Never."

After breakfast Melissa told the children. "We're goin' to have to leave lots of our belongin's with the folks. We cain't carry 'em." As Benjy started to speak, she said, "Benjy, we don't have no room to tote Ol' Tom. He kin git the rats in Granny's barn."

She heard the Holmans pull into the yard; Ben Baker walked away. "Damnation and hell's fire. That ol' man come just to whittle. We could've got goin' without them. Never thought I'd have to ask a favor of them—asking Jimso to drive one wagon."

The leave-taking was full of tears. Shug hugged the baby a final time and added another jar of tomato preserves to the lunch. Melissa promised to write. Ben Baker was grim-faced. At the last, Shug pulled her sister aside and said, "Now, Melissa, if you get in the family way, I hear tell that slippery elm—" Melissa shook her head and vowed that she was never going to have another baby. With waving and more tears, the wagons pulled away from the Filaree Ranch.

The three wagons crawled across the flat Mesa, which showed the effects of the summer's heat in drying plants and browning lands. Finally the caravan reached the river. It was edged with dry quicksand, and Ben Baker halted the wagons and ordered the riders out. He wedged tarpaulins under the wheels and directed the children to add limbs and brush and weeds under them. Taking the leather whip from the wagon, he positioned himself in a wide stance by the front wagon wheel. Sweat made creases of dust on his cheeks. He called to the others, commanding them to push, push. His whip cracked. The team moved. The wagon groaned and labored until the wheels found the solid footing of the opposite bank. Then they pushed the other wagons across in the same way.

Now they moved into unfamiliar country. Melissa looked at the exposed mountainsides, with the strata of colored rocks and dirt, the layers of blues, reds, grays a reminder that eons ago a turbulent sea had washed against a shore here. But the children had grown too tired to notice, and they dozed until a loose boulder jarred the wagon and jostled them alert.

Melissa held Baby until her arms rebelled and called for rest. She laid the child in the box on the wagon seat. She stared ahead, lost and far away and submerged in a fantasy that now only remotely concerned Ike Talbott.

Ben Baker slouched silent on the seat, letting the horses set a steady pace. He cleared his throat of dust and phlegm. The air grew sultry. Clouds multiplied. The humid breeze was stifling. Ben slapped the reins. "Helluva rain comin'. We kin camp at Granite Creek if we kin make it."

At Granite Creek, the men set up camp on a high spot of land, shoveling trenches around the tents to drain the water. The family ate a cold meal and waited for the night to bring the storm. Ben and Melissa slept in one tent, the children in another; Jimso made a bed under the wagon.

As the rain rolled off the canvas, Benjy poked an experimental finger toward a place where the water caused the tent to sag. "Don't touch it, Benjy. You'll have the whole water come down on us," Hannah warned.

The wind threatened and the rain assaulted. The children snuggled together. In the other tent the man and woman did not. "That roan horse's scairt of thunder. Hope he don't bust that rope." The wind increased.

"Mama!" Melissa was awake instantly. She saw Hannah's form outlined in the tent doorway. "Mama, the tent blowed down on us. I tol' the others to stay till I come got you."

Melissa shook her husband. "Git up. Younguns' tent blowed down." The snoring stopped. "What the hell?" He yanked on his pants, reaching for his slicker and the lantern.

The tent flap opened, and the other children straggled in. "You drownded rats! Look out, don't splash no water on that lantern." Melissa rummaged through a box. "Take off yore clothes. Here's something dry. Climb into this bed."

Benjy said, "I gotta pee."

"Cain't you wait? It's comin' daylight. Still pourin' outside."

"No!"

"Come over by the tent flap and try to keep dry."

"Them girls is watching me."

Melissa turned to the snickering girls. "Cover up yore faces." She pushed Benjy to the open tent flap, and he faced his shivering body outside.

Ben Baker returned. "Cain't fix the tent in this rain. We'll wait here till day."

In the morning, Melissa had the children hang the wet clothes on the bushes. The sun had come up and cleared the sky. Ben said, "We'll haveta wait here a few hours. Cain't travel with every dadgummed thing wet. I'm going ride down the road, see what there is. We're not too far from Habe's store."

Habe's store—and saloon, Melissa thought. But she said nothing as he rode off. She and the children turned the clothes over, and by late afternoon most articles were dry. She said, "I guess I'll haveta pack a few damp things till we git to stop again."

Melissa waited out the day. That night she lay in the dark, her mind on The Mesa. The Filaree Ranch already seemed so far away. It was late when Ben Baker stumbled into the tent and kicked off his boots and forced his body against hers.

2.
By midday the road to Tempe brought them to low desert country. The people in the wagons could bow their heads and narrow their eyes against the glare, but they could not prevent the sun from reddening their skin. The wheels crushed on and rolled onto a dry lake. The sinking water, evaporating, had leached the soil, the salt residue deadening growth and turning everything a sterile white. Heads down, the horses forced one hoof ahead of the other across the alkali flats.

The woman and girls turned down their bonnets and secured the black stockings on their arms. The men and boys no longer bothered to wipe away the sweat that seeped from their hat-bands. Alkali dust crept into their throats, and they choked and coughed and spat and hacked. Melissa's hair was whitened with it. She covered the baby's face, but the cloth could not keep the dust from filtering through. The woman turned burned eyes to the man hunched on the seat. "Couldn't we pull off and git ourselves a drink?" she asked her husband. "The younguns is askin' fer water. I wanta wash off the baby's face."

"No. You-all kin wait. The younguns shoulda drunk up good 'fore we left. We'll be hittin' the farm area purty soon. When we git there, we'll be nigh to Boer's Ranch. We're rentin' one of his houses."

The team jolted on, and by late afternoon they came to scattered green fields. Ben pulled the team to the shade of a cottonwood tree by an irrigation ditch. The children jumped from the wagon, running to splash in the water. Melissa, too weary to move, rested before she alighted to put a dipper in the running water so that she could give the baby a drink and refresh herself. Ben and Jimso unharnessed the horses to water and rest them.

Melissa inhaled the coolness of the shade. The alfalfa field was bordered by a line of huge cottonwood trees on the ditch bank. "Strange, these trees in such a line," she said.

Ben splashed water on his face. "They wasn't meant to be that way. The first farmers to come to the Valley didn't have no fence posts. They went to the river and cut limbs off cottonwood trees. The posts took root and growed into trees."

Melissa watched the bees that flitted among the purple alfalfa blossoms. Yellow and white butterflies swarmed over the field. Spider sailed a rock at a bird in a tree; startled blackbirds rose like a black blanket.

"We better be gittin' on," Ben said. "We don't haveta drive through town. We turn off somewheres up here. I see a house down the road a piece. I'll stop and ask the way to Boer's place."

They came to a man in the irrigating ditch lifting shovelfuls of wet dirt to tamp against the bank. Stopping the team, Ben walked over to get directions. Melissa saw the man point down the road.

Ben Baker started the team. "We cain't miss the house. Should be around the next turn. Has a green frame and big date palms in front."

They made the turn and came in view of their new home.

Ben Baker stopped the team in the front yard. A dark-skinned man emerged from an adobe building and hurried toward them. "Señor. I am told to watch for you. You come to leeve at thees place? The boss man tell help you. My name ees Manuel."

"My name is Benjamin Baker. This the Boer place?"

"Seguro que sí." The white teeth were exposed in a smile in the brown face. "I weel show you where to put the horses, how to make the pump run for water. Señor Boer say I am to come to town to tell heem when you get here."

"I'll wanta unload and take care of the horses first."

"Sí. *Mi esposa* clean the house so that everytheeng be good when you come. I weel tell my wife to help you put the things een the house, no?"

Melissa smiled. "Thank you. I could use help. We're tired and hungry. How far is this ranch from Tempe?"

"I theenk three, four miles."

The children ran around inspecting the new premises. "Mama, what is this? What kind of tree? Look."

Melissa answered. "That's a mulberry tree. A pomegranate." She swept her arm toward a tree whose drooping limbs reached the ground. "A weeping willow. By the ditch, that's a fig tree." Spider climbed the fig tree to grasp a bug drooling over the fruit.

Melissa walked around the yard. "Nothin' but Bermuda grass."

Melissa sat down on the porch to nurse the baby. With a sinking feeling, she looked at the peeling green paint on the frame building that was to be her new home.

3.

Jimso had returned to The Mesa. The Bakers had been moved into the green frame house on the Boer Ranch for a week. Melissa found few furnishings in the house but told the children, "We'll make do." She was pleased that the rooms had unbleached muslin tacked to the rafters for a ceiling. "Keeps the bugs from fallin' down." She had found a centipede on the porch the day they arrived.

Melissa was sewing when Annie came into the room dragging Benjy by one hand. The boy's other hand was dripping blood. "Benjy, what in the—?"

"Mama, he g-g-got cut. He was playin' with a butcher knife in the t-t-tub of grain outside, and he cut hisself." Annie still stuttered whenever she got excited.

Melissa tried to keep her voice calm. "Let me wash it." She poured cold water over the wound. "I'll put some iodine on it."

"No! That hurts—that medicine."

Melissa held him tightly, putting a bandage over the cut. Benjy, jerking loose, ran outside. "Oh, it burns, burns!"

Melissa returned to her sewing. She looked up at the sound of wheels outside. Stopping in front was a black buggy. A man, a woman, and a girl whom Melissa surmised to be near Hannah's age, got out.

Melissa went to the porch. "Howdy do. Come in."

The three walked to the porch. Melissa thought them well dressed, as she later described them to her husband. "City folks." The man supported the woman on his arm. The woman walked slowly and watched her feet as she stepped.

The visitor raised his hat, and said in a low voice: "We're your neighbors down the road, in the red-brick house. We stopped by to get acquainted."

Melissa turned to Annie to fetch some chairs. She faced her guests. "I'm Melissa Baker. My husband's in town. It's warm this morning. Would you like a drink of water?"

The man took the chair from Annie and seated his wife. Melissa noted that the straw hat with the veil that the woman tossed back revealed her eyes—like a fawn's, she thought.

When Melissa looked at the woman's soft fingers, she put her own stubby hands behind her back. She was glad she had put on a fresh percale dress that morning.

The man smiled. "We're glad to have new neighbors. I'm James McBride. This is my wife Elizabeth and our daughter, Roselyn. We moved here from Chicago for my wife's health. Been here six months. Our girl finds it lonesome with no young folks. She's in high school."

Melissa said, "We have two girls in high school, or will have, come fall—Hannah and Mary Belle."

The man was clean-shaven. Melissa noted his skin was not burned like Ben Baker's. He spoke: "It was lonely for Roselyn this summer with no young folks around. Last year I drove her to school. She doesn't drive. We thought perhaps this year we could make arrangements for the children to ride to school together."

Melissa brightened. "We'd like that. I think we could work out something."

The man leaned toward his wife. "Are you feeling all right?" When the woman nodded, the man said, "Elizabeth doesn't go out often. Tires her. We bought this ranch for the quiet."

Hannah and Mary Belle had come from behind the house to stand on the porch. Melissa said, "These are my girls, Hannah and Mary Belle."

The man held his hat in his hand. "We're glad to know you girls and hope you'll come down the road to visit us. We don't want to keep you, but we wanted to invite you to our house tonight to get acquainted."

"That's mighty neighborly of you. I cain't come on account o' the baby has been poorly all week. And I cain't say when my man will be home."

"Perhaps the children could come. I could drive over and get them." The man looked at his wife. She nodded and smiled.

"I'm sure they'd like to come, but they kin walk."

"Since they're walking, they could come while it's light. I would drive them home." The McBrides rose to leave. The woman smiled wanly and pulled the veil down over the brim of her hat. The man bowed slightly to Melissa and carefully guided his wife down the steps.

When the McBrides left, Melissa said, "You-uns better start gittin' cleaned up if you are goin' fore dark. I don't want you stayin' too long. Be shore you mind yore manners. And bathe good—none o' your spit baths."

Ben Baker did not get home until night. "I got a job renting my span of mules. Met some new people. Not like The Mesa or Stone Springs folks—but good."

He was eating a late supper when the children came back from the McBrides' house.

Mary Belle said, "We had fun. We made popcorn."

"They got wallpaper with red roses on it!"

"We looked at something—they calls it a stereopticon. Saw pictures of Niagara Falls and 'The Saviour's Life Before the Crucifixion.' "

"Roselyn's nice. She don't talk much. She played their talking machine. On the front in gold letters it said Gramophone Gem."

"Mr. McBride had a accordion and he played for us. He showed us a tambourine and he hit Benjy on the head with it and he let Benjy shake it."

"The mother played one piece on the piano. Then she was tired and had to go to bed."

"Roselyn's father drove her to school every day last year 'cause she don't know how. We tol' her Hannah drove a team all the way from The Mesa here. Her father said that was wonderful and you must be proud. Hannah got red in the face when he said that."

"Roselyn's mother has to stay in bed most of the time. Roselyn and her father do the work."

Ben Baker poised his fork in the air. "You-uns hush a minute. Cain't make out half what yore tellin'. Henry Boer says the McBrides is fine folks. Sold a furniture store in Chicago and come here: The woman's sickly. Boer said he knowed McBride would wanta hire my mules for plowing his fields."

When school began, Hannah drove the McBrides' canopy-top surrey to school with all the children. Melissa fretted. "We don't wanta be beholdin' to no one. We wanta do our share." She was gratified when it turned out that she could sew for Roselyn. Mrs. McBride bought cambric and nainsook, and Melissa made underclothes and dresses for Roselyn. From the remnants she made a dress for Annie and a shirt for Benjy.

All that fall and winter Ben Baker found work for himself and his mules, but it seemed there was never enough money to cover all needs. Occasionally he would mutter about wanting to "git enough ahead to take a trip back to Texas."

"We ain't got that kind of money even with savin'. I'd like to go to The Mesa to see Shug and Pa and Ma. Shug writes that Ma ain't been very peart this last winter."

Ben Baker did not listen to his wife. He was thinking of the visit to Texas.

4. The next year, 1912, passed for Melissa with much the same hardships and deprivations she had known on The Mesa. She had little contact with the townspeople, her one outlet being her neighbors, the McBrides. Melissa grew thinner, her body losing some of its vibrancy. She noted that the flesh under her arms hung loosely. A few gray hairs appeared in the long brown coil held by bone hairpins. Ben still refused her permission to cut it.

In the third year she received a letter from Shug. "Melissa, I hate to give you the bad news. Martha Brownell passed away in her sleep. Guess it was her heart. She had got so fat. . . ." The letter started Melissa thinking about the mound in the burying ground. She wondered if the filaree still grew rank at the Big Mesquite thicket. She became homesick.

Soon after, Mary Belle came home to inform her, "Ma, Hannah's got a fellow at school. Name is Joe. He walks her to her classes."

When her father came home, Mary Belle repeated the news. Ben pursed his lips and narrowed his eyes. "Hannah's got her a beau. Now he'll be over here sparkin' her, I 'spose." Hannah hung her head and ran out of the room.

Melissa flared. "Pa, ain't you got no feelin' fer a youngun? You hurt her. She don't take kindly to that rawhidin'."

"A little joshin' never hurt no one. She kin take a bit o' funnin'. What does he do fer a livin'?"

"He works after school at the livery stable. He's one o' the Ladlee boys. Comes of a good family, God-fearin' people. Wouldn't hurt fer some o' that to rub off on this outfit. Now, you leave her be."

Ben walked out. Melissa heard the door slam and her husband's voice, "Damn, a man cain't even say 'a feller's come a-spooning.'"

The next Sunday afternoon Joe drove to the Baker house in a shiny black buggy with red wheels; it was pulled by a bay mare. He came to the front door and stood awkwardly, his cap twisting in his hand. "Missus Baker, I wonder if I have your permission to take Hannah driving?"

As Hannah and Joe drove away, Mary Belle said, "They already had that ride made up. He asked her at church."

"Yessum, I 'spect he did."

Ben Baker became more irascible with the passing of the years, and Melissa realized that time was slowing him. He was nearing fifty-five. The calls for his mule teams were diminishing. Employers preferred the new trucks and tractors that were beginning to appear everywhere. Ben was alarmed. He simply could not come by the money to purchase one of the new machines.

But both parents found consolation in the success of their children at school. Though they maintained the Filaree tradition of nightly work at the kitchen table, Melissa had been forced to relinquish her dream of keeping up her studies. She sought compensation in her association with Baby, but her youngest child seemed forever remote. The other children, mainly Mary Belle, cared for Baby. Melissa felt the estrangement and sometimes wondered if the feeling was punishment for her resenting the child's birth.

The fourth year came, and it was time for Hannah to graduate. Melissa began to think that the move from the Filaree Ranch might almost have been worthwhile. Though Ben Baker had missed out on some clearing jobs, and there was no money, Mrs. McBride bought material for Hannah's and Roselyn's graduation dresses. Melissa did the sewing in return. Ordering the material from Sears, Roebuck Company, the girls chose white dimity. Each evening Hannah requested to go to the McBrides' house. "Seems peculiar," her mother said. "You see Roselyn every day at school. Ain't like you to go off. I cain't seem to git the energy to finish yore graduation dress. I got Roselyn's done, and her underdrawers and petticoat. The baby does tire me."

Melissa continued to nurse the child. Shug had said that so long as Melissa "let the baby suck" she would not "git in the family way." Melissa's breasts had dried up years ago, and it embarrassed her to have a child of five seek her out several times a day for suckling.

The day before graduation, Hannah's dress lay unfinished on the sewing machine. The day had been hard for Melissa, her head ached, and her "innards fussed her." The children and her husband were in bed when Melissa lit another kerosene lamp and sat down at the sewing machine. Hour after hour she pushed the treadle up and down. Her eyes blurred and burned. Her head had hammers beating inside. Her neck "cricked" and her back muscles stiffened. She pushed the treadle into the early hours. As the east began to lighten, she bit off the last clinging threads and laid aside the completed dress. Going to the kitchen, she made a quick fire and boiled a cup of coffee. She closed her eyes and put a damp cloth over them. The sun was up. She called the children. Ben rose and went outside to feed the stock.

When Ben and the children left, Melissa put the irons on the stove and pressed the graduation dress. She washed and ironed the lavender-flowered cotton dress with a high neck and long sleeves, which she saved for special occasions. She wished she had a new one, of silk perhaps. This dress was too tight around the waist, where her body sagged and had begun to settle.

After the baby had eaten lunch and taken the breast, pulling on the lifeless, empty teats, Melissa took the opportunity to lie down. Her exhausted body, crying for rest, gave in to sleep even before the baby napped.

She was awakened by the children. Spider's voice assaulted her sleepy nerves. "We got outa school early 'cause o' graduation. We got the whole afternoon off."

Melissa rose quickly. "Then we better git started for the doin's tonight. Spider, you get your papa's good boots and shine 'em. Brush off his Stetson hat, the tan one, in the closet. Mary Belle and Annie, give me a hand fightin' out these flies. Bad as they was at the Filaree."

She stirred the fire. "When the water biles, I gotta rench the milk vessels. They smell plumb sour. Then you take the suds and wash out the slop jars. They needs a good scrubbin', Mary Belle."

They had an early supper that evening, and the house became a chaos of activity. Hannah and Mary Belle left early to ride with the McBrides. Ben Baker demanded his pants. "Where's my britches? A man works all day, and then cain't have his clothes ready."

"Hold yore horses, Mr. Baker. I'll have 'em pressed in a minute."

By the time they arrived at school, the auditorium was already filled with people. Melissa, ill-at-ease in her simple cotton dress, noted the fine wear of the other women. A few nodded to her. But her exhilaration at being at the graduation overrode her embarrassment. She and her husband took seats at the rear of the room, in the most inconspicuous spot they could find. Melissa and Annie took turns holding Baby on their laps. Green draperies across the front of the room hid the stage. Members of the school band were seated at their playing positions in front of the curtain. Although the windows were open, the air grew warm and moist.

Ben Baker fidgeted in the hard-backed seat. "Hell to damnation. Wish they'd git started." The band struck up with music, and the crowd grew silent. In the small enclosure, the band instruments blared and resounded. The introductory music ceased. Slowly the green curtains parted, exposing a double row of twenty-three graduates stiffly sitting on their chairs.

Melissa craned her neck to peer above the heads in front of her. She searched for Hannah's face. Her daughter was in the center seat in the front row. Roselyn was in the second row. Melissa thought their white dresses looked just fine. She wanted to wave to Hannah, but the thought made her blush.

Melissa recognized some faces on the stage. She whispered to her husband. "That boy on the right, ain't that the doctor's son? The girl on the end, that must be the lawyer's daughter. I seen her at the typing contest—the one that Hannah won."

A small man in a black suit came forward on the stage. Melissa again whispered to Ben, "Ain't that the Christian Church minister?"

The minister asked the audience to lower their heads for the invocation. Melissa listened to the man's droning words and thought of Dudley Schmelz's soft voice on The Mesa. Ben Baker twisted, as if the minister's words confined him. At the word "Amen," her husband lifted his head and sighed.

Melissa knew Mr. Lowe, the high school principal, would be the next speaker. He came briskly to the front and Melissa caught fragments of his talk, "The young people of today . . . leaders of tomorrow . . . our hope for a better world . . . four years of toil to complete . . . It is with pleasure and pride that I announce the student with the highest academic achievement for the four years, who will give the Honor Speech . . . It is my privilege to introduce the valedictorian . . . Miss Hannah Isabel Baker."

Melissa caught her breath and she heard her husband gasp. Had she heard right? *Miss Hannah Isabel Baker?* Melissa raised up in her seat, lifting her head higher to see the platform. She watched Hannah, in the white dress with the three rows of ruching and pink satin ribbon, rise and timidly walk to the front of the stage. Melissa felt cold, and then warm. She looked at her husband. He was staring straight ahead, his breathing heavy. His brown calloused hands were clenched in his lap.

Melissa heard her daughter's voice, high and thin and hesitant, the first few words almost squeaking. "To our principal and our teachers," and then the voice was stronger, "we offer our appreciation in reaching this platform tonight. To our friends whose support has sustained us, we thank you . . . To those to whom we owe the most, whose deprivations were made for us, to them we give our thanks and our love—our mothers and our fathers . . ."

Melissa heard no more. Tears gushed down her cheeks. Her heart pounded. She lowered her eyes and saw Ben's hands clenching and unclenching. The audience applauded and continued clapping long after Hannah had taken her seat. To Melissa the rest of the program became a blur. A graduate sang

a solo. The music teacher accompanied the class in singing
"America." A short closing speech was made by a boy in the
front row, and then the graduating class stood. The green
curtains closed.

The audience rose and gathered in small groups around the
room. The graduates came from backstage and surged into the
crowd, seeking their parents. Parents kissed graduates, and the
graduates laughed and kissed them in return. Beaming faces
nodded to one another.

Melissa and Ben Baker left their seats and pushed their way
through the excited groups to a corner where they stood alone,
waiting for Hannah. They saw their daughter walking toward
them, and Melissa raised her hand. Hannah's face was flushed,
causing her freckles to show against her skin.

Melissa put her arms around Hannah. "My daughter, you
didn't tell us. I'm so proud—" Then she stopped, her throat
choked, and the tears again washed her cheeks. She dropped
her head.

Ben Baker took Hannah's hands awkwardly, but he could
not speak. Hannah's sparkling eyes held his, and she smiled.

Mary Belle rushed up. "I knew all the time she was the
winner. We kept it secret. That's why she kept going to
McBrides'—to practice her valedictory speech. The McBrides
knew it." Then she turned to her mother, "There's Joe over
there—the one who likes Hannah." The boy noticed them
looking in his direction, and turned his head in obvious embarrassment.

The Bakers rode home that night holding their joy within
them. "Our girl has done us proud, Mr. Baker," Melissa said.
"You was right to leave the Filaree Ranch."

Her husband's voice was tight. "I don't regret it. Tonight
was payment in full. None of my kin ever went to high school."

"Tonight was my proudest time—"

"Now we got this one graduated," Ben Baker broke in,
"maybe we kin save for a visit to Texas."

Melissa listened in disbelief. "Ben, you been hankerin' long time to go to Texas, but we got other younguns."

She did not speak again. There was something in the way he spoke that dimmed the aura of Hannah's achievement.

5. The summer after graduation was the hottest ever in Tempe—or so the old-timers said. The Bakers rose at dawn to work in the cooler part of the morning, remaining inactive in the blistering early afternoon, and enlivening themselves in the late afternoon when the sun's fierceness had abated.

"This house is an oven," Melissa said. Benjy sought relief in a dampened hole under the porch. Melissa told him, "I do declare, yore jist as smart as an ol' hound dog. You got yoreself a scroochin' place—heap cooler than in this house." Benjy took Cheep Cheep with him, a pet chicken that rode on his shoulder.

It was that summer that Elizabeth McBride took a turn for the worse. Each day Melissa would bring a dish of food to her neighbor, but the sick woman's appetite was noticeably fading. Many times Melissa saw the doctor's buggy go past to the McBride ranch. The sultry days of August arrived, and Elizabeth had to be hand-fed.

Melissa, standing at the open window, fanning herself with a folded newspaper and planning a dish to entice Elizabeth to eat, heard her husband scraping the manure off his boots on the iron plate bolted to the porch. "Damn country—hot as hell. No work. A man ortn't to have to face it." Then he raised his voice. "Melissa, look, here comes McBride."

The black buggy stopped at the Bakers' gate. James McBride jumped from the seat and came with great leaps to the porch. "My wife, Elizabeth, she's—" He covered his face with trembling hands.

Melissa was the first to speak. "Mr. McBride, I'll go over with you to the house. Let me git my bonnet."

"I'll go to town and notify—" Ben Baker walked off the porch.

McBride stood up and measured his words. "Thank you. I appreciate it. I went in to give her a drink of water, and I found her. She was gone." He stared out across the irrigation ditch.

The next day McBride came to see the Bakers. He was composed. "I'm taking Elizabeth back to Illinois for burial. Roselyn and I will stay with my sister in Chicago for a while. Roselyn can go to college there."

Melissa looked at the suffering in the man's face. "We'll miss you," she said.

"I'm goin' to sell the ranch. I'll come back later to straighten up my affairs here. Don't know when. We leave tonight on the late train." And he was gone.

September came with humid heat. "I feel like a dead fly," Melissa said. Lightning played on the horizon in the evenings but the promise of rain was not kept. The place was lonely for Melissa now that the McBrides were gone. She had depended on their friendship and on the help they had given the family in the green house by the irrigation ditch.

It was Ben Baker's custom to stamp his feet when he was angry. One night Melissa heard his noisy striding on the porch before he opened the door. He removed his clothes as if his wrath could be relieved by tearing at them. "We gotta git off this place." He threw his boots across the floor. "Boer's goin' to let his brother's family move in here. His brother's offered to buy it, and Boer wants to sell. We'll haveta find a house in town to rent. Don't know where I'll keep my mules—"

"Mebbe it's jist as good. The younguns'll be close to school. They don't have no buggy now to git to their classes. It's been lonely without the McBrides."

Ben Baker snorted. "I don't know where we kin find a place.

I asked in town, and I understand the old Hudder house's empty. Wish I was back in Texas."

Melissa knew it was no use to offer consolation. Her husband would refuse it.

Ben Baker came home the next week to announce he had rented the Hudder house in Tempe and that they would move as soon as they could get their furnishings loaded. He was in a lighter mood when he told Melissa he'd found pasture close to the house where he could care for his mules.

In three days the family went into town to view the Hudder house. They walked up the sidewalk. The cracks made jagged patterns in the concrete; through the fissures grass had forced up withered blades. Ben pointed to the house.

"There she be. We's lucky to git any place a-tall to rent fer the price we kin pay. Wouldn't-a got this but Boer knowed the owner." His habitual scowl engraved his forehead. He swerved to face his wife. "Well, woman. Speak yore mind. You gotta bellyache about—"

"Don't be edgy. You done the best you could." Melissa looked at the yard, the hardened dirt broken by patches of dried Bermuda grass, the wire fence nagging at the staples that held its rusted form. She made an exploratory kick at the earth, raising a show of dust. "Ain't been watered for who knows how long. I do thank the Lord there ain't no irrigation ditch for Baby to fall into." She jerked her hand toward two ash trees supporting their trunks against a fence post. "I'm glad fer the shade o' them trees—scrawny as they be. What's that tall tree with the white bark?"

"The owner said that was a u-cay-lyp-tus. They's plantin' lots o' them in California." Ben walked over and crushed a leaf between his fingers. "Smell that."

Melissa stepped to the porch that sheltered the south and the west sides of the house in deference to the seasons of prolonged heat. The place was built of pine board—cheap, common, and uninteresting. The original yellow color had faded to a near-white. Melissa reached up and touched the curling paint; it crackled and fell into bits at her feet.

But one thing she could not complain about. Instead of an outhouse there was an inside water closet, a white hopper with a dark oak tank high on the wall, and a nickel-plated chain that released the water. Spider pulled the cord experimentally, liberating a horrendous flushing that resounded throughout the empty house. The children grinned, pridefully accepting the sound as an indication that "We's a-comin' up in the world." Melissa walked into the kitchen with the Michigan Hardwood Ice Box. She filed away the thought that in the summer she would purchase ice for special occasions.

Once again, the Bakers began a new life. Ben Baker found work clearing raw land of creosote, mesquite, and palo verde in Scottsdale where farmers were planting cotton and orchards of apricot trees. Melissa took in a girl from the normal school, who shared a room with Hannah and Mary Belle and returned on weekends to her parents' cotton ranch ten miles away. They needed the money.

The town of Tempe, on the banks of Salt River, was surrounded by farms of cotton, alfalfa, and grain. Ben said, "Folks here is different from Texas—even different from The Mesa folks. It galls me workin' my mules with these farmhands. 'Tain't like ridin' after my own cattle."

Hannah started her first year at the Tempe Normal School, a training school for teachers; Mary Belle, Spider, Annie were all in high school; and Benjy was in the fifth grade. Melissa was asked to enroll Baby in the normal school's prekindergarten group to demonstrate "the learning process for the teacher-training program." Melissa had continued to nurse Baby because she thought it would prevent pregnancy. But now that the child would be away at school in the mornings, Melissa decided that she had no choice but to wean Baby.

She painted her nipples with ink. Baby crawled on her lap,

and from habit closed her eyes and began to suck. After two pulls on the nipple she jerked away. She looked at the nipples. Black! She howled. "What'd you do to my titty?" She jumped off her mother's lap and kicked at her. "I hate you. I don't like black titty. Tastes bad." She ran outside and sulked, sitting under the eucalyptus tree.

That afternoon Baby returned and tried again at Melissa's breast, which was still inked. She bit down on the black nipple. Melissa screamed, bumping the child off her lap and slapping her. She pressed her hand over her throbbing breast. Baby lay on the floor, screaming and kicking. Melissa washed off the ink: Baby never again took the breast.

Hannah came home from school to announce that she had won two firsts in typing, for speed and for accuracy. "Our typing teacher told me they wanted someone to type on Saturday at the bank. She recommended me. Mr. Hanes, from the bank, came to school. I am to work this Saturday. I'm scared." She hugged her mother.

The telephone company accepted Mary Belle's application for after-school duty at the switchboard. She worked until past suppertime, and when she came home found little to eat, sometimes a cold potato or biscuits or corn bread. She made no complaint. The other children maintained their good schoolwork, and the teachers complimented them on their conduct.

Melissa's satisfaction in her children was darkened by her husband's increasingly ugly disposition. He became even more tyrannical than usual, and constantly exploded into profanity. With the move into town, the Bakers' home life began to change. Melissa could feel the old closeness of the ranch slipping away. Hannah spent more and more time with the boy who worked at the livery stable. The older girls, exposed to school and to new associations, became aware of the limitations of their background, their ungrammatical speech and their lack of manners. Mary Belle, who wanted to be a teacher, was an intense missionary in bringing enlightenment to the household. She would tell Baby, "Don't say 'ain't' nor 'he don't.' " Baby took to correcting the other members of the family.

At supper one night, Ben Baker ate silently, loading his knife with mashed potatoes and carrying the food to his mouth. Baby lifted her fork and said, "Papa, aren't you afraid you're going to cut your mouth with that knife?"

The family stopped eating, full of apprehension. But for once Ben Baker's face relaxed. "Missy, I ain't no more likely to cut my mouth with this here knife than you are to jab yore gums with that there fork." Everyone laughed; such moments seemed too rare lately.

When Hannah was graduated from the two-year Normal course, she and Joe slipped off to Phoenix and were secretly married. Just as quietly they left for the mining town of Hayden, forty miles away, where Joe had a job, like his father, in the copper mine. Ben Baker was shocked and disappointed. He told Melissa that he had been betrayed. She tried to calm his anger. "It's just that young people want to git married and start out on their own," she said. But her husband was unconsolable.

Mary Belle was graduated the following year, and secured a teaching position in Scottsdale. She was enthusiastic. "The first thing I'm going to do is to save my money. I'm going to buy a set of encyclopedias. When I have enough," she joked, "I'm going to India to see the Taj Mahal. Mama, do you remember when the teacher told us about the Taj Majal?"

That year Annie finished high school, but her father's income had so diminished that she had to take a job in a lawyer's office, filing and doing errands. At her noon hour, she took classes in shorthand and typing. She moved to Phoenix. Melissa was disappointed that Annie had been forced to stay out of school. She said to Ben, "Mebbe, though, the others kin go on."

Ben's voice was resigned. "That's all I've spent my days fer

—younguns in school. A man gits powerful tired gittin' nowhere fer hisself. I'm about to the end o' my rope. I'm a-
hankerin' to git back to Texas 'fore I die."

That same summer Spider found a job working on a friend's
ranch; he did not return to school. Only Benjy and Baby were
left now. Ben often worked out of town with his mules, taking
a bedroll and sleeping at the work place: To Melissa's relief, he
spent less and less time at home. The money he gave Melissa
was not sufficient to live on, and she supplemented it by taking
in sewing.

The terrible heat of southern Arizona summers didn't help
Melissa's spirits. People who found their houses too uncomfort-
able for sleeping took to setting their cots and beds outside for
the night. Melissa learned a great deal about her neighbors that
way: which dogs barked, which families quarreled. The man
who lived next door to the Bakers would get up in the night,
and in the quiet dark his whispered words could be heard:
"Elmer, peepee for Papa." But it embarrassed Melissa to think
that her neighbors could also hear Ben Baker's profanity. Sleep
did not come easily to her. Sometimes when the desert air
retained its heat, it was nearing morning before she dropped
off—and the Bakers were always up before the first light.

Of late Melissa noticed that it took more push for her to do
her work. Her step had lost its spring. The aching in her
abdomen was always there to remind her of her "female trouble." She talked about seeing the doctor but never went. When
she washed her heavy hair, the deep resentment toward Ben
revived. She had hours of melancholia. But the worst times
came when she allowed herself to think about what was hap-
pening to the family. It seemed to be disintegrating, and her
whole world with it.

6.

Melissa hurried to close the windows against the dust that was filtering inside the house. Beyond the butte she could see the dust clouds roiling, coming closer.

"Probably just a dust blow," she said to Baby, who was her most constant companion now. "No rain. Heaven knows we could use some. Them dust storms is always foolin' us, spittin' and blowin' dry." Baby said nothing, but continued to cut out pictures from the Montgomery Ward sales catalogue for her paper-doll collection.

The sky darkened. Melissa watched Benjy outside, holding his head back with his mouth open, catching the first drops of rain on his tongue. He opened the door, and a whiff of wet-smelling wind preceded him. "Shut the door. Quick. What for you stand in that dadblamed dust? Yore head's a-reekin' with dirt. Yore hair's a sight. Go comb it."

The rain increased, falling throughout the day and into the evening. It was nearly dark when Ben Baker clumped into the house, his wet boots leaving smudges on the floor. He took off his hat, and trickles of water splattered on the wooden boards. Stamping his feet, he released lumps of mud. He was in the foul mood that Melissa had come to expect and accept. His voice was petulant. "Damn rain. Wait all year. Then comes a gully washer. Won't be able to git the teams to the fields. I'll lose work."

The rain kept up into the next morning. It wasn't just a noisy storm that rattled the loose windowpanes, or beat the leaves off the eucalyptus trees, or slammed the back screen door on its loose hinges. It was a downpour confined by no breeze, making a pond in the yard and turning the road into a stream.

Ben Baker glared at the sheets of rain which obliterated his view. He limped to a chair and rubbed his leg. "Damp weather plays hell with my rheumatiz. Gits worse each year. Hell fer a man to git old and crippled."

He took out his pocket knife and began making holes in the leather of the harness that lay by his chair. "This is damn near past mendin'. Need a new outfit." He repaired the leather and the frayed edges of a rope, working silently, but with the scowl that scarred his forehead.

Melissa sensed that something was wrong. Though her husband seemed pleased with the mended harness, she knew he felt no real satisfaction. Ben Baker had a restlessness that was destroying him.

They saw a shadow pass by the rain-obscured window and heard a knock on the door. The town constable stood on the porch, water running from his slicker and his drenched hat.

"Baker, we're in trouble. Salt River's rising. Looks like it'll overflow and flood lotta folks outa their homes. We're filling sacks with sand to hold the water at the banks, and we need you and your teams. Gotta hurry on. I got lots o' folks to warn." The man rushed back into the rain.

Ben put on his old clothes, and reached for his slicker and gloves. "Don't know when I'll be back. Depends on the river risin'."

Melissa waited all day with the children in the house. The novelty of confinement began to pall on Benjy and Baby, and they bickered. By late afternoon, the rain abated. Melissa said, "Seems to be clearing a mite. If we could git through that water, we might go to Miz Ralson's house and see if she knows anything."

Benjy said, "Oh, let's go. 'Tain't cold. We're tired o' stayin' in this house. We'll put on ol' clothes. We been wadin' before."

They bundled themselves up and walked through the water to the next block, where they stood on their neighbor's porch. Melissa declined to go in. "We won't bring mud into yore house. Have you heard any more 'bout the river risin'? I was thinkin' maybe now that the rain's slackened, we might walk down to the bridge and find out. It's awful upsettin' sittin' at home."

"Wait'll I git a jacket and I'll go with you. Glad you come. I'm full o' fidgets myself, here alone."

"Mr. Baker done taken his mules and went to haul sand and rocks to the river's edge. Constable come this mornin' to git him. I was thinkin' mebbe there was somethin' we could do. Wonder if any folks is washed out and needs beddin' or food."

"Harry's been gone too. He said it was the rain in the mountains that come down. Might wash out the railroad bridge. Men up all night watchin' it. If they don't bank them low places, lots o' homes is goin' to go."

The women and the two children ploughed out into the mud, sloshing the muck over their shoe tops as they walked. The sky was still ominous, but the rain had stopped. Reaching the river's shore, they found pandemonium. Mud-caked men feverishly filled gunny sacks, and horses and mules pulled wagonloads of earth and rock to stay the onslaught of the water. As Melissa, standing on a high bank, watched them, she thought of frightened ants scuttling hither and back, overrunning one another in their frenzy. She did not recognize the Salt River. The gentle stream where she and the children had waded and rested on the sandy beaches was no more. An angry stranger flowed there, and she was reminded of Mary Belle stranded on Big Rock in the flash flood—so long ago, it seemed now.

Melissa saw Ben with his mule team, whipping through the bogs of mud, fighting the sucking water to inch forward and unload the rocks. She watched nervous women bring baskets of food and set them down for the men. They came forward, knocked the slime from their hands, and ate standing up. A five-gallon can of coffee rested on a fire on a protected rock. A woman stood and ladled out cupfuls. The men swallowed the liquid and returned to loading sand and rock into the gunny sacks.

That night Ben stumbled into the house after dark. He shed his muddied clothes on the porch and came in to huddle in a chair by the fire. Melissa brought a blanket to wrap around him. She warmed his supper, and he sat chewing huge mouthfuls of food and gulping cups of hot coffee.

"River's stopped risin'. Bridge held. Roadway leadin' to it washed out. Sutters' house is one of them that's gone. If this rain'd kept up, there'd been hell to pay. My leg's achin'."

"Did you have 'nough to eat? Coffee?"

Ben ignored her. It was as if he were talking to himself. "Damn this country. I'm plumb sick o' it. Heat kills a man in the summer. Too many people in this valley. Gittin' too crowded. They suffocates a feller. Smothers him. Not enough work to feed a man."

Melissa scraped bits of biscuit off the plate. "Most likely you need a good dose o' salts. Might be a cold yore catchin'."

"Woman, sakes alive, you got no understandin'. It's this country I'm sick of. The only thing good 'bout this flood is I got paid tonight for using my teams."

"I'm glad you got that money. Rent's due."

"Wish you'd put out some dry clothes fer me, and my other boots."

Melissa made sure that Benjy and Baby were asleep, and went to bed. It was dark and an hour before dawn when she heard Ben get up. He did not light a lamp but dressed in the dark. She heard him rummaging in the bureau drawers and in her sleepiness wondered the reason. She pulled the quilt over her head and drifted back to sleep. She heard him pull again at the bureau drawers and then heard him say "Goddam." She dozed.

Melissa awakened startled. It was light and she had overslept. Jumping out of bed, she called the children. There was no fire in the kitchen. Ben was not there. Her attention was caught by a piece of paper on the kitchen table. It was a note. She read and reread the three scribbled words:

"Gone to Texas." There was no signature.

Uncertainty overwhelmed her. The rent had to be paid. Where would she and the children go? The few dollars she had in the coffee can behind the flour sack would buy food for only a short while. She was owed some money from her sewing. She would have to call on Mary Belle at Scottsdale, but the need angered her. The world was blank. Her husband had not even said goodbye.

She was to remember for years the last word she heard from him: "Goddam."

7.

Melissa applied herself to the business of surviving. She became "the widder" who took in sewing, did housecleaning, and was the town's washerwoman. She found an old house, dirty and in need of repair. With cleaning and the addition of braided rugs and calico curtains to hide the cracks in the windows, she made the place respectable enough to rent rooms to two workingmen. By cooking their evening meal, she earned a tiny bit more.

Although never a churchgoer, Melissa wrote to Shug that "I got 'religion,' and I got 'affection' for the church. The Ladies' Aid Society of the church give me the privilege and some pay fer doing their dishes after their Wednesday Night Chicken Suppers." These affairs were to raise charity money to send to the needy in foreign countries.

Melissa explained to the children, "You-uns kin come with me. Part of my wages is our supper. We git to eat what's left."

Baby boasted to her friends about how "besides chicken, we git to lick the ice cream can—and sometimes there's some left for all of us." She and Benjy counted their life from one Wednesday night to the next. Benjy glowed on the big evening, "Tonight we eats high on the hog." The two children would wait in the church kitchen while their mother scraped plates and washed huge amounts of white crockery, enameled pans, and heavy cooking utensils—but they waited happily amidst the garbage of potato peelings, discarded lettuce leaves, and fried chicken grease.

The church ladies followed a rigid routine. The tables were not cleared, the dishes not removed, and the leftover food not returned to the kitchen until the completion of their business meeting. Sometimes social conversation further delayed the end of the dinner. One night Benjy, rubbing his stomach, lamented, "I'm so hungry I could eat a dadburned bear." Baby wearily sat on a chair, her head spasmodically dropping on her chest as she dozed. Melissa put Benjy's coat on the floor in the corner and laid her on the floor. Benjy waited for the food. When the platters finally came back to the kitchen, he surveyed the chicken remnants. He foraged among them, pulling skin from a chicken wing. "Mama, they shore done eat a lot tonight. I wish they'd leave a leg or a breast or a wishbone. They don't never leave them."

By the time they started to walk home, the streets were dark, the night cold, and Baby's legs crumpled when she tried to push them forward. Melissa and Benjy tried to form a saddle by crossing their arms to carry her. It didn't work. Melissa's back and arms ached. "I cain't hold her," she said. Benjy hefted the child on his back and carried her piggyback. Melissa thought she had never known such a tiring walk, the blocks seeming to grow in length as she forced her lagging feet forward.

Several days later, Benjy disobeyed his mother by going swimming in the river. "The boys—they done dared me." He came home blue-skinned and shivering. Melissa was wrathful and told him it was "plumb foolishness—you'll catch yore death o' cold." To punish him, she put him in the clothes closet without any supper. Exhausted, she went to bed.

Next morning when the breakfast was ready, she called him,

and when he did not come, sent Baby to go to his bed and get him. Baby returned to say he wasn't there.

In disbelief Melissa remembered. She ran to the closet and opened it. Benjy lay curled up on the floor, his nose edged toward the opening under the door. Full of remorse, she awakened him. "Benjy, I'm plumb sorry. Oh my Lord, I forgot I put you in here. I was so tuckered out last night I jist didn't have my wits about me."

When Melissa packed lunch for school with peanut butter and jelly sandwiches, Baby complained. "Peanut butter sticks to the roof of my mouth. Other children in my room have apples. Sometime kin we have a apple?"

Melissa wished that she had something else to put in their lunches. It did seem that Baby wasn't growing as fast as she should, and Melissa admitted that she was "a mite scrawny looking—plumb puny, in fact." The child, with her straw-white hair and her thin face dominated by eyes too large, made her look, as Melissa put it, "bug-eyed." Melissa discussed this with Addie Hankins, whose washing she did each Monday. Mrs. Hankins had become Melissa's closest friend in Tempe; she, too, agreed and added that Benjy looked "peaked." Melissa "laid to Benjy's pore blood" as the cause of the sores that broke out on his sallow skin.

Benjy scrounged the town for jobs. Sometimes he swept out the grocery store for Mr. Hankins and delivered bread for the Powers Bakery. He kept his money in an empty Bull Durham sack, taking out and counting and re-counting his coins. Adept at marbles, he added to his bank by selling his winnings in the game, an aggie or a steely for a penny.

Melissa was not much larger than the children, and her clothes were no better, but she accepted this. She believed in the work ethic, and she would tell the children that to toil was to be good. It was better to work and do without than to accept charity. Charity was a shameful word. She told Benjy and Baby, "People what are too ornery to git out and hustle come from poor stock. Some folks is no 'count 'cause they got pore bree-din'." As if to support her words, she smoothed her faded apron, clenched her worn hands, and repeated, "You younguns remember that you come from good stock."

Melissa's two boarders lost their jobs and moved to another town. Now Melissa could not pay the rent. She wrote to Shug. "We are moving into the attic above Addie Hankins' house. We don't take nothing free. I do her washing and ironing. Folks across the way has grapefruit trees and they give us a tub full."

The attic was barren and lined with rough lumber that gave splinters if one touched the walls carelessly. The weather had become cool. The heat for the attic came from the stovepipe that led from the Hankins' stove below. Melissa cooked on a kerosene stove. Sanitary facilities were outside. Benjy carried water from a faucet in the yard.

Melissa started to look for a better-paying job. Hearing that there was need for cotton pickers outside of Tempe, she de-cided to give up trying to find work in town. As she explained to the children, "It won't be fer long. Cotton pickin' season is on now. When it's over, we'll come back for you to go to school. We gotta work while the cotton is ripe for pickin'."

Melissa had not heard from Ben, and presumed he was in Texas. Her headaches had diminished. She contemplated cut-ting her hair but could not release herself from her years of oppression. At night as she combed the long strands, she pro-mised herself, "Someday, I'll whack it off, short, like a man's." She noticed a dull ache in one of her teeth, but she knew she could not afford a dentist.

Life, she felt, was passing her by. She thought of The Mesa and longed to visit again to see her folks. Sometimes the vision of Ike Talbott intruded, but it seemed so vague to her now.

One afternoon she went to the trunk by her bed, reached into the bottom, and took out a heavy object wrapped in a cloth. Unwrapping it, she looked at Ike Talbott's gun for the first time in years. As she ran her fingers over the weapon, the memories rushed back, painful but somehow reassuring. She knew then that she had not lost the strength to go on.

8.

Melissa stood in the doorway of the tent-house the cotton owner had assigned her and surveyed her new surroundings. The tents of the cotton pickers lined the banks of the irrigation ditch, white scars on the gray earth. A fig tree grew nearby, its roots exposed by water, its limbs twisted and disfigured. Beyond stretched the cotton fields with their rows of browned plants. Leaves, crushed by pickers' feet, filled the depressions with moist decay.

A sudden wind swept clouds across the wintry sky and shook the still-dormant buds on the cottonwood trees. Melissa shivered. Tomorrow would be her first day picking cotton.

She turned inside and set about arranging the room. Its canvas top and sides were anchored to a three-foot siding and a wooden floor, still splattered with grease and dirt from the previous tenants. Bare boards formed a doorless cupboard on one wall. The pipe of the Supreme Wood Heater thrust its rusty neck upward through the roof. Lighting the fire, she heated water and began scrubbing. Benjy brought in cottonwood sticks.

"I know you say these don't burn so good," he said, "but I cain't find nothin' else." He walked by the shelves. "Ma, look at them rat turds. They smell."

"I'm cleanin' 'em, Benjy. I'm cleanin' it all. You and Baby unload that box and help me make the bed." She lifted heavy quilts onto the metal bedstead and springs. "We'll all haveta sleep here together till I can find a cot for you, Benjy. It'll be warmer, though, together. Tomorrow we gotta git up early. We git paid for as much as we pick."

The sun declined behind the cotton field, and the air grew

colder. Melissa heated two bricks on the stove, wrapped them in a cloth, and put them between the blankets. The children moved their bodies close against her and slept. But Melissa lay awake with worry. Could she pick enough cotton? What about the children's missing school? Where was Ben Baker?

She listened to the wind outside, slapping at the canvas, whipping the dead winter leaves along the ground, whistling a requiem. A noise inside joined the wind's talk: mice scuttling. Somewhere, a rooster's crowing announced the dawn; Melissa stirred. Her breath vaporized in the chill. Putting her feet on the rug by the bed, she hurried to snatch a shawl. By the light of the coal oil lamp she pulled on a pair of men's overalls and heavy, high-topped laced shoes. "Benjy, Baby," she called. "Time to git up. We wanta git to pickin' early."

By the time Melissa and the children set out for the field, light was spreading in the east. Their lungs ached from the cold air. Benjy pulled his cap over his ears and hunched his shoulders. Baby, a scarf tied over her head, held her mother's hand and trudged along on the frozen earth. They came to the darkened stalks topped with white cotton bolls. The dank smell made Melissa sneeze. She stamped her feet. "Feels like my feet'll crack off. You pore little younguns, near froze to death."

Benjy puffed on his blue fingers, tucking his hands under his armpits. "Jump up and down," Melissa told him. "Git yore circulation movin'. Won't be so bad once that ol' sun comes up. By noon, we'll be peelin' off these coats." She unfolded a quilt she carried. "Baby, I'm gonna wrap you in this. You lie here at the end of the row till it gits warmer."

Melissa fastened the canvas loop of the cotton sack around her neck and one shoulder, and letting the bag trail behind her, she started up the first row. With numbed fingers she reached high for the top bolls and crouched to ferret out the cotton near the ground. Benjy silently pulled his sack in the adjoining row.

When Melissa had picked back down the row, she walked

over to where Baby lay on the ground. The child pushed back the covers. "Mama, I got to go diddly."

"Go squat in that ditch behind the cotton. Ain't no one near." She blew on her hands as she unwrapped the child. "Hurry, 'fore you freeze."

The child returned, shivering. "I'm hungry."

"We'll eat come noon. Cain't stop now. Lie back down."

By noon, the sun had warmed and dried the cotton patch, and Melissa removed her heavy coat. Together with other pickers the Bakers sat at the end of the cotton rows eating their lunch of cold biscuits, fried meat, and sorghum. Down the way Melissa recognized the man who lived with his family in the tent adjoining hers. Baby kicked at the damp earth. "I wanta go with you, Mama. I'm tired waiting here."

"The stalks is still too wet and cold. You stay here where the sun hits you. Mebbe tomorrow it'll warm up. Look at my britches. They're wet." Bits of mud fell from her pant legs as she shook them.

At the first signs of approaching darkness, Melissa and Benjy joined the line of pickers waiting to weigh their cotton. She dragged her sack to the scales, her back sore and aching, her head throbbing. The weighing master upturned it on the table. "You musta been out early. Cotton's wet. Makes it weigh more." He was not unpleasant, though.

The weeks that followed were like the first day. Melissa and the children became acquainted with the family in the next tent. She told the mother, "I'm glad Benjy's got yore boys to pick with." At night the boys gathered dried tumbleweeds from the fence and lighted them in a bonfire. One Sunday the Bakers were invited to chicken dinner by their neighbors. It was a relief from the salt pork, cornbread, and beans that were their usual fare.

Benjy began picking cotton with the neighbors' boys. When the days grew warmer Baby wanted to follow them. "Mama, cain't you keep her with you?" Benjy objected. "Them boys say words she ortn't to hear."

"Then you ort not to say words she shouldn't hear. I'll tell her to stay far back of you. She's just lonely."

She gave Baby a pillowcase, and the child trailed along behind. She picked as high as she could and squatted to get the low bolls. Soon she stopped to rest. She saw her brother and his two friends reaching down now and then to pick up a small pebble which they tossed into their sacks. Feeling that her own sack held little cotton, she found a rock and dropped it in. By late afternoon Baby had added several more rocks to her pillowcase. She followed the boys into the weighing station.

The owner, taking her bag, turned it upside down on the table. The rocks tumbled out with the bolls of soiled cotton. The man's voice was stern. "Seems you put extra weight in your sack. We pay for cotton, not rocks." Baby's eyes clouded over. None of the men in the line laughed. She said, "I saw the boys—" Benjy grabbed her and pulled her out of line, "Mama wants you."

The owner smiled. "Just a minute. Come back. Don't you want your pay? How old are you?"

"Seven years."

The man wrote on a piece of paper. "Take this paper to that man at the table and he will pay you."

Baby's face lit up. Running to the table, she held out the paper. The paymaster dropped the money in her hand.

Counting the coins, she ran to her mother. "Look. I earned seven pennies—one for each year old I am."

Melissa said, "You done fine—for your first day's work."

One evening Baby came into the tent with a cat in her arms. "Mama, can I keep this kitty? Them Mescans that moved away give it to me. They give Benjy that hat he's wearing."

"Cat? Looks sick to me. Mangy."

"I'll put medicine on it."

"Cat's sick. We cain't hardly feed ourselves. Cotton pickin' season is nigh over. Folks movin' out. Not enough left in the field."

"Kitty can eat rats." Baby carried the cat outside and Melissa saw the animal clawing for release.

When Benjy came in, she said, "Baby's picked up a sick cat. I want you should get shut of it. Take a gunny sack and—"

"You mean . . . ? No. I cain't drown no cat."

"Benjy, you gotta. You're the only man we got in this family."

That night Baby took the cat to bed with her, smothering the animal against her chest. In the morning when she awakened, her arms were empty. "Where's my cat?" She ran outside. "Kitty, kitty, kitty." But it was nowhere to be found.

The cotton fields closed, and the tenant pickers moved out. Melissa, preparing bacon, pulled her butcher knife across her finger, testing. "So dull it wouldn't cut butter." She ran the blade back and forth across the metal stove. "You need a whetstone, Miz Baker." The neighbor's wife stood in the doorway.

"Come in," Melissa said.

"I can't stay. We're packing up, gittin' ready to leave. Just wanted to know if you had any plans."

"I ain't rightly sure. No place to move to. No work."

"We're movin' to Brawley. There's work in the melon fields fer men. Here's a newspaper my husband had. In the advertising, there might be somethin' fer a woman."

"Thank you. The owner is wantin' us out of this tent. They're ready to plow the fields." She called to Baby. "Come here." She pointed to the bare spot on the child's head. "What does that red spot look like?"

The neighbor woman examined the bald area. "Miz Baker, 'pears like ringworm to me. Put iodine on it. I've got some that ain't packed."

"I knowed that cat was sick. You done got it from that dadblasted thing, Baby."

The next morning Benjy was scratching his head. "My head itches like the devil."

"Needs washin'. Come here, let me see." Melissa parted the boy's hair. She frowned. Pulling a hair from the boy's head, she ran her fingernail along and felt a roughness on the strand. "My Gawd, Benjy, that's a nit. You got lice. Where's that hat them Mexicans give you? No tellin' how many's wore that hat." She sighed, "Hope our troubles don't come in threes. We've got two already. I'll haveta cut off all your hair."

"No, Mama, don't want my hair cut all off." Benjy screamed. "Just wash it."

"Hush up. We don't wanta catch them things from you."

Melissa got the big shears and took Benjy outside. When she finished she put coal oil on his head. All that day the boy sulked under the cottonwood tree, holding his clipped head between his hands. He stared at the hawk flying above him and wished that he too were flying away.

The next morning Melissa's neighbor came to the door. "We're fixin' to move on. Wanted to say goodbye. Do you know where yore goin'?"

"Not rightly. I done wrote a letter to an ad I seen in that paper you give me. Wanted a cook at a mining camp in Quartzsite. Ain't had time for no answer yet."

"What'll you do about the children?"

"I've give it thought and worry. I can send Benjy to my daughter Hannah. She lives in a mining town in Pinal County. Her man might not like it, but I'm gonna ask if they'll keep him. My daughter Mary Belle teaches in Scottsdale, and mebbe Baby could stay with her. I just don't know what to do. I'll have to work out somethin' if the man gives me the job."

At the supper table, Benjy spread his fingers apart. "I got a burning in my fingers, in between."

Melissa examined the spots. "Let me see yore belly. Stop scratchin'." She looked at Benjy's waist. "Benjy, I do declare. You got the itch." She scowled as she examined the irritation caused by scabies.

"Is it catchin'?"

"It blamed sure is. Everythin's a-happenin' to us. I gotta send to town for sulphur. Put that and lard on you."

"Does it hurt? That sulphur?"

"No. We're goin' boil yore clothes and that bedding. I'll burn these old socks you got on."

A knock sounded at the door. Melissa saw the cotton owner outside. "Missus Baker, could you tell me when you'll be moving? My men need to start ploughing where these cabins are."

"We gotta be here a little while. My boy has the itch. I need some sulphur.

"All right, I'll have my men hold off on the ploughing a bit. I can bring your sulphur from town. I'm going in for the mail."

Melissa spent the next few days doctoring Benjy. Her tooth had been aching, but with her other problems, she ignored it.

On the fourth night she lay in bed thinking. *My hard luck has come in threes, for sure.* She sighed, and the sound echoed in the still air. She thought of Ben Baker. Her feelings were as cold as the ashes in a campfire after an all-night rain. For a fleeting moment the image of Ike Talbott passed before her. It seemed so long ago that he had held her in his arms. But the memory was as comforting and warm as the few embers that still glowed in the cookstove.

She planned to leave in the morning.

9. Melissa sat on a stool in the Quartzsite Cafe. She had received an answer to her application for the cooking job at the mine. Reading the letter again, she replaced it in her pocketbook. She had looked at the signature several times and wondered about her new employer. *Jason Herrick* . . . According to his directions, he would meet her here, at the stage stop in Quartzsite, Arizona.

Facing the window, she gazed at the Mojave desert country and at the ochre-colored mountains to the north. Her thoughts centered on the past two days. She had left Baby with Mary Belle and had sent Benjy to the eastern part of the state to stay with Hannah and her husband. *It was all I could do*, Melissa justified herself.

On the wooden counter before her lay a week-old issue of *The Arizona Republican*. "General Pershing arrives in Paris," she read. But she did not follow the war news. She pushed the paper aside. At the moment, her own survival was more important.

Except for a man in working clothes, she was the only customer in the Quartzsite Cafe. He sat at the other end of the counter taking large bites of apple pie. Seeing Melissa looking at the paper's headline, he poised his fork in midair. "Lady, with Black Jack in Europe, them Huns'll run. They ain't even human. Them Huns been putting ground glass in the cornmeal we Americans buy."

Melissa felt uneasy. She imagined a piece of corn bread in her digestive tract, glass fragments cutting the intestines, the blood seeping. She shuddered.

The man brought the fork to his mouth. "Them Huns been killing little babies. Little innocent babies in Belgium. Sticking swords in their stomachs and hacking the bodies. And cuttin' out the babies' eyes."

Melissa tried to black out the image. At the cotton patch where she had worked, the pickers knew little about the war across the ocean. But she had heard a few talking about "the horrible things the Germans did."

The man swallowed the last of the apple pie. "And what's

more, the Germans in our own country been sneaking around putting poison in the tanks that hold our drinking water."

The only Germans Melissa knew were the owners of Kruger's Grocery Market in Tempe. She had always thought them fine people. She had bought the sauerkraut that Mrs. Kruger made. She recalled the storekeeper's kind face. *Miz Kruger always give me an extra ladle of sauerkraut and never charged me.*

Shoving his empty pie plate away, the man pointed to a calendar on the wall. Below a picture of an azure lake surrounded by bright-green trees and a blue sky, Melissa saw the date: 1917. The man shook his finger. "Before this year is out, Black Jack will have the Germans whipped. Them dirty Huns . . ." He walked out the door, muttering.

The talk had disquieted Melissa. Running her hands over the front of her print dress, she smoothed the wrinkles. She felt as drab as the cactus wren in its nest on the cholla cactus outside the cafe. She raised her shoulders. Her back ached from the eight-hour ride in the old open Cadillac which served as a stage on the Phoenix–Los Angeles route. With both elbows on the counter top, she cradled the coffee cup in her hands and sipped. The heat of the coffee sent a throbbing reminder of her tooth, still aching.

The cafe owner, a white round cap on his head, came through the door of the kitchen. Standing in front of her, he swished a soiled rag across the counter. Sweat glistened on his upper lip. There was no one else in the cafe. "Waitin' for someone?" He made another slap at the counter with the rag. Two flies escaped to settle on the specked window, with its uncertain view of the dull hills beyond.

Melissa placed her feet on the multicolored valise. "I'm to meet a Mr. Jason Herrick here." She swallowed the last of the coffee. "I got a cookin' job at the Lost Hope Mining Camp."

"Yep, I know. Jake comes to get supplies here. Stage only brought part of his order this time. Couldn't get some of it on account of the war."

"Did Mr. Herrick say he was comin' here?"

"Last time he was in, he said for me to look out for the lady cook comin' in by stage. I figured you was her. Not many folks stop off here. Mainly they're on their way to California. Jake'll be tootin' in any time now in that flivver of his—if it don't break down or bust a tire."

The man wiped the moisture from his forehead with the back of his hand. Picking up a toothpick from a glass on the counter, he stuck it between his front teeth. "Road to his claim is hard on tires." Melissa noticed the teeth, stained brown. The man chewed aimlessly, moving the wood from one side of his mouth to the other. He snatched the cloth and lunged at a returning fly. "Jake's camp is yonder, by them hills. That's as far as the road goes. Then a trail takes off to the mine." He gestured. "See that saddle between them peaks? That's where the trail goes." The owner jerked his chin toward a haze moving from the hills. "That must be old Jake coming." The dust cloud came closer and settled in front of the cafe. A worn Ford chugged to a stop.

The man who opened the door looked to be Melissa's age. His face and clothing revealed years of exposure to the outdoors. He took off his hat, giving it a quick slap against his khaki trousers, and silt filtered to the floor. He lifted his hand toward the man behind the counter. "Hi ya, Bill."

Walking toward Melissa, he lowered his voice. "Missus Baker? I'm Jason Herrick." Melissa liked his smile. The teeth gleamed white against the rugged brown skin of his face. She nodded.

Herrick looked at the valise on the floor. "This all your belongings? Soon's as I get a cup of this rotten stuff Bill sells as coffee, we can be on our way to the mine. Like a cup?"

Melissa Baker sat beside Jason Herrick in the front seat of the Ford. Her body shook as the car bumped along over the uneven dirt road. She laid her hands in her lap, folding the swollen knuckles one over the other. Occasionally she gripped the seat to lessen the jolts. Her tooth ached.

"In about an hour we reach the base of those hills," Herrick said. "Road ends there. I've got a couple of horses and a mule tied up. I'll get your valise and the supplies on the mule. We'll ride to the claim. It's not far. You ever ride a horse?"

Melissa smiled. "Yes. Used to ride in Texas. Then later we had a cow ranch in Gila County, here in Arizona." *Ride a horse?* For a fleeting second, she recalled riding bareback in her nightgown to Big Mesquite Thicket.

"Good. I only got a small mine. Work three men. We may get a cold supper when we get there."

Melissa liked the way he turned to her when he spoke, his brown eyes soft. She found herself enjoying the talking. "How long you been at your mine?"

"Four years. Was partners with an old prospector. Bought him out last year. He preferred looking for gold to digging it. That's what keeps a miner going—looking for that color."

Melissa wanted to know more about Jason Herrick. "You Arizona born?"

He looked at her before answering, his eyes only slightly darker than his tanned skin. "Missouri. Left our farm on my sixteenth birthday. Thought that day turned me into a man. Had restless feet. Rambled and roamed. Did lots of different kinds of work."

"A life free from care, Mr. Herrick?"

The man tossed back his head and laughed, his lips strong and firm. "Not precisely. I've had my ups and my downs. Never had time to settle. Never married. Wouldn't want to force my life on any woman. Hardly stayed in one place long enough to meet any girls."

"And your folks?"

Herrick threw the car into low gear and the Ford climbed a sharp, bumpy incline. "My parents passed away in Missouri, long time ago—on the farm. No use for me to go back home now. Only shirttail kin left. Someday I'd like to stop roaming, squat on farmland. Always wanted to try my hand at cotton growing. I hear it's a good business in the Valley now."

Melissa listened to the easy-flowing voice and liked its warmth. Already she felt she knew a great deal about Jason Herrick. "Do you get lonely at the mine?"

He took his foot off the clutch. "Don't have time to think of that. Too much work. Seven days a week. I'm doing well bringing out the ore—and for a small claim. Lonely? I guess I could be."

Melissa found herself telling Jason Herrick about The Mesa and her folks. "My sister Shug does beat all. Best company there is. She's younger than I am but she's gettin' white hair already. Don't bother her none though. And it don't make her look old. Guess it's 'cause she's most times laughin'. And that's what folks see, her good humor and her spunk."

Melissa eased her body down into the seat. She felt relaxed with Jason Herrick. She set her eyes on the gap in the mountain where the road ended and they would continue on horseback.

It was early evening when Herrick and Melissa rode into the camp. They reined their horses to a halt near a frame cabin. Herrick took Melissa's hand to help her alight. His grip was firm, and she felt the strength of his fingers. "Missus Baker, there is the cook shack. I'll call the boys to put away the horses. We'll go see if there's a bite left for us to eat."

The mine owner held her arm as they walked to the cabin. Melissa's legs felt as if they had been starched. It had been years since she had ridden horseback, especially on a mountain trail.

In the kitchen, Herrick introduced her to the three men sitting around the table. She saw them only as vague faces. He carried her valise to the adjoining room. "This is your sleeping quarters. I'll show you where to wash up. I'll hustle and get us something to eat—if these boys left anything. They'll be glad to get your cooking after my meals!"

. . .

In a few days Melissa came to distinguish the faces of the miners and to learn their names. They all expressed appreciation for her cooking. She remembered to place the chili pepper by Jose Hernandez's plate. He sprinkled the red powder on his beans and smiled at her. *"Muy bueno, señora. Me gusta mucho."* Billie Bassoon, not more than twenty, was always hungry for something sweet, and she made him macaroons. She was at ease with all the boarders except Bear Hobbs, so named, the men told her, for his brutish strength, his lumbering walk, and the black hair that covered his arms and chest.

Hobbs had a voice as big as his physical proportions, and he dominated table conversations. She noted that his eyes followed her as she filled the plates and walked from the stove to the table. She avoided looking at his coarse, pitted face.

One evening after supper, Hobbs returned to the kitchen, where she was washing dishes, and asked for coffee. Melissa became agitated. It was not the custom for the men to come back to the kitchen and her sleeping quarters after supper, nor to ask for service other than at mealtimes. Uneasily, she poured coffee from the pot. Reaching for the cup, he brushed his shoulder against her. She walked into her room and shut the door. She heard Hobbs leave the kitchen. Thereafter, she never spoke to him nor looked at him when she placed food on the table.

Her days settled into routine. She was up at five o'clock each morning, starting the fire in the cookstove, getting breakfast, and packing lunch for the men. The remainder of the day she cooked, washed dishes, swept, and scrubbed. She carried buckets of water from a nearby spring.

The men paid her for washing their clothes, and although the work of heating water, using a rubbing board, and hanging the clothes on the bushes exhausted her and left her hands raw and burning, she needed the extra money. She made a schedule, doing some laundry each afternoon before she started the evening meal.

She fought an unending battle with the armies of small black ants that invaded the kitchen in search of food crumbs. She wiped and swiped. They got into the sugar bowl and paraded on the syrup pitcher. She put the table legs into cans of water, hoping to "drown them piss ants."

The miners worked until dark, and she saw little of them. There was scant socializing in the evening. The men came in for supper, ate, then retired to their tents for the night. "The men work long hours," Herrick told her, "but I pay them well. Then we take off for a spell, several weeks, before we start again. Seems to work better that way." There was no respite from work on Sundays. Each day was like the rest: cooking, washing, cleaning. Herrick asked her if she could stand the tedium. "We have to do as much as we can before the heat of summer comes. Gets unbearable. Then the men go back to their families. We resume in September when it cools."

Although the days were filled with limitless rounds of work, the solitude depressed Melissa. Sometimes when she had supper ready and waited for the men to come in from the shaft, she stood in the cabin doorway staring at the desolate course of the canyon below. She had always found consolation in nature, but here she sensed no relief, no pleasure in the rocks and the scrub growth. Only Jason Herrick's kindness softened her feelings of isolation.

When she went to the spring for water, she heard the mourning dove's forsaken call. She remembered hearing the same song by Tonto Creek, near The Mesa cemetery. She wrote to Shug. "Sure would like to see you all. Sometimes I want to run away—where I don't know. This is a good job, though. I don't want to lose it. I'm saving my wages. I don't know where else I could get work. Mr. Herrick is a fine man, comes from good stock."

She had also written to Mary Belle in Scottsdale. Baby was in school and doing well, her daughter had answered. But

Hannah's husband, Joe, had complained about Benjy's living with them. Melissa fretted.

The nights increased her loneliness. As she lay awake in the dark, her conscience punished her with painful memories and fears, doubts and self-accusations. She longed for companionship and for a stop to the aimless fading away of her existence. At night, too, the ache in her tooth became worse. She could feel the skin on her underarms and neck becoming flaccid, and she was frightened by the signs of age.

It was on one such night of sleeplessness that she sensed, rather than heard, a noise. *In the kitchen.* Her heart pumped against her breast. Rising, she tiptoed toward the door. Before she reached it, the hinges whined and a huge form was outlined in the dimness. She steeled her voice. "Get out! Get out of my room, Bear Hobbs!"

She ran to the kitchen and out the door. She heard Hobbs' footsteps pass her as she fled down the pathway, her screams echoing in the canyon stillness.

A light appeared in the tent down the way, and she saw a man's figure emerge. Jason Herrick was panting as he hurried toward her. "What's the matter. Did you scream?"

Melissa was shaking. *What should I say? Will I lose my job?* Perspiration seeped under her arms. She tried to quiet her breathing. "I'm sorry. I thought I heard somethin' outside. Sounded like an animal around my window. I must have had a nightmare. Sometimes I dream. I didn't want to cause any trouble or awaken anyone." She was glad the darkness hid her nightgown.

Herrick walked around the cabin. "Don't see anything. Might have been that mule wandering around. He can lift the latch on the corral gate. They're no wild animals around here. Are you all right now?"

"I'm fine. Sorry I disturbed you." She felt assured with the presence of Herrick. "Thank you," she said again, and hurried back to her room.

Thereafter Melissa did not eat at the table with the men, as had been her custom. She filled their plates and retreated to her room. When the men were gone, she came out and ate her meal. She told Jason Herrick that she had a "nervous stomach" and ate better alone. She noted that Bear Hobbs was quieter, and his talk with the men more reserved when she served the table. He kept his eyes away from her.

One afternoon in the following month, the miners came in early. Melissa saw them walk down the trail from the mine shaft and go into their tents. Herrick came into the kitchen and sat down with her. "Bad news, Missus Baker. Machinery broke down. Can't fix it. Needs a new part. I have to send for it to California. May be weeks, even months, before I can get it. I told the men we'd lay off until the replacement comes. They need the rest. They get cabin fever when they're penned up here too long. When we get the machinery, I sure do want you to come back. Be hard to get along without you.

She looked at his rugged face as he sat across the table. It was not a handsome face, but it was strong and kind, with eyes that were brown and soft as they looked at her. "Missus Baker, let me know your address. Write to me. Keep in touch."

The next morning Melissa packed her worn valise of flowered carpet material. As she was leaving the mine, her thoughts were of Jason Herrick. She recalled how he had carried water from the spring and filled the black wash pot for her. She thought fondly of the cooler he had built for her food storage, a wooden frame covered with gunny sacks she could wet so the air would cool the food inside. No man had ever shown her such consideration. Now Herrick took her to the stage stop. As the converted Cadillac pulled away she repeated to herself the miner's final words, "Write me." She hoped she would see him again.

10.

Melissa trudged down the dirt street to the Scottsdale boardinghouse where Mary Belle rented a room. She knocked, and Mary Belle came to the door. "Mama! I wasn't expecting you. Only got your letter last week, and you didn't say anything about . . ." She put her arms around her mother.

"I'll tell the story soon's as I get my breath. Just got off that stage." Melissa bent to wipe the dust from her shoes and loosen the laces. Weariness stooped her back. She sneezed. The rooms were heavy with the odors that old houses accumulate.

Mary Belle pointed to a chair. "Sit down. You look ready to topple over." She looked at her mother's worn gingham dress and straw hat. "Did you come on the stage in that dress? Same one you had in Tempe. It's so . . . As always, Mama, you make do."

"I didn't have no sewing machine at the cotton camp nor the mine. I've had to save what little money I got." Merciless sunlight slipped through the curtains, accentuating the lines of strain in Melissa's face. "How is Baby?" She reddened at the memory of the child's birth and of how she had wished it dead in her womb.

"She went to the store for thread. I'm making her a new dress." Mary Belle handed her mother a glass of water. "Don't worry, Mama. She's doing well in school. Happy here with me."

Melissa relaxed. "I'm powerful glad to hear that. Have you heard from Hannah?"

Mary Belle began folding the dress scraps scattered on the table. "Yes. She and Joseph have rented a house. It's small, but is all they could get." She waited before she continued. "Hate to tell you this, Mama, but she says Joseph doesn't want Benjy to stay with them. Crowds the house. He sleeps on a cot on the porch. And he hasn't fit in well at school. Some boys chased him home with rocks."

Melissa sighed. "We'll just have to wait and see."

"Hannah writes that Benjy can stay until school is out and then . . . she doesn't know."

"I'll write to Shug. Maybe he can go to The Mesa for the summer. Ma and Pa ain't able to care for no youngun." She paused. "Any word from your papa?"

"Had one card. Said he was in Stone Springs. Annie came to see me Sunday. She has a beau and he drove her over. She likes her job in Phoenix and expects a raise. She had her beau drive her to The Mesa so she could check on Spider. She said he looked all right, and the folks like the work he does on the ranch."

"Mary Belle, I just feel shook up—all our family is scattered. I cain't hold 'em together. I'm goin' to have to find work. Mr. Herrick said he didn't know when the machinery would be fixed. Could be months. I can't wait that long."

Mary Belle put her arm around her mother.

"I'll keep in touch with everyone, Mama. We'll find some way."

Melissa rubbed her cheek. "Tooth's sore. Been botherin' me somethin' terrible lately. Gotta to git to Tempe to the dentist . . ."

Quick steps sounded on the porch. The door opened and Baby rushed inside. Seeing the strange figure in the rocking chair, she stopped. Melissa reached out her arms. Rising, she walked to the child and hugged her, kissing the top of her head. But Baby pulled away from the embrace and ran to her sister's side.

Melissa grew pale. She watched as Baby picked up her schoolbooks and sat in a corner, turning the pages.

Mary Belle cleared her throat. "Mama, I'll get a wet cloth for your tooth." She continued hastily. "And I'll tell the landlady you'll be here for dinner."

Melissa's voice was strained. "Don't go to no bother. I ain't hungry. She walked slowly back to the chair and sat down.

"You have to eat."

"Coffee'll do me."

"You've been on the stage for hours." Mary Belle walked toward her mother.

"I don't wanta put you out none."

"I'll get a cot in this room for you to sleep."

"Oh, a quilt or two is good enough. I'll make me a pallet to lie on the floor. Tomorrow I've got to go to Tempe. See the dentist. I can stay with Addie Hankins. She's alone now, and got room. I'd like to visit with her anyway."

Mary Belle walked to the bed and pulled a pillow from under the covers. "Come over here and lie down. You've had a long trip. I'm going to take Baby outside on the porch and help her with her lessons. We won't bother you. Supper's at five."

"Thank you. I guess I'll lie down. Rest my eyes for a spell. My tooth hasn't let me . . ."

Mary Belle motioned to Baby, and the two tiptoed outside to the end of the porch. "Why did you treat Mama like that?" Mary Belle whispered. "You didn't even kiss her." She took Baby gently by the shoulders.

Lowering her head, the child stared at the floor. "I don't know. I don't want her to hug me, kiss me."

"But you love Mama. She loves you. Someday when you're older, you'll understand that Mama has had a hard time. When I was your age, I used to feel like . . ." The woman stopped. She was remembering her own childhood on The Mesa.

"I don't love her. I love you, Mary Belle." Tears appeared on the child's face. She clasped her arms around her sister's waist.

Mary Belle's voice was as soft as the feather mattress she and Baby slept on. "And I love you." She put her arms around Baby and felt the small body shaking with sobs.

The following morning Melissa boarded the stage for Tempe. As soon as she arrived she hurried to the dentist's office. The doctor frowned as he examined her mouth. "Missus Baker, why haven't you had this tooth extracted? No wonder it's paining you."

"No chance, doctor. Been in the hills cookin' at a mining camp. My problem now is to git work. Have you heard of any around here?"

"Open wider. I'm going to pull it. No work here. But I read that in California fruit was ripening. Man in here the other day told me he'd been working in the packing sheds in Mar Vista, California. Said the war has taken so many young fellows that women are working in their places." The dentist adjusted the light into Melissa's mouth. "I'll try not to hurt you."

"Yank away, Doctor. Won't hurt no worse than what I've had."

The doctor arranged his instruments on the white cloth covering the dental tray. Melissa sat in his office for an hour, and then, with throbbing jaw, she walked to visit Addie Hankins.

Addie Hankins invited Melissa to move her chair deeper into the shade of the porch. "You're a sight for sore eyes. Mighty glad to have you visit. Tell me what you've been doing."

Melissa held a handkerchief over her twinging jaw. She talked about the mining job and Jason Herrick. "I don't have much use for men, but that Mr. Herrick is different from Ben Baker and others."

"Have you heard from Mr. Baker?"

Melissa wiped away bloody spittle from the edge of her mouth. "Nary a word. He orta send some money to help with the younguns. They needs clothes. Orta send Hannah somethin' for Benjy. I jist can't make it on my own."

Addie Hankins lunged with her swatter at a fly buzzing

overhead. "That's jist like a man. I had one same as yours. Always thought about his own enjoys."

"Yes, Miz Hankins, Ben Baker allus did take care of his own delights. Wimmenfolk and the younguns come fer the hind part—and there never was much hind part left." Melissa's voice rose. "Most men is no 'count."

"Cain't say I blame ye nary a bit fer feelin' like you do. You've worked hard. What d'ya reckon you'll do now?"

"I jist don't rightly know. Dentist tells me he hears there's work in California—packin' fruits and vegetables. When my tooth's a bit better . . ."

"Aren't you leery goin' off by yourself to California?"

"I sure am. I hates to go off to a place I don't know. But there's nothin' else to do. My family's splittin' up, and I got to get work. I'm goin' hang on to the few dollars I saved at my cookin' job."

Melissa stayed five days with Addie Hankins, and then returned to Scottsdale to tell Mary Belle that she was going to California. Her daughter assured her that Baby could stay with her and that she would let her mother know about the other children. "I'll write Aunt Shug myself and make some kind of arrangement for Benjy when school is out. Maybe one of the ranches could use him."

Melissa put on her hat. "Might' nigh stage time. I'll write you from California—soon's I git settled."

Mary Belle picked up her mother's valise. "I'll carry this for you. Whew! It's heavy. What in the world do you have in it? Your few clothes could never weigh this much."

Melissa didn't answer. But she knew the weight in the valise was a Colt .45. As she walked beside her daughter toward the stage depot, she felt her hopes rise. *Maybe life will hold more for me in California.*

11.

From the front seat where she sat next to the driver, Melissa saw a frame building with the letters PACIFIC COAST TRANSPORTATION COMPANY painted on a panel above the door. The stage, a converted automobile with the passengers' baggage tied on top and on the running boards, drew to a stop. The driver pulled himself from behind the wheel. "All passengers out for Mar Vista, California." He unloaded several suitcases.

Stepping onto the sidewalk, Melissa arched her back to relieve the stiffness. The cold air tingled her nostrils: salt from an ocean breeze. She had been thoughtless not to wear a coat. But it had been nearly a hundred degrees when she left Phoenix, and she could think of little besides the problem of finding work. She looked at the abundance of grass and trees, at the automobiles in the street, at the Oriental faces. The strangeness of the place made her apprehensive.

The man behind the desk in the stage office pointed his finger to a building in the next block. Lugging her dust-covered valise, Melissa made her way slowly down the sidewalk. She stopped at a sign in a smudged window: ROOMS FOR RENT. DAY AND WEEK RATES. Her heel caught on a loose nail as she struggled up the steps.

A full-figured woman, with a coarse complexion and gray-streaked hair wrapped in cloth curling rags, opened the door. Her eyes traveled from Melissa's face to her feet, and rested on the valise. "You want something?"

"The man at the stage depot said you rented rooms. I need the cheapest you have."

The woman continued scrutinizing Melissa, shivering on the steps. "What's your business here?"

"I'm lookin' for work. Heard there was jobs in the packin' sheds."

The woman scratched a pimple on her chin. "Money in advance for the room. How long you stayin'?"

"Depends on gettin' work. I'll pay for a week in advance."

The door opened wider. "Come on in. Lotsa people looking for work. Though you don't look strong enough to do field work." The two walked down a narrow hall.

Melissa surveyed the small, sparsely furnished room. Against one wall stood a narrow bed with an iron frame. A wooden stand supported the porcelain pitcher and washbowl. On a repainted dresser, a missing drawer handle had been replaced with an empty spool, held by a nail.

"Somethin' wrong?" The woman scratched again at her chin. "My cheapest. You want it?"

Melissa nodded, wrapping her arms around her chest.

"You cold? Got no sweater?"

"Just seems damp. It's been hot where I come from in Arizona." She opened her purse. How much for a week?"

"Two-fifty. I'll bring the change. Toilet's down the hall. I furnish one towel a week."

Melissa heard the sound of the woman's footsteps recede down the hall. She stared at the dingy lace curtains, mildewed where the edges touched the casement. A cockroach halted on the window sill, then slid into a crevice that seemed no thicker than Melissa's fingernail. Her window looked out on an alley. She sniffed the air. A stench of decaying onions seeped in from the fields. "Might mean work, though," she consoled herself.

A sharp knock sounded on the door, and the landlady entered. "Here's a key. And your change."

Melissa felt the emptiness of her stomach. "Any place to eat near here?"

"Cafe down the street. Jim's Eatery. I don't allow no cooking in the rooms. No smoking. No drinking. No loud noise. No carousing." She nodded her head, the curls dangling. "And no men in your room!" She left.

At Jim's Eatery, Melissa found herself the only customer. The place consisted of small tables covered with figured oilcloth and a long counter at the rear. Across the back wall stood a shelf with glasses, cups, and a coffee pot.

The proprietor came toward her, sipping coffee from an agate cup, balancing a cigarette on his lower lip. With stained fingers he motioned toward a folded cardboard sheet. "Want to see our bill of fare?"

"No, thanks. Coffee. You have soup?"

"No. Got pie, though. Apple-cherry-peach." Leaning closer, he took the cigarette from between his lips. Melissa saw the swarthy skin of his face. "You new here?"

Melissa felt her appetite disappear. "No pie. Just coffee."

The man took a step closer. The armpits of his brown shirt were stained with sweat. "You must be one of Missus Gael's roomers. Any new person is always from her place. I get 'em all here to eat." He walked away and returned with a cup of coffee.

Melissa drank. "I'm here lookin' for work. I heard they were hirin' in the shed."

"Little lady, you come to the right place. Old Jim knows 'em all." He rubbed his hand across his nose. "The boss eats here. I can put in a good word for you."

"No, thank you. Where do I find the office to apply?"

"Not far from here. Up the road a-ways. Where d'you say you was from?"

"I did not say. But I came from Phoenix. Can I walk to the sheds?"

"If you'll wait, I'll—"

"I'll walk." Melissa frowned, rose, and started toward the door.

"Wait. I didn't mean no harm. Don't get huffy. It's lonesome this time of day. I just wanted to get acquainted."

Melissa turned. "I forgot to pay you. How much for the coffee?"

"Application office closed now. Open in the mornings only. And you don't owe old Jim nothin' for the coffee. Introduction to a new customer. Worth it just to talk to you. I get lonely."

Melissa handed a nickel to the man. "I pay for my coffee."

"Don't get sore." He followed her to the door. "Come in the morning. The boss eats breakfast here. If you need old Jim, just call on—"

Melissa was out the door, hurrying toward the rooming house.

12.

Melissa tossed anxiously in her sleep. She moaned, and the sound awakened her. She pulled the quilts over her, trying to keep out the breath of the fog. She had been dreaming that she was struggling to wash her long hair, and then had been trying to cut it. Daylight was beginning to creep in under the mildewed curtains. Today she would ask for work at the sheds. She dreaded the task, but her timidity was not as great as her fear that she would be forced to accept help from the cafe owner.

She dressed quickly and counted the money tied in her handkerchief: one five-dollar bill and a quarter. She went outside, her heels clicking on the sidewalk. A storekeeper stopped his sweeping and leaned on his broom to watch her. Melissa hurried past him.

She went into Jim's Eatery. The haze of cigarette smoke suspended in the air made her sneeze. Men in work clothes sat at the tables. They all seemed to be talking at once. They pounded the tables, shook their fists and waved their hands. Only the owner noticed her entrance. He came toward her, cigarette hanging from his mouth. "Coffee, my little lady?"

"And a doughnut. I'm on my way to see about a job in the shed."

He leaned toward her. "See those men? They're on strike. That's why they ain't at the shed. They're mad. If you go to the sheds, might be trouble."

"How can they strike? The war needs their help. I am goin' to go to the shed."

"If this strike keeps on, these men are goin' to hang around here. I'll need help." He moved his face closer and she felt the heat of his breath. "Why don't you work for me?"

"No. I'll try the shed."

He drew in on the cigarette. "These men'll stay here till they eat and drink up their money. Strike might go on for weeks. The job is yours. You'll have to come down off that perch, little lady."

A voice bellowed from across the room. "Jim. Give us eggs and bacon. More coffee." He went to fill the order.

Leaving the cafe, Melissa directed her steps toward the shed. As she neared the packing building, she found the sidewalk lined with groups of agitated men.

She walked up the steps and into the office. Before she reached the grilled window, the man inside shook his head. "Office closed."

"I wanted to ask about work."

"Not hiring. Strike's on." He turned his back.

Melissa retraced her steps. The men, still in belligerent clusters, scowled at her.

Back in the rooming house, she took a tablet of lined paper from her valise. "Dear Mary Belle," she wrote laboriously. "I'm in Mar Vista, California. No work in the sheds. Strike is on. I hear there's fruit picking up north. I may try my luck up there. I'll let you know my address when I settle. Will stay around here for a few days trying for other work. I don't want to use up my little savings by traveling." She signed the note "Mama."

At the drugstore she bought a newspaper and checked the "Help Wanted" column. Returning to the rooming house, she asked to use the phone.

"Well, dearie, I don't want you tying it up. With that paper in your hand, you might be a long time."

"Only two calls." She picked up the receiver, and a tremor went through her. At The Mesa there had been no phone, and in Tempe she had only called the doctor once. She firmed her lips, "I wonder if you'd show me how to call this number."

"Why sure. You do it this way." The landlady spoke into the black mouthpiece. "Give me number five-oh-two." She stood and watched while Melissa called another number.

"No jobs, huh?"

"I'm going to go and check on this other ad." Melissa left.

When she walked into Jim's cafe, the owner came toward her. "How's the job huntin' going? Any luck, little lady?

Melissa sat down, stretching her toes inside her shoes. "I've walked all over this town. No work. Tried all the ads in the paper."

Jim sauntered closer and she noted the puffed skin under his eyes. His voice was close to her ear. "Why not work for me? Better than starving. I ain't hard to get along with. I'm fond of ladies."

Melissa shook her head. She wanted to get away from the dark face, the coarse voice. "No. I don't want to work here."

Jim continued talking. "I can get lots of help. Cheap. But they'll steal you blind. I've been busy all day. These strikers hanging around. Haven't had time to even wash the dishes. Sink's full. You wanta start now?"

Melissa rose. "I cain't think. Cain't hardly move I'm so tuckered out." Forcing her aching feet toward the rooming house, she thought only of going home to Arizona.

For three days Melissa hunted work, asking at shops, talking with people she met in the street. She counted the money in her handkerchief. On the fourth morning she stood, hesitating, outside the cafe door. The air was motionless, gray and clammy with mist. Her spirits were as leaden as the overlay of clouds. Shivering from the dampness, she forced her hand against the doorknob.

She walked through the empty dining area to the kitchen at the rear. She found the owner standing at the grease-marked stove. The glow of a yellow light bulb accentuated the sallowness of his skin and the grubbiness of the interior. Dirty containers of mustard, chili, pepper, and salt were arranged on a shelf above his head. Nearby, next to a dented garbage can, lay a sack of potatoes.

He looked up. "Thought you'd be comin' in one of these days. No work? You got a job here." Holding a safety pin, he jabbed at the palm of his hand. "Splinter. Broom handle. Been threatening to throw away the damn thing."

"Guess I'll take that job you offered," Melissa said, "at least for a while." She pushed her pocketbook behind the gunny sack of potatoes. "Don't use no pin. Get a needle. Put the point over a flame."

Jim stabbed at the splinter and blood showed on his palm. "I'm tough. Don't need no care. I got it." He lowered his eyelids at Melissa. "We better cook up a batch of stew for today. Got some vegetables gettin' old. Stew goes a long ways."

Melissa, an apron around her waist, sat at the work table with mounds of onions, potatoes, celery tops, and carrots. Cutting up the vegetables, she added them to a pot of meat boiling on the stove. Jim came in with trays of dirty dishes. She washed them and he brought more.

Carrying food scraps to the garbage can, she lifted the lid. The stench repelled her. Rolling the heavy can out the back door to the alley, she poured the contents into a larger container and cleaned out the can with a hose. Dirty water and decayed food drained down the alleyway.

Inside, Melissa washed her hands and began shredding cabbage. The strikers' loud talk filled the dining room. A voice reached her. "I ain't going back to work till the bastards give me a raise. War or not. '

Jim hollered to her through the narrow window separating the kitchen from the front counter. She hurried to fill his orders. The kitchen grew hotter. She wiped perspiration from her face. Hair, escaping from the pins, fell on her forehead. Brushing it away with one hand, she pushed orders through the opening to Jim.

Late in the afternoon the rush subsided. When all the strikers had left, Jim came into the kitchen. "You did good work. Lots of business today."

She didn't look up from the stove she was wiping. "Cookin' ain't new to me. Done it all my life. Cow camps. Ranch. Mine. In Tempe, too."

Jim helped himself a bowl of stew. "Good cookin', this stew. Tomorrow we can mash up the vegetables, add lots of onions, and have soup." He wiped his bowl with bread, then licked his fingers. "Don't want to get personal, but are you married? Or workin' at it?"

Melissa did not answer. She had come to earn money and be on her way north to the fruit orchards.

She went in search of the toilet. In the small room behind the back door the air was rank from stale urine. Holding her breath, she used the stool and returned with some Fels-Naphtha soap. She scrubbed the wash basin and the toilet stool. "If I'm goin' work here, I cain't stand this stink." She thought of Shug, who swept her dirt yard with a broom and put old newspaper on her splintered cupboards. *Oh, wouldn't Shug have a conniption fit at this filth?*

Returning to the kitchen, she saw Jim putting pepper in the remains of the stew. "I say, add lots of seasoning and lots of water. Customers won't miss the meat. It's quittin' time, little lady."

Melissa took off her apron and pushed back her hair. Reaching for her purse behind the potato sack, she felt Jim's hand on her shoulder. His voice was thick and slow. "I'll just walk home with you."

"No. I been out after dark before. Keep your hands to yourself!" She dashed out the back door.

In her room, she pulled off her shoes and rubbed her aching feet. She brushed her hair. "Needs washin'. It will have to wait till a sunny day comes along. Never get dry in this fog."

She worried about her work at the cafe and distrusted Jim. "Damn men. I got to keep the job long enough to get stage fare north to pick fruit." An insect buzzed above her and she slapped at it in the falling darkness.

13.

Melissa had been working at Jim's Eatery for almost a month, and still the strikers did not return to the packing shed. She heard that some had moved on to find work elsewhere. Business in the cafe slackened. Jim took to closing on Sundays.

"Men are using up their savings," he told her. "Now they spend what they have on liquor. They think that'll take their cares away."

Melissa responded with coolness to his continued familiarities, and she sensed a growing irritability. Then, at closing time one Saturday night, Jim turned out the front lights, locked the door, and came into the kitchen. Melissa had already put on her sweater and tied a scarf over her head. She was at the back door when he grabbed her, forcing her against the wall. "Little lady, I've had enough of your leave-me-alone airs." His arms fastened her. The scarf slid from her head, dislodging the hairpins and loosening her hair. Her purse dropped to the floor.

"Damn you!" She screamed and fought to pull away.

"No use to holler. No one can hear. You been ignoring me for a long time. A man can stand only so much. And I've had it. Tomorrow's Sunday. You and me's goin' to make a night of it. I been wantin' to get after you for a long time. What you savin' it for?"

Wrenching her arm free, Melissa remembered reining a horse on The Mesa. *If you pull hard on the bridle, he'll fight it. Rein him easy. He'll respond.* "Perhaps you're right. But I cain't breathe. You're crushin' my ribs. You're hurtin' me. Please." She smiled.

"You been hurtin' me for a long time." But feeling Melissa relax, the man loosened his grip.

Melissa flung her head forward and thrashed her hair against his face.

He stepped back. "My eyes! You hellcat!"

She brought her knee heavily into the man's groin. He groaned. His body sagged and he crumpled, moaning, to the floor. Grabbing her purse, Melissa sprinted out the back door.

She ran all the way to the boardinghouse, locked herself in her room, and sat down on the bed. Her breath came in irregular spasms. She made a decision. Leave now. Jim owed her a week's wages. She would not get it. She had paid a week's rent in advance, and she would lose that. Her savings were little more than sixty dollars, tied in a handkerchief.

Stuffing her belongings into the valise, she started for the door, then stopped and returned. Suppose the landlady reported her absence to the police? On a piece of lined paper, she scribbled: "Here is the key. I had a call from Arizona. Am going home. My daughter is in the hospital." She signed her name.

Outside in the cool air, Melissa breathed more calmly. She looked up and down the highway and started north. Soon she was at the edge of town and in the countryside. Few cars passed in the night. Her feet became sore. The valise was heavy, and she shifted it from hand to hand. She forced herself on, not knowing what to do except to keep going, hardly thinking, intent only on putting distance between herself and Jim's Eatery.

She could walk no farther and stopped to rest against a tree trunk. A car slowed down as it passed her, and she heard the brakes. It backed up until it had drawn even with her.

The man behind the steering wheel leaned across the empty seat toward her. "Going far? Want a ride? I'm headed up the coast, all the way, past San Francisco." He waited.

Melissa moved closer and peered at the man. He was small, clean-shaven, dressed in a dark business suit and a small-brimmed hat, which he wore pushed back. She hesitated, and then spoke. "All right. I do need a ride. I'm so tired, I just cain't walk another step." She walked back to the tree and picked up her valise.

Inside the car, she listened to the droning of the wheels and knew she was wearier than she had realized. Her head fell forward and she jerked it back. The man kept his eyes on the road and pressed down on the accelerator. She wished he wouldn't drive so fast.

He leaned toward her. "Kinda late for a little one like you to be out alone. "What's your destination?"

"I'm going to . . . Los Angeles."

"It's not my affair but—"

Melissa flared. "That's right. It is not your affair."

The man laughed. "Don't get testy. Just making conversation. Maybe we'd better introduce ourselves. Name's Henry."

"My name is Adelaide. Adelaide . . . Hartley." She rather liked the sound of the name. "Just got word my mother died. I'm rushing home. Couldn't wait to get a bus." Melissa felt pleased with the falsehood.

"Oh, I'm sorry," said the man. "I didn't know. Didn't mean to pry."

"Of course you didn't. It's all right. I'm sufferin' so with the death that I don't rightly know what I'm sayin'. I'm in a hurry to get to Los Angeles."

The driver searched for a new topic. "I travel this road every week. Go north to take orders. Los Angeles and so on. Anything that cuts—that's my business. Knives, scissors, tools." He looked sideways at Melissa. "In fact, I'm quite a cutup myself."

Melissa did not laugh, ignoring the invitation. "You must spend lotsa time drivin'."

"I do. Gets tiresome. Lonesome. That's why I pick up passengers. I'm afraid I'll go to sleep driving at night. People give me someone to talk to. Passes the time. But I never picked up a woman before."

"Oh." Melissa could think of no response. "Do you travel lots at night?"

"No. Had a little trouble with the car today. I'm trying to make up time."

The car was open, and the cool evening air blew back her hair. She noted the cultivated fields passed into a wildness of untouched country as the automobile pulled farther away from town. The road was graveled but wide enough to permit the passing of the occasional car that came by. Melissa hardly bothered to answer the driver's attempt at conversation.

"Uh-huh," Melissa listened to the rhythm of the turning wheels, and her eyelids grew heavy. "I see." She fought the drowsiness. Her head fell forward. She straightened up. Leaning back on the seat, she swayed with the motion of the car. Everything darkened.

She was awakened by a light. The car had stopped. Beneath the light swung a sign advertising TOURIST ROOMS. She saw a row of numbered rooms with a concrete pathway connecting them. They had reached the edge of a town.

The man opened the car door on her side. "Is my baby sleepy? Thought we'd stop here for the night. It's past twelve. I can see my baby can use a little rest."

My baby? Melissa's torpor passed in a flash. She felt her heart pound. *What did the sonofabitch mean?* The man walked toward the office. Melissa dragged out her valise and followed. A frowzy-headed woman sat behind the desk. She looked up from her magazines. "Wanta stay all night?"

The man ignored Melissa. "A room—for my wife and me."

Smiling, Melissa stepped forward with money in her hand. "I've been sick all day. I'll take a room by myself. Don't want to bother anyone." She began to cough and pushed a two-dollar bill into the woman's hand.

"Number five. Two doors down." Melissa grabbed the key and hurried out. She heard the woman say, "Mister, I got number eight for you, across the way."

Melissa entered number five and locked the door. Putting down her pocketbook and valise, she began to set up a barricade. She pushed the back of a chair under the doorknob. Straining, she moved the bed against the chair. She locked the window and, dropping a metal ashtray inside the tin wastebasket, balanced it against the window sash.

She lay in bed listening. Sleep did not come. She heard steps, someone fumbling at the door, then a noise at the window. She sat upright, her heart pounding. She had been dreaming. All was quiet. She lay back and dozed.

The next morning she awakened to full daylight. She dressed and cautiously peered out the window. Only two cars were parked in front of the rooms. The man's car was gone. Across the pathway the door to number eight was open. Grasping her pocketbook and valise, she stepped outside. Number eight was empty. She breathed easier.

In the security of daylight she no longer felt the terror that had throttled her the night before. She walked toward town, found a restaurant, and ordered breakfast. When the waitress came to pour her another cup of coffee, she asked, "Any work around here?"

"No ma'am, not that I know of. But a customer told me there was work in Peach Valley. Fruit is ready there. Jobs in the packing sheds."

"How far is Peach Valley?"

"About fifty miles."

"How can I get there?"

"If you wait at the post office, you can ride up with the man that takes the mail. He carries passengers sometimes. He leaves about noon."

Melissa paid her check and lugged her heavy valise toward the post office.

14.

Melissa arrived in Peach Valley and rented a room in a private home. She liked the small town, with its huge walnut trees shading the sidewalks and the yards of flowers she had never heard of on The Mesa: purple bougainvillaeas, pink hydrangeas, giant scarlet geraniums that grew high as the fences. The grasses were many and different, but none like the filaree.

She found work sorting peaches. The area outside the packing shed was busy with loaded trucks coming in from the orchards. An aroma of ripe fruit hung in the air. The voices of the drivers and other workmen mingled in talk and laughter, bringing a twinge of homesickness to Melissa. She would save her money, and someday, she would go home.

She sat at a long bench, with fruit rolling in front of her on a moving belt. Her fingers, though slightly stiff with arthritis, were nimble enough to sort the impaired peaches and push them into a side box. She felt the strain on her back. Taking quick glances around her, she saw the faces—brown, white, black, yellow—all hunched over the tables, and hands operating in a mechanical rhythm.

The brown-skinned woman next to her spoke softly. "Señora, you work too hard. Your back is straight. Do like me. See?" She slumped her shoulders and settled back. Melissa saw that she was pregnant.

"Thank you. I'm new at this job."

"*Sí.* I know. I been here long time. Soon I quit. Going to have a baby." The woman clutched at her abdomen and

Melissa caught the peaches that slipped past her. "I got pain —bad. Baby comin' soon."

Melissa wished she could do the woman's sorting for her. "Yes. Babies are pain. I've had eight." The memory flashed back: Hannah, Mary Belle, Annie, Spider, Benjy, Baby—and the baby left in the Texas grave. She felt a dull ache. *And Carter in The Mesa grave.*

Her neighbor nodded. "Eight? I only have three, and that is too many. Life is hard. My man is not good to me, not good to the babies. All men—the same. I have been weeth two husbands. Same life. Same pain. Same work. *Trabajo mucho.*"

The quitting whistle released Melissa from the bench and the unending flow of peaches. The next morning at work, the seat next to hers was empty. She wondered about the Mexican woman. Soon the space was filled. Taking covert glances at the new worker, Melissa gauged her to be in her late forties. Her face was heavily powdered, her cheeks tinted with rouge, her mouth bright with lipstick. Her henna-dyed hair gleamed artificially. She wore a too-tight skirt and a blouse that strained at the buttons over voluptuous breasts that had started to sag.

Melissa liked her at first sight. Was it pity or understanding she felt for the woman who sought to hold back the years, to cling to a youth that was no longer there? The woman maintained a theatrical pose, with a stretched smile and a posture that forced her neck upward.

At the thirty-minute lunch break, Melissa made her way to the end of the shed where sandwiches were dispensed. The woman moved beside her. "Mind if I eat with you? It's my first day."

"Surely. I'm new too. You cain't learn much from me. Pleased to have company, though. Let's sit over here." The woman carried their lunch to a vacant bench at the other side of the room.

"My name's Evelyn." Talking fast between bites, the woman told Melissa about herself. She was divorced and lived alone, moving up and down the coast and working at different jobs. She laughed often. At the end of the lunch period Melissa knew she had made a friend. The assurance of a companion made her feel less lonely.

After three weeks Melissa and Evelyn took living quarters together. The two-room apartment had a bedroom with two single beds separated by a striped curtain strung on a wire. The other room was a combination of kitchen, dining, and living areas. The kitchen had a two-burner gas stove, a small sink with an overhanging brass water faucet, a wooden drainboard, a folding-leg table, two straight chairs, assorted dishes, and mismatched cutlery. A worn sofa with weak springs and a faded covering dominated the parlor end.

In the following weeks, Melissa came to know better the woman with whom she roomed. Evelyn's cheerfulness helped to raise her spirits.

They had Sundays free, and Evelyn spent the mornings refurbishing herself, putting buttermilk and cucumber packs on her complexion, buffing her fingernails, washing her clothes. She took time out to show Melissa the new foxtrot dance her friend had shown her. She told Melissa, "That new style, bobbed hair, is what everybody's wearing. I might even cut mine, but right now I want you to help me put this henna dye on it. Just the roots. Touch 'em up a bit. Don't need much. Look there in the sack I brought from the drugstore."

Melissa read from the package. "Take two parts of henna to—"

"Sweetie, you don't need to read the directions. I done this so many times, I can do it both eyes closed. Here. Give me that bowl. Pour this much peroxide into this white powder, and then the henna." Evelyn mixed the dye components and handed the bowl to Melissa. "Now, part my hair in the middle, begin at the crown, dab it on like this." Go easy. Don't scratch my scalp. This stuff burns like fury."

Evelyn talked much and laughed often, and Melissa found

herself joining in. Encouraged by Evelyn's interest, she reminisced about her life on The Mesa, her husband Ben, and Jason Herrick. She did not mention Ike Talbott, although she thought of him occasionally.

"Men? I love 'em," Evelyn said. "They're out for what they can git—but I'm on to 'em, and I'm takin' care of Little Evelyn first."

"I'm goin' to cut my hair when I get divorced from Ben," Melissa told her.

"Ain't you divorced, honey? Why not? I was only fourteen when I ran away and got married the first time. I didn't know nothin'—not even where babies come from. I soon found out. My husband left me. He was just a young one himself. He loved to go dancing. I was no good at it then. He had women, and I was home alone. Then one day he just up and went his way. That was in Kentucky. The baby died. Guess it was for the best. Pore little thing wouldn't had no life with me, and no daddy. Then I went my own way. Come out here to California. I made up my mind that no man was ever goin' to hurt me again— and they haven't." Evelyn's eyes became thoughtful, and then bitter. "Oh, maybe they have—a little—once or twice."

She often brought home a bottle of whiskey and mixed a hot toddy as the two women sat at night discussing their lives. Melissa found it hard to accept some of the off-color stories that Evelyn told. "A dirty story ain't no harm. You see, there was this traveling sa—" She stopped. "Oh, I told you that one?" She began to rouge her cheeks. "I'm goin' out tonight. Got me a new sweet daddy. Whyn't you make yourself a little drink, and one for me too?" Melissa shook her head and prepared a glass for her roommate, but not for herself.

She had slowly begun to accept Evelyn's free living, her disregard for the conventions that had always guided her own life. She did not approve, but neither did she condemn. The one thing she did find offensive was Evelyn's choice of her numerous men friends.

Her roommate explained it. "I'm free. I like 'em young. Makes me feel young myself. I don't want no old, worn-out codger with his toes on the edge of a coffin. He'd probably have the gout and the chiggers and the wheezies."

"But Evelyn, the ones you choose are young enough to—"

"Sure, they are. Go ahead and say it. Young enough to be my son. It's the young ones that keep me young. I wanta git outa this life all I can. Of course, some of them don't have any money—but they got good bodies."

When the knock sounded on the door, Evelyn quickly inspected herself in the mirror. She pulled at a lock of hair and let it curl over her forehead. Melissa looked at the youthful face of the blond caller. *This one is not much past the pimple stage,* she thought. He grinned at her and acknowledged the introduction weakly. "Howdy."

The door closed, and Melissa heard their voices fading away. She listened to Evelyn's laugh, forced, childlike, but merry. With Evelyn's exit the room seemed to grow as colorless as it really was. In spite of their differences, Melissa had come to depend on her roommate's company more and more. Evelyn never gave Melissa time to brood. But when she was alone, depression settled in. Her thoughts turned invariably to the uncertainty ahead. Her life remained unfulfilled, her sense of destiny was fading. She got up to make herself a hot toddy.

It was on nights such as these that Melissa wrote letters to Shug, to Mary Belle, and to Addie Hankins. Shug told her about the changes on The Mesa, how some friends had died, how others had moved away. Mary Belle, who had become a supervisor in the Scottsdale school system, was keeping in touch with the loosely connected Baker family. Hannah had a baby now, she informed Melissa, and Benjy had long since gone to The Mesa and was working with William Brownell at the El Bar ranch. Annie was engaged to a young man who worked in her office in Phoenix. Baby was doing well in school and was happy living with Mary Belle.

But, Mary Belle added, there was no letter from Jason Herrick.

15.

The peach season ended, and Melissa and Evelyn moved to new towns. In Pomona they worked in the citrus sheds. The next year they traveled to Salinas and found work packing vegetables. The war was over but it made no difference to them. The following season they moved south to Banning to the cherries, and on to Beaumont to the apricots. Then they traveled north again to the San Joaquin Valley, working with fruits and vegetables.

Melissa continued to think about returning to Arizona, but whenever she had saved enough, the money always seemed to be needed for something else. Many times it went to keep them between jobs. When Evelyn's teeth became such a problem that they had to be extracted, and her vanity dictated that the dentures be only the best, Melissa was again left without funds. Five years passed.

She received a letter from Shug that her mother and father had both died, within a month of each other. Since the mail was slow and Melissa's change of address so frequent, several weeks elapsed before she received the news. "Pa fell and broke his hip," Shug wrote. "When Ma moved him off the ground to a chair, the bone pierced the flesh, and seems trouble set in then. We got him to Roosevelt to the doctor, but it was no good. Jimso has a Chevrolet car now, and he drove him into town. They brought him back to The Mesa, where he just stayed in bed. But Ma seemed to get younger taking care of him. Then he took pneumonia. Didn't last long. And Ma just let down after Pa died. She couldn't seem to eat nothing."

Melissa pained as she read the letter. Regret flooded her that she had never had the chance to return to The Mesa. Now they were gone. Too late, too late.

Melissa began to notice that she had periods of "feelin' out of sorts with Evelyn." "Melissa, I got no time for the blues," her friend proclaimed. But Melissa hurt inside as she observed her roommate's desperate efforts to conceal the ravages of the years. Most of the support of the household fell on Melissa. When Evelyn worked, she spent the money on clothes, cosmetics, and to Melissa's great resentment, on her "men friends." She bought them gifts, paid for movies and dancing.

Melissa was cleaning rooms in tourist cabins.

Evelyn had been without work for two months. She had lost her job at a dry cleaner's because she came in late too often, as she invariably did on the mornings following one of her dates. Her usual good humor frequently gave way to irritability. "Melissa, why do you hang your wet stockings in the bathtub? Drips on my hair. Hang 'em on the porch." "I'm sorry," Melissa said. She felt her depression growing.

One evening Evelyn borrowed a dollar from Melissa. "I'm going out with Tom. We want to beat the blues. There's a dance place just opened, out on that new road to Los Angeles. Tom's got no job and he's a bit short on that old do-re-mi-fa-sol, and I told him I'd help pay."

Melissa stopped ironing. "You pay? On my money?"

Evelyn threw her hairbrush across the room. "Well, if you can't lend me a little cash . . . Long as we've been friends! You think you're too good for the company I keep. Tom says he could get you a swell feller."

"That's not it. I just don't have no extra money. My savings is about gone. I don't know how long they'll want me cleanin' them rooms."

"Melissa, Tom says he has a friend you could go with tonight

—with us. Says he's a swell looker. Dresses keen. We could make a foursome. Have a drink. Dance. Go somewhere . . ."

"Evelyn, you don't understand. I just don't *like* those men."

The next morning, Melissa knew even before Evelyn spoke that her roommate was in a sour mood. She pouted. "Listen, Melissa, you missed a fine time last night. Tom's friend had a new Hupmobile. They asked me if you was too stuck-up to go. Because of you, Tom may not come back to see me. Says if you don't like his friends, you don't like him."

A week passed and Evelyn again brought up the matter of Melissa's refusal to go out. "Melissa, I've had just about all I can take of your high-and-mighty airs. Tom says he can get me a job in San Jose."

Melissa put her arms around Evelyn. "Evelyn, please. We've been friends for a long time. You've helped me out in times of my loneliness. We need each other." She went to her bureau drawer and untied a handkerchief. "Here is five dollars. Take it. Go out and buy yourself something you want. Cheer yourself up. We don't have much to eat on, but you need a change. I still have my job." Melissa tied up the remaining coins.

The next afternoon when she came home from work, she saw Evelyn with her suitcase packed. "Where are you goin'? What's the—"

Evelyn put on her hat. "Tom is taking me to San Jose. Says there's work there. I just cain't take no more of this. I guess you think I ought to pay you back the money I borrowed—"

"No. Keep the money. Don't go. You'll find work here. We can get along."

Evelyn shrugged her shoulders. "Cain't. Made up my mind. Tom's waiting in the car for me, in that Hupmobile." At the door, she turned and said, with a tremor in her voice, "Goodbye. You've been good to me. I'm sorry. Melissa, there's never been a meeting but what there's been a parting." Then she ran from the room.

The next day, before going to the corner grocery store, Melissa went to the bureau drawer and untied the handkerchief. It was empty.

16.
The days without Evelyn were bleak for Melissa, and the house seemed a lonely prison. The two women had made few acquaintances, depending on each other for company. Now Melissa wanted Evelyn to talk to, wanted to hear her laugh again. Her nights were sleepless. She ate little. Her thinking was dull. She was nervous and afraid of staying alone in the apartment. Sorrow settled on her. *I must save money and return to Arizona.*

She tried to relieve her loneliness, but the other women where she worked cleaning cabins offered little companionship. She took to walking in the park. As she sat on a bench one Sunday, a man walked by—someone to talk to, she hoped. She smiled. The man smiled. She waited. The man's smile widened and he nodded. Melissa moved her head. A girl in her twenties, hair glistening in the sun, was playing with her dog as she loitered along the pathway. The girl returned the man's smile. Melissa rose and walked home.

The sound of the wind that evening only increased her depression. Putting on her coat, she walked to the drugstore. She ordered a cherry Coke and sat at the counter observing a man at the magazine rack. He thumbed through several papers, then went to the postcard stand. Melissa surveyed his blue suit, tan hat, polished shoes, his small mustache. She rose and stood next to him. She coughed. The man did not look up. Picking up a card, she said, "They sure make them purty nowdays, don't they?" The man frowned and went out the door.

Melissa followed outside. She saw him a few feet ahead. Perhaps she could pretend to be lost. She wanted someone to

talk to, anyone. The wind blew mournfully, sweeping papers
from the sidewalk into the gutter. She hurried until she was by
the man's side. Her heart beat uncertainly. "Sir, could you tell
me where—"

The man hastened his steps. "Sister, I don't want any. Get
lost. Get going now. I'll call the cops on you!"

Melissa blanched. She turned and ran to her apartment,
squeezing her eyelids to keep back the tears. Inside the door,
the first thing she saw was Evelyn's half-empty perfume bottle
on the dresser. She ate supper and went outside to sit on the
narrow porch. There were no people about, and Melissa stared
vacantly at the lifeless street. She began to sit each evening on
the porch. Anything was preferable to staying alone in the
house from which Evelyn's presence and gaiety were gone.

Another time she nodded to the bald-headed man she had
seen behind the meat counter at the grocery store. Julius
Wentz returned her greeting. For a week the two nodded and
smiled at each other.

One day he stopped at the porch. "You are the lady that
comes to buy meat, no? I haven't seen you at the store for a
long time."

"I haven't been in. My friend who lived here with me went
away. I don't need much for one person."

"Oh, you live alone here?"

"Now. Evelyn moved to San Jose."

"Is she the one with the red hair that used to come to the
butcher shop with you?"

"That's Evelyn."

Several days later Julius Wentz stopped by again. He told
her he lived with his only son and his daughter-in-law but that
he did not like having to be in the same house with them. He
had no freedom, and his three grandchildren were noisy.

The next evening Julius accepted her invitation to come
inside for coffee and a piece of pie. She eyed him closely. With
his slouching shoulders and large belly, he was hardly attrac-

tive, but at least he was pleasant. Soon he was spending every evening with Melissa, often staying past midnight. She grew bored with his endless stories about the meat business. "Now, you take round steak, and—" She blocked out his monologues by thinking of Arizona. She still missed Evelyn, and Julius' presence helped to fill the emptiness.

He brought over a phonograph and records. They played music while Melissa cooked dinner. He left a pair of slippers in the apartment so he could change after work. When he told her he took his laundry out because his daughter-in-law complained of the extra washing, Melissa said, "Bring it over. I'll do it for you." After dinner Julius dried dishes for her and took the garbage out to the alley. Sometimes he brought her hard candies. He kept the kitchen supplied with meat from the butcher shop. Melissa worried that he would soon mar their friendship by familiar talk or gestures. But time went by and Julius made no move toward a greater intimacy.

One day at work Melissa's employer called her over. "Missus Baker, I've sold my business. The buyer will be taking over soon. He says times are changing and he's going to renovate all the cabins. He won't be needing cleaning help for a while. I'm sorry. You've been a good worker."

That night Melissa poured out her woes to Julius. "I can help you," he consoled her. "I'll pay your rent till you get a job and get straightened out."

Melissa sighed and thanked him. It was good to have a comforting friend. But since Evelyn's departure she had succeeded in putting away some savings and could manage on her own—at least for a while. She wanted a few days to look for new work.

The next evening Julius did not come by, nor the evening after that. Melissa began to worry. Going to the grocery store, she saw a new man standing behind the meat counter. She asked for Julius. "The old man had a heart attack. Sudden. He's at his son's house. Don't expect him to be back. They say he's awful bad off and they're going to put him in the hospital."

A week passed and Melissa was still without work. She decided to take what savings she had and return to Arizona. She would see Julius first, to say goodbye. The new butcher gave her the address. Coming to the prim, white clapboard house, Melissa knocked. A young woman answered. "You want something?"

"I'm a friend of Julius Wentz'. I heard he was ill. I—"

"Papa can see no one." The woman's voice was cold. "He doesn't even know my husband, his only son. If he comes to his senses, I'll tell him you called." Melissa felt the rush of air as the door closed.

That night she packed her few belongings. In the morning she bought a ticket for Arizona. As she sat in the bus, at last headed home, she mused about her sojourn in California. It seemed to her now as if she had spent all that time in a limbo, just existing, day after day, month after month, year after year. And she saw that she had needed this emptiness. Now, Melissa told herself, she would begin to live again.

The bus traveled through the orchard country, where the white-frame farmhouses had porches covered with flowering vines. And always there were the waxy-green citrus groves. The graveled road brought the bus to the endless hills of sand dunes, and on into the oasis-like Indio Valley, green with irrigated fields. Beyond lay the sweeping miles of burned hills and sparse desert vegetation. The bus continued into the night; Melissa slept fitfully. She awoke as the first light splintered the edges of the eastern mountains. The bus sped past a highway sign, and Melissa saw the words STATE OF ARIZONA. Tears slid down her face. Seven years it had been. Now she was coming home.

The bus turned onto the narrow twisted road that led through the flats to Quartzsite. The thought of the Lost Hope Mine, somewhere in those blue hills, excited her. Where was Jason Herrick? Had he moved away? Had he found that farm he always talked about?

The bus driver braked the vehicle, the wheels spitting gravel. "We stop here for snacks. Toilets are to the right of the building."

Melissa stepped out and stretched. The Arizona air was more invigorating. She recognized the place despite a few changes that had taken place. The sign over the Quartzsite Cafe now read "Mojave Inn," and there was a new gasoline pump in front. The countryside remained exactly as she remembered it, the chollas in the distant flats reaching to the hills. Had Jason Herrick found "the color" he was always looking for up there?

Inside the cafe, a waitress brought Melissa coffee and a piece of peach pie. Gripping the cup until her knuckles turned white, Melissa asked, "Do you know a man named Jason Herrick who lives around here?"

The girl shook her head. "I only been working here a month. The boss might know. He's owned the place for a long time. I'll ask him."

The owner came to Melissa's table. "You the lady asking about Herrick?"

"I'm a friend—used to be. I cooked for him a long time ago. I was wonderin' if he still worked his mine?" She felt her heart flutter.

"Jake's still got his mine. He don't work nobody. Just been keeping it open himself. Lately he's been taking some men from Chicago out there. They want to buy. Jake's getting a little stove-up and wants to sell out. Says he wants to buy a cotton farm."

"Do you see him often?" Melissa folded and unfolded her hands.

"Sure. Been here lots since he's been carting those Chicago buyers up to the mine. I save his mail for him."

"His mail? Maybe I could leave a message for him."

Melissa finished her coffee and pulled out a writing pad from her purse. "Dear Mr. Herrick, I hope you remember me. I am looking for work and hoped you might know of a job. I am returning from California. I'll give you my daughter's address in Scottsdale if you ever have need of a cook."

She gave the letter to the owner. "Would you see that Mr. Herrick gets this when he comes in?"

"Sure thing, lady. He's a fine old man, that Jake is."

Happier than she could remember, Melissa got back on the bus for Scottsdale.

IV

1. Melissa sat in Mary Belle's living room. The meeting with Baby had been strained. The child, now fifteen, had suffered her mother's embrace and then escaped to the Scottsdale library. As she closed the door behind her, Melissa had been reminded of the unwanted birth.

She now brushed her long hair, preparing for bed. Streaks of gray had appeared amidst the brown.

"Mary Belle," she said, "when the bus come through Quartzsite I left a message for Jason Herrick. He was the one I worked for at the mine. He may be sendin' me a letter to your address."

"I'll watch the mail for you."

"After you wrote me from California, I called the lawyer. He contacted Papa in Stone Springs. The papers are nearly ready."

Melissa smiled. "That's a heap o' relief. Been embarrassin' all these years, being married and then not married. I want to be shut of that part of my life. I couldn't have done this paper work without your help."

Mary Belle straightened the stack of school notebooks she was grading. "It's for the best. You couldn't go on like this."

Melissa put down her brush. "Right now, I want to go back to The Mesa."

"Now?" Mary Belle slashed the red pencil across a page. "You just got here. Better rest up a few days. You hardly make a shadow, you're so thin."

Couldn't Mary Belle understand?

Melissa lusted for the land, The Mesa land. It had been fourteen years since the wagon had taken her from that valley cradled between the Sierra Anchas and the Mazatzals. She wanted to tell Mary Belle about the hurting inside her, which

compelled her to go back, to see the country that had taken
so many years of her youth. Melissa longed to see Shug, to hear
her laughter, to feel her love of life, her warmth, her caring,
the support of her strength. She wanted again to see the distant
jagged peaks, the endless sky, to touch again the broad flat
earth cut by Tonto Creek, to walk in the country she had
pushed from her thoughts for so many years.

Mary Belle looked at her mother, then folded the school
papers. "You seem determined to go. We'll write Aunt Shug,
and she can meet you at The Store. But it'll be a couple of
weeks before you get an answer. You could visit with Addie
Hankins at Tempe. That would give you time to see Spider.
He's there, too. Annie could come over from Phoenix."

"Guess you're right. I could get this blamed hair washed and
my clothes cleaned up."

Melissa boarded the bus for Globe. From there she would
change vehicles for Roosevelt, and then on to The Mesa. Shug
had written that she and Jimso would be at The Mesa Store
to meet her. Since their parents' death Jimso had moved in
with Shug, at the house by the creek, and his Chevrolet gave
them a chance to move around the country.

In Roosevelt the stage crawled along the narrow one-way
road leading over the dam that held the waters of Salt River
and Tonto Creek. It passed the shimmering lake, then continued up, up and on, to the beginning of The Mesa country.

Melissa leaned out the window. She was astounded at the
bountifulness of the countryside. The Mesa had always been
an unpredictable land, a land of change, contrast, and surprise.
When the Baker family had left in 1911, the winter had been
nearly rainless, and the land burned dry and barren. Melissa
recalled the miles of dried grasses whipped by the wind, a
landscape desolate and scarred. The memory pained her. *Dear
God, what emptiness it was.*

This year the winter had been a wet one. Wild flowers

covered the land with splashes of color. Trees were lush with leaves, and the gutted road green with spring grass. It was just such a spring that must have brought the first settlers here.

As the stage swayed along the dirt road, Melissa's thoughts turned to what history of The Mesa she had heard. She saw the Indian mounds by the river's edge, where the Salado people had lived some hundreds of years ago. In their burial grounds Melissa had once found broken pottery, woven mats of yucca fiber, stone arrowheads, and the metates where the women had hand-labored the grain, rock against rock, to grind the seeds. The stage passed within a mile of the abandoned soldiers' fort where, before the turn of the century, the government troops had failed to quell the Apache rebellion. She saw a long-abandoned mining claim. The first prospectors had come into the land with picks and shovels and dreams. The dreams had produced only promissory notes, and the prospectors had left the diggings for new territory.

Melissa's attention was caught by a comical, tail-heavy bird running beside the stage. She smiled. *A roadrunner.* Her eyes searched the countryside. Gambel quail, ready for spring mating, had quitted their winter coveys and now were consorting in pairs. She watched the bobbing, alert, black-tasseled heads. The stage passed through a creek bed, the bordering cottonwoods blocking out the sunlight, the soft sand overspread with a layer of damp leaves. The familiar smell of rank water weeds assailed her. It was a fragrance she had long forgotten. Melissa was coming home.

There it was—The Mesa Store—it had been rebuilt since her departure. A Chevrolet car stood in front by the roadside. She saw Jimso and Shug. Her heart bounded, her throat felt tight. The stage stopped, and Melissa was out almost before the car doors opened.

Shug's arms were around her, and they both cried unashamedly. Turning from her sister, she stretched her hands toward Jimso, who stood quietly on the side, controlling his own tears.

Moving back to Shug, Melissa looked at her sister. Her long white hair was parted in the middle and braided on each side, the ends tied with pink knitting yarn. Her complexion was the color of golden leather. "Shug, you do look Indian, brown as you are, and with your hair that way." She saw the laugh lines around her sister's eyes. It was Shug's laughter that always made her face look so alive. Now she was grinning broadly, showing the gap in her front teeth. She never had the time nor the money to get a false tooth, but it made a handy place for the mesquite twig she constantly chewed. *Beautiful Shug!*

Melissa listened to Shug's voice, vibrant, strong, rippling with zest and confidence. She looked on as Shug lifted her valise, and she admired her sister's legs, lithe and slender as a girl's. "I got them legs from usin' 'em," Shug always claimed, "from chasin' them damn goats all over Tonto Creek."

Jimso started the car. Melissa and Shug rode in back, clasping hands and hugging each other. "Melissa, you do look a mite peaked. You need some of ol' Shug's frijole beans and goat milk." She grinned. "But you always was the pretty one of the family. You still got that little-girl look. And your hair ain't hardly gray a-tall." She pursed her lips. "Guess it's the easy life you've had." She burst into tears again. "Melissa, my joke ain't funny." But Melissa did not mind. She was happy just to be back again.

The Chevrolet topped a rise, and Melissa saw the flat Mesa. "Jimso, stop the car!" She pointed. Miles and miles of green filaree, crowned with purple blossoms, covered the earth. Springing out, she reached down and gathered a handful of lacy green leaves and tiny lavender flowers. She held them close to her face, closed her eyes, and remembered—remembered the Big Mesquite Thicket, and the tall, long-limbed cowboy. *But to him I am grateful. He came at a time when I needed something to cling to, to survive.*

The trio arrived at Shug's house, Melissa still clutching the plant, now crushed and wilted. The place was as she remembered it, only somewhat more rundown. The screen on the front door was rusty and needed mending. Shug and Jimso had set up cots in the yard for cooler summertime sleeping. The garden was full of chard, black-eyed peas, turnips, tomatoes, cucumbers, and chili peppers.

Inside the house Shug set out food. "Soon's as we eat and rest a bit we want to git ready for the doin's tonight." She passed corn bread to Melissa.

"A party?"

"I ain't had time to tell you, but there's a political fellow what's giving a shindig at The Store tonight. He wants your votes and he's willin' to pay for 'em with vittles. A barbecue supper. Band music is comin' from Globe. They clear out the pool tables for dancing."

Jimso came in from outside. "I don't git no chance to say much. Shug here hardly never stops talkin'. Did she tell you she likes to go to these political meetings for that happy water? She's got a friend with a still hidden up the canyon."

"Jimso Holman, one of these days you're goin' to be talkin' when you shoulda been listenin'. I'm goin' kick yore butt all the way from Tonto Creek to the Four Peaks. That likker that comes outa them corn squeezin's is so damn weak it never hurt no one. I do it just to be sociable. Just a drop or two."

"But, Sis, you don't stop at a drop or two. You're the only woman on The Mesa that takes any at all."

"Them wimmenfolks would be better off if they did take a drop or two. They say it ain't legal. They're scairt a prohi-man might sneak up into this country. I admit I go out in the back to take my snort."

Melissa found herself laughing, tears wetting her cheeks. She wiped them away with the back of her hand. "Shug, Shug. Didn't you run off your last old man for drinkin'?"

"Oh," Shug wrinkled her nose. "That's different. I just take a little nip. Not because I like it, but to make friends. Besides that, wimmen ought to do more for their own enjoys."

Jimso sat down at the table. "Melissa, you ain't never goin' out-talk or out-figure that woman."

"Enough sass outa you, Jimso Boy. Melissa, we oughta leave here well before dark. Give you time for a little nap. Go in there to the bed. I'm goin' go out chasin' down that ol' nanny goat. She's probably run all the way up the hill to kingdom come."

That evening when they stopped the car in front of The Store, they could already hear the noise from inside. "Quite a commotion," Shug observed. "They got a head start on us."

Melissa spent the time greeting old friends and learning about others who were not there. Shug was drinking that "drop or two" by going out behind the store, surrounded by friends who enjoyed her talk and antics. She came over to Melissa with a wavering gait. "Melissa, you gettin' to see old friends?"

"I want to ask about so many. Dudley Schmelz? How about John Brownell?"

"Them old-timers ain't able to stay up with us young ones." Shug shook her white braids. Her eyes were glazed. "I'll tell you all about The Mesa folk when we get home. Tonight's the time for playin'."

Melissa watched her wander to the middle of the floor, soon to be surrounded by others. She heard her singing: " 'Tis the last time, darling/He gently said/As he kissed her lips/Like a cherry red/Tomorrow high up/The bells shall ring/A joyful peal/Was there ever a king/So truly blest/On his royal throne-/As I shall be/When I claim my own." Melissa hurt as she listened, her mind slipping back to the years when she had learned the song from her mother. Sarah Holman now rested beside Carter in the burial ground on the hill. Melissa wished she could push away the sorrow which enveloped her.

The dance music started. Shug was the first one on the floor.

She walked to the side of the room and grabbed an old man. Melissa did not know him, but someone said he was a prospector hunting the country for any sign of mineral. Melissa could see the man resisting, but Shug insisted. She put her white head against his grizzled beard and pulled him onto the floor. Soon she turned him loose and continued dancing by herself. Encouraged by the applause, she ignored the beat of the music and did in turn the schottische, the polka, the varsovienne, and some improvised steps of her own.

When she finished, she wandered to a chair and was instantly surrounded. *Everybody loves Shug. She makes people forget their worries. Shug, who has so little, gets so much living out of nothing.*

The party ended. On the way home, Shug slept, her head on Melissa's shoulder. She was too exhausted to pull on her nightgown. Melissa had to help.

"Shug," Melissa comforted her, "we at least have some good memories of tonight."

Shug dragged herself in-between the sheets, and raising her head said, "Hell, Melissa, I'm ready to make new memories."

A few days later Jimso drove the women to the El Bar ranch to visit Benjy. At twenty-one, he had grown into a handsome boy, tall and strong, tanned by The Mesa's sun. Melissa was happy to see that he cowboyed with his old friend, William Brownell, doing work which he knew and enjoyed.

At the Schmelz ranch, Melissa talked with Dudley. His voice had the same soft, soothing tone that she remembered from Carter's funeral service. She was grieved to see that he needed a cane to help him walk. His wife cared for his needs. Their son Skeeter had married and lived in Globe, working at the copper mine. Shug gave her sister other news of The Mesa. Since Martha Brownell's death, her husband John had "failed, plumb lost his senses," she said. "No one to care for him. Had to be sent to the insane asylum at Phoenix." Melissa thought often of Ike Talbott but she refrained from asking about him. It was for her too intimate a memory.

"Before I leave," she told Shug, "I want to go to the graveyard." Jimso took them in the Chevrolet. Spring had brightened the area with white mariposa lilies and blue lupine. Melissa was glad. She saw the Mazatzals in the background and heard The Mesa breeze whispering through the mesquite brush. Shug showed her the crosses Jimso had made: "Sarah Holman, Our Mother" and "Silas Holman, Our Father." The mounds were outlined with river rock.

Melissa walked to another wooden cross: "Carter Baker." She knelt by the green mound. She stayed so long with her head bowed, clasping her hands, that Shug came and gently lifted her up. "We must go, Melissa."

The next morning Jimso drove his sisters to The Mesa Store, where Melissa was to board the return stage for Scottsdale. She had spent a week visiting, smiling, and laughing at Shug's liveliness. It had been years since she felt so good.

As the stage pulled away, Melissa waved and remembered Shug's parting advice. "Melissa, I'm glad to see you finally got some spunk. Don't never act like a egg-suckin' dog, tail twixt your legs. Don't you never again take nothin' off no damn man. Just keep a-whippin' and a-spurrin'.' "

2. When she arrived in Scottsdale at Mary Belle's house, Melissa spent the first few days recounting her visit to The Mesa. One morning, as she was telling her daughter about Shug's final admonition, the postman knocked on the door. He held a letter addressed to Melissa.

Even before she opened it, she knew. Turning it over in her hand, she held it until Mary Belle left the room. Then, carefully, she tore open the envelope: "Dear Mrs. Baker, I was surprised to get your message. How many years has it been? I never did replace the machinery that broke down. The war kept all materials tied up. So I worked the mine by myself. Since I was making wages that way I kept on alone. I nearly starved to death at times and wished I had your good cooking. I been trying to sell the mine. Now I have some buyers from Chicago looking at it. Next month I'm coming to the Valley to see a lawyer about drawing up the papers for the sale. I would like to see you. I can come to Scottsdale. Let me know. Very truly yours, Jason T. Herrick."

Melissa smiled. She hurried to find the lined tablet in her valise. Mary Belle would have a stamp.

When her daughter returned, Melissa hastened to explain the letter. "And I'm going to Tempe," she concluded, "to stay with Addie Hankins. I need to get work. Addie says there's need for help at the hospital there." Mary Belle thought she had never seen her mother so excited.

"Mother, I didn't want to give you the news when you first came back, but I feel I can tell you now. Papa is coming here."

"What d'ya mean—Ben Baker? Here? Melissa's spirits fell. "Why? When?"

"He's been staying with his ranch friend, that man Boer— where we used to live. He came to sign the divorce papers, and I think to visit—and to see you. He said he had a message for you."

"I have nothin' to see him about, nothin' to say." Melissa felt a resurgence of the old animosity. "He hightailed it to Texas and now he has a message for me. Never sent no money for the younguns. You had to take care of Baby . . ."

"He'll be here today."

Melissa mused. "You've been the lead mule, pullin' the weight and keepin' this ragtag family together. Ben Baker's burden fell on your shoulders. When you were a youngun, you caused the greatest ruckus. Turned out to be you're the hub of the wheel."

"Seems I'm the only one left free to do it. Hannah married. She's tied up with her own family. The boys are gone away. Baby's in high school. She's young, needs someone to cling to. But don't get upset, Mama. We're doing fine. I'm putting away a little savings for her to go to college."

"Mary Belle, it ain't fair. Time passes faster than you think, and life passes you by in that time—"

"You get so morbid sometimes, Mama."

"Well, if you hadn't had this weight, you'd most likely have a family of your own by now."

"Never! No man, no children, no marriage for me. I want to travel. Maybe someday I'll even see the Taj Mahal."

"That Ben Baker gallivantin' around . . . Spendin' money for travel what ought be sent to his younguns." But somehow the familiar bitterness that had accompanied Melissa for all the years of her marriage had lessened.

Late that afternoon the doorbell rang and Mary Belle admitted Ben Baker. Melissa faced him. *How many years?* How old was this man, standing awkwardly and clutching his wide-brimmed hat? *He must be nigh on to sixty-six years old.*

Mary Belle kissed her father, indicated a chair, and went to get him a glass of water. Melissa stood back and observed. The tobacco-stained mustache was gone. His hair, fine as silk when he first courted her more than thirty-three years before, had thinned to a gray mat and lay plastered against his moist skin.

But, as always, he wore good boots, shined and sharp-toed. He had told her many years ago that one judged a cowman by his boots. *Bet they cost a purty penny. Money shoulda been sent to care for his younguns, 'stead of them fancy-stitched things.* Yet she was surprised at not feeling more anger. Where was her despair and frustration, her bitterness and resentment toward this man who had sired her eight children? She was grateful for the indifference she felt.

The man sat stiffly in the chair, still clenching his hat as if for support.

"In Texas, I—" He hesitated.

"Speak up, Mr. Baker. Mary Belle said you had a message for me."

He noted her impatience. "I left Stone Springs and come to stay with some friends in Silver City, New Mexico. I run across an old acquaintance of ours. From The Mesa. He's constable now in Silver City. Job of respect and importance. I got a message for you."

"Why should you give me a message?"

"I gotta keep my word."

A Baker's word is good? Too bad you didn't keep them highfalutin' ideals when you was saloon drinkin' and cussin'— and abandonin' your younguns.

"The name's Ike Talbott. You remember him? Worked at the El Bar. Disappeared after Neeson was killed. He told me, 'When you see your missus, tell her if she ever needs a friend, I'll come.' Wonder what he meant. Guess he liked your cookin' when we all rounded up together."

Melissa's voice was cool. "Mr. Baker, there are more important things about a woman than her cookin' on roundup." For a fleeting second she recalled the long-limbed cowboy and the ride to Big Mesquite Thicket. She was surprised that the recollection caused so little change in her emotions. Seemed like a dream, a faded dream she no longer needed.

Facing Ben Baker, she said, "It's been a long time since them days, and much water has gone down Tonto Creek. I 'spect we've finished our business." She walked to the door and held it open for him. She heard him say hesitantly, "Goodbye, Melissa." She watched his bowed legs as he stepped off the porch, and out of her life. She felt no remorse, only relief to find that she no longer burned with bitterness.

She sank into a chair, remembering, for the first time in years, it seemed, the lonely ranch house on the treeless Texas prairie, where she had started married life. She had been fifteen when Ben Baker brought her there. He was thirty-three and he was old, old as were the other men who grew up too soon under the hardships of the frontier. "My young filly's got lots of spirit," he had said. "Green broke. With training, she'll rein."

Melissa's thoughts turned to the trip from Texas. She recalled the canvas-covered wagons, the buggy, the mules and saddle horses, the three months of dirt, heat, exhaustion, uncertainty—and hope, always the hope of something better that lay ahead. She shuddered, remembering the interminable miles of hills and barren red cliffs, the baby's illness, the scorpions, the flies. Then there had been that magical night when they camped in a juniper thicket in New Mexico. She could almost smell again the aroma of the campfire and feel the lure of the black night where mysterious silence was punctuated now and then by a coyote's call.

She listened now in the quiet air of Scottsdale. She smelled the citrus blossoms. She thought of the letter from Jason Herrick, now hidden in her valise, and felt cleansed of Ben Baker.

3.

In Tempe Melissa Baker began her new job at the hospital. Her duties varied. She cleaned rooms and helped in the kitchen, preparing vegetables and arranging patients' trays.

In the year that followed, Jason Herrick came often to the Valley to confer with his lawyer on matters related to the selling of the Lost Hope Mine. Those were joyous times for Melissa. Jason drove her to Scottsdale to visit Mary Belle and Baby, and to Phoenix to see Annie, now married to a young man from her office. Spider had recently started work at the Desert Zoological Gardens in the same city.

Melissa rented a room from Addie Hankins, and the two women spent many hours together. One day they were looking in store windows. "I'd like to go into the Ladies' Dress Shoppe," Melissa said.

"You want to buy a dress?"

"I might as well tell you the news now. Jason and I are gettin' married soon's as the mine deal is completed."

"That's not news. I been expecting it. For more'n a year now he's shown it every time he looks at you. You show it when you see his car coming up the driveway. A wedding dress?"

Melissa flushed. "I wouldn't call it that. I just don't have nothin' decent to wear. I want somethin' practical I can wear after the ceremony, all the time."

Addie Hankins took her friend's arm and steered her toward the dress shop. Melissa explained to the saleswoman, "Size? I don't rightly know. Haven't had many boughten dresses in my life. I weigh a mite over a hundred pounds." She pointed to a rack of dresses. "How 'bout the voile with the long sleeves, the tan-colored one?"

Pulling the dress off the rack, the clerk peered at the label. "This is much too large for you. I have another one here—blue, with the pleats and lace. Would fit you right."

Melissa hesitated. "I had thought tan would be a sensible color. The long sleeves would hide my ol' arms."

"Nonsense, Miz Baker." Addie Hankins turned to the clerk. "Help her try on the blue. Fits her eyes. She needs something light and pretty."

The friends left the store, Melissa carrying a package with the blue voile dress. "I never thought I'd get married again. Jake's different. Kind. Gentle. Soft-talkin'. Somehow I believe in him. Hope these old eyes of mine are not blinded by love. I don't wanta jump outa the skillet into the blaze."

"You ain't makin' no mistake. I can't tell by lookin' at a frog how far he can jump, but I can tell by lookin' at Jason Herrick that he'd jump any way you pointed. You won't have to work no more at the hospital?"

"No. We'll live on that cotton farm Jake's been talkin' about. Last time he was down, we drove down to see it. Three miles from that new town they call Coolidge."

"Coolidge isn't more than a one-horse stop on the way to Tucson."

"Jason says it's the comin' place for cotton. Lots of wells are being dug there for irrigatin'. The place he likes ain't got no kind of house on it. But I've lived in worse." She laughed. "Evelyn used to say she'd rather live in a tent in an oasis with a man she loved than in a mansion of gold on a mountain with someone she didn't care for. That's the way I feel about Jason. He's the only man—" She stopped. "There was only one other man I ever thought about—and that was so long ago—in another country." Her eyes grew distant. "It was a hundred years ago . . ."

Addie Hankins took her friend's arm. "I'm just powerful glad for you. I thought Mr. Herrick just knowed mining."

"He was raised on a farm, and he's always hankered to go back. He's smart. He can learn. Been readin' up on cotton and talking to farmers in Coolidge. Went to see that university agriculture professor. He's got some ideas he wants to use."

"How does he take to your family?" Addie Hankins raised her eyebrows.

"Like a hound dog to cold biscuits. Snaps it up. Says he always wanted a family of his own. Never been married. His folks are dead. No kin. A cousin in Missouri is all. Jason says he's proud to have ready-growed children."

"I'm happy for you. You deserve a good man. You've had your share of hardships over the years. But what do your children say about this marrying up?"

"They want me to have a home. Sometimes they even show more affection toward him than me. Especially Baby." Melissa's face clouded. "She's always held a sorta aloofness from me. Lately, though, she's coming closer."

"Missus Baker, sometimes when you talk 'bout that man, you just look like a sixteen-year-old with her first beau.

"Perhaps he is my first beau. He calls me Honeybee." She blushed.

"You look plumb red, Miz Baker. Be proud he calls you that." She opened the screen door to her house. "Come in quick, 'fore the flies do."

4.

Melissa stood outside her Coolidge home, dipping a bucket into the clear water that rushed by in the irrigation ditch. She spoke to the frog that lived in the weeds on the bank. "Little froggy, this ain't like the pretty windmills on The Mesa, but it is sure easier on a woman." She looked out across the dark green of the cotton plants that covered the Herricks' 160-acre farm.

She had been Melissa Herrick for ten years now, and it seemed that each year was happier than the one before. She no longer felt her old frustrations and resentments. The headaches had disappeared. And there was always Jason, "Sweeter by knowin' him," she wrote Shug.

Jason had taken the raw desert land and built it into one of the finest farms in the Coolidge Valley. The Herricks were respected landowners. Melissa liked being Jason Herrick's wife and she liked the sound of her new name, Melissa Herrick. "Music-like," she said. But their neighbors and the Coolidge merchants with whom Herrick traded knew her as Honeybee Herrick. "My wife, Honeybee," Jason always introduced her. Even the Elkins' children, who lived a half-mile down the road, called her Aunt Honeybee.

The first year the Herricks had settled on the land, they moved into a two-room frame building. The floor of the combination kitchen-dining-living area was covered with pine boards. The bedroom had a dirt floor and open windows. Jason gave the only other building, a tent-house, to the man he had hired to help him cultivate the farm. He was distraught by the crudeness of both living quarters. "Honeybee, it won't be long.

First thing I'm gonna do is build you a good house."

"It doesn't matter," Melissa assured him. "I've lived in much worse. Like when I picked cotton outside Tempe. Why, Evelyn used to say—"

"I know what Evelyn used to say, but those days are over."

Every few weeks Melissa's children came to spend Sunday on the farm. Baby was working in a Phoenix newspaper office. She brought along a Kodak on these Sundays and took pictures of the family, the cotton fields, and the house. Mary Belle gave her mother a book entitled *Death in the Afternoon*. But Melissa said she "in no way liked that blood and bullfighting —wasn't what cattle was made for."

Jason bought a tractor and a Model A Ford. Several times a year he took her to Phoenix to the movies. After seeing a Johnny Weissmuller Tarzan movie, Melissa took to calling her husband to lunch by going outside when the tractor neared the house and giving a jungle yell. Jason smiled. "Aren't you ever going to grow up, Honeybee?" Melissa told him she guessed she never had any growing-up when she was young, and she was enjoying it now.

One day Melissa had washed her hair and was drying it in the sun when Jason came in from the field. "I'll get out your lunch in a minute," she said. "This heavy hair plagues me. Takes so long to dry the danged stuff." Tossing her head up and down, she fluffed the strands with her fingers. "Aggervates me no end, and always has."

"Why don't you cut it?" Jason walked inside and stretched himself out on the couch. "You've wanted to cut it ever since I've known you."

To talk about cutting her hair was one thing, but actually to cut it was something altogether different. "You . . . wouldn't mind?"

"Why should I? If it bothers you, get rid of it." A grin wrinkled the corners of his eyes. "Fact is, I'll cut it for you. I'm handy with scissors. I've done some sheep shearing in my time."

"But I'm no sheep." Melissa tossed back her hair. "All right, farmer boy, I'm callin' yore bluff. Git them scissors off my sewing machine."

"You mean, I'm calling your bluff."

"Jake, I do want it cut but—"

"I'll cut it now before we eat." He held the scissors high. "Sit here. I need good light."

"Outside, Jake. Don't want no hair in my cookin' room." Melissa walked to the ditch bank.

"Are you sure? In five minutes, it'll be too late to change your mind."

Melissa put an old shirt around her shoulders. "Of course, I am sure. Been wanting it cut for more years than I can count." She seated herself on a box. "Jake, are *you* sure you don't mind?" Melissa compressed her lips. "Go ahead, then. Bob it. I've cussed it for years. I don't use it as no excuse. It frets me."

Jason placed the scissors to the side of Melissa's ear. "You want it about this short?" She nodded. He closed the scissors. Great hunks of gray-brown hair fell to the ground. Melissa gulped. "Go ahead, Sheep Shearer. Hack away. Cain't be too short to suit me." Around and around her head he went. The pile on the ground grew larger. With a final clip, he stepped back and observed his work. "That's it. Shall I get the looking glass?"

Melissa stood up and shook her head. She looked at the pile at her feet. "Goodness, I had enough for two women. I don't need no glass to know I like it." She ran her hands through the cropped hair. "Feels so light. Took pounds off my head. I feel freed. Free as a mockingbird I be."

5.

Melissa and Jason took to sitting outside after supper. They propped their chairs against the side of the house nearest to the irrigation ditch and talked, watching the sun sink over the western mountains and listening to the birds bidding good-bye as they sought refuge in the trees for the night.

One evening Jason pulled out a can of Prince Albert tobacco. Melissa watched him remove the brown wheat papers from his shirt pocket and roll a cigarette. "Jake, give me a cig."

Jason let his chair drop on all four legs. "Is my little Honey-bee going to take up smoking?"

"I would do it to keep you company. Most of all, though, it shows a woman's right to independence."

The man's weathered face crinkled with laughter. "Haven't you ever got over that independence idea? You got your hair cut. You've always done what you wanted since we've been married."

His wife looked toward the pink clouds in the sunset. "You never did put blinders on me, or a rein, and for damn sure, no quirt. Guess my feelin' is a holdover. For so many years I was shackled down. I like that free feeling—to do what wimmen-folks in my day weren't allowed to do." Her eyes narrowed. "Wimmen were just like . . . slaves."

"You go right ahead, Missus Herrick, and have all the smokes you like." And Melissa did just that, although for her it meant having only one cigarette a day with Jason in the evening. She really did not like smoking.

The days, the months, the years began adding up. She wrote to Shug: "Wish we could come to The Mesa. Want to see you bad. Seems Jake can't get away. Too many things can go wrong on this farm. Funny, sister, how one year can follow another, just about the same. Then one day you look at the calendar, and you wonder where has the time passed away."

The newspaper was delivered each morning at the gate. Their new Philco radio brought entertainment and news. For the first time Melissa began to take an interest in events that occurred beyond Coolidge and the cotton farms. In 1938 she read how Howard Hughes had flown around the world in three days and nineteen hours. "What's this world a-comin' to?" she asked Jason one evening as they sat by the irrigation ditch. "It took us more'n three months to get from Texas to Arizona."

They started to hear the name Hitler more and more, but Europe seemed as remote as ever. Then Pearl Harbor changed their lives. The war was on. For a time, there was panicky talk of a Japanese invasion of California, and Japanese were interned behind barbed wire in a camp nearby; later on, German prisoners were shut up in another camp near Phoenix. Pilots were trained in the Arizona desert, and the Herricks became accustomed to the sight and sound of warplanes buzzing their fields. And the sudden booming demand for cotton was making them unexpectedly well-off. Melissa felt she was lucky that her own family were not called to serve in the war. Benjy was engaged in the "essential business" of raising beef; Spider had signed up for the draft, but his number was never called because he was overage.

Mail was now delivered and placed in the metal box fastened to a post by the roadside. Several months after the end of the war a letter came from Mary Belle. The children planned to come to the farm for Mother's Day. "Don't cook anything," Mary Belle wrote. "We will bring the lunch. I've called Annie. She's coming with her husband and both children. They'll bring Spider and his wife. I will drive my car with Baby. Hannah can't come."

Melissa was excited. "It's been a long time since they been here—what with the war rationing and everything. I gotta clean this place. That Mary Belle is as fanatical as Shug about cleaning."

On the Mother's Day Sunday the Herricks were up early, waiting. At ten o'clock two cars pulled up in front of the farm.

With much shouting, kissing, and embracing, they all walked into the house.

Jason took the two grandchildren for a ride on the tractor while the women began preparing a large table on the ditch bank to hold the picnic lunch. "Keep the younguns out from under foot," Melissa instructed him. "I swear, livin' alone as we do, I'm just not used to 'em—and on The Mesa I hardly noticed younguns. Give me a chance to git caught up on the family news."

Mary Belle said her mother asked questions faster than she could answer. Yes, she knew that Addie Hankins had passed away. No, she hadn't heard that Spider had been made head man at the Zoological Gardens in Phoenix. And she embraced her daughter all over again when Mary Belle told her that she was about to become principal of the Scottsdale school. Mary Belle said that she had written to Benjy asking him to come down with Shug for the Mother's Day reunion. He answered that Shug had recently fallen on a rock, breaking her arm and several ribs. "And I can't leave now," Benjy concluded. "Roundup's ended and I'm waiting for the cattle buyers to come to the El Bar."

Baby still lived with Mary Belle. It was with this child that Melissa noticed the greatest change. The estrangement between them had lessened. Her youngest daughter put her arms around her mother and laughed with her. She explained her newspaper job. "I write for the woman's page and do some feature work, mostly photographs. Everybody at work calls me Baby, although I tell them it is Velma Marjorie."

Melissa looked with fondness on her youngest daughter. "How old are you now? Do you have any boy in mind? How come you haven't married?"

"Oh, Mom, guess I'm just lucky." She grew serious. "Really, I don't have the time. I'm so busy and wrapped up in my work. Marriage would interfere."

"Take away your freedom? How about Benjy, Mary Belle?"

"He writes that he has a girl who works at The Mesa Store. I was afraid he was going to be an old bachelor."

Melissa snorted. "Look who's talkin'. How about yourself? You still married to the Taj Mahal?"

"I really am planning a trip there one of these days. I'm satisfied with my life, Mama. Never wanted a man or children. I had a feeling of achievement when I bought that encyclopedia set with my first pay check."

Melissa turned to Baby. "Couldn't you cut my hair? You always was handy with the scissors. I want to keep it short, short."

"Absolutely not, Mother." Mary Belle objected. "It's nearly up to your ears now."

"Let Mother have it the way she wants, Mary Belle. This is not the schoolroom where you rule. Come outside, Mom, and I'll cut it by the ditch bank."

Spider walked through the house. "Mama, you and Jake are living like peons. You've made more money off that cotton than you'll ever spend. Why don't you build a decent house?"

"Jake would do whatever I want. But I got as good a house as I need. He's bought me lots of gadgets. See that new refrigerator? Kelvinator. Electric lights. I don't need anything fancy."

"I'm talking mostly about that bedroom. You never did put in those windows. You could just as well be sleeping out in the open. Whether you like it or not, I'm going to take that plywood I found in the barn and board up that northern wall. Give you some protection." He spent the next hour sawing, hammering, and nailing, filling in the openings.

After the picnic lunch Mary Belle packed away the remains and put them in the refrigerator. Then she asked her mother if they could talk in private for a moment.

"Mama, I had a letter from Aunt Hetty in Texas. Papa is . . . dead." Her voice broke. "Wasn't sick. Aunt Hetty wrote me that he just didn't eat his supper one night, and passed away in his sleep. Buried in Stone Springs in the pioneer cemetery."

Melissa did not speak. She was surprised at her own compo-
sure. Thinking of the broad expanse of green farmland that
stretched beyond the irrigation ditch, she was reminded of the
summer heat on The Mesa, and the miles of barren brown
earth. "He must've been eighty or more. It's a strange thing,
Mary Belle, how all those years I felt such anger and bitterness
toward him, resentin' my life, and now those years don't even
seem to belong to me. Seems they happened to someone else.
I just feel indifferent—like we were talkin' about someone we
just once were acquainted with. My life began with Jason."

"As I grow older," Mary Belle said, "I've begun to feel that
perhaps he did the best he could." She held back a sob.

Melissa spoke without emotion. "I am glad that your papa
got back to Texas. He lived in Arizona but his spirit was always
in Stone Springs."

"One more thing, Mother. You know we all love Jason
dearly. Baby and I were talking. We both feel he looks thin and
worn. He coughs. He should have a thorough physical checkup.
He's a few years older than you, so he must be past seventy.
Time he was taking it easy. Why don't you sell this ranch and
move to Phoenix? You've made lots of money here. It would
be no problem."

Melissa frowned. "I've been worried about him too. He
don't hardly eat nothin' some days. Works all the time. I'm
going to see that he gits to that doctor in Coolidge. We
wouldn't have no trouble sellin' this ranch. These real estate
men are always comin' out here, makin' Jake offers. This is one
of the best places around here. Jake's done a fine job buildin'
it up. Fact is, I guess he's just about plumb worked hisself to
death."

Late in the afternoon Melissa's children and grandchildren
drove away from the Herrick farm. Melissa and Jason stood by
the road, waving. After the cars had disappeared from sight,
Melissa walked into the bedroom. She shook her head. "I know
Spider meant well, but he ruint this room. I cain't sleep with-

out fresh air. Cain't stand to be fenced in." Taking a claw
hammer she began to remove the nails, stacking the plywood
on the floor.

A grin lit up Jason's face. "Anything to please my Honeybee." He began to help her pull out the nails.

When they finished, Melissa turned to her husband. "Let's
go outside, sit by the ditch. "I love them younguns and I want
to see them. But havin' the whole caboodle at a time does tire
me. Guess I ain't used to it, livin' here with you in all this quiet
and peace. Jake, roll me a smoke."

6. Melissa watched her husband talking to a well-dressed
man as they stood at the end of the cotton field. He gestured
with his arm toward the green acres. The men shook hands. As
the visitor drove past her, Melissa noted the words "Hightower
Realty Associates" painted on his car door.

Inside the house, Jason slowly eased himself into a chair.
"Honeybee, that real estate man is putting pressure on me to
sell. Has a client with two-thirds cash down. I told him I'd have
to talk it over with my wife."

Melissa looked at her husband's tired face, his slumped back,
and white hair. "Jake, I think the time has come for you to ease
up."

"Man said a large farm cooperative was buying up all the
land they could around here. Even if we sign now, we'd have
months to get off the place." He coughed. Several seconds
passed before he could regain his breath.

"You ain't never seen that doctor in Coolidge. Mary Belle
says she worries about you. She's been lookin' for a place for
us to buy in Phoenix." Standing above her husband, Melissa
noted his weathered face, brown as the land he tractored, and
the deep lines on each side of his nose. She felt a constriction

in her throat. "Day after day you're up at dawn. I say, let's sell."

The doctor in Coolidge examined Jason. "Doc says it's malnutrition," Jason reported. "Gave me some pills and wrote me out a diet. Said he didn't have the equipment to give me a thorough goin'-over."

"You don't hardly eat nothin' at all. Your teeth need fixin' bad. No wonder you cain't chew nothin'. You ain't took time off this farm to get your teeth fixed."

In the following months the Herricks made several trips to Phoenix, looking for a house to buy. Mary Belle always had a list of possible purchases. One day Spider showed them a two-acre plot with a red-brick house on the outskirts of town. Melissa decided. "This place would give us breathin' space. And I like them pomegranate bushes. House is kinda old, but I never did live in a fancy dwellin' noway."

Sitting in the evenings by the ditch bank, the Herricks began making plans to sell and move to Phoenix. Jason inventoried his farm equipment. Melissa gathered empty boxes for packing. The first item she placed in her valise was a folded cloth, heavy with an old .45 pistol.

The Herricks moved into the brick house with the pomegranate bushes. Jason's health improved. Melissa said it was "the rest that's done him good—and gittin' his teeth pulled." Mary Belle drove them on Saturdays to do their week's shopping at a new supermarket. Spider brought them three rabbits and built a hutch in the backyard. In a short while Melissa said, "I got rabbits runnin' outa my ears. I sure hate to kill them for eatin', but Jake cain't hardly find room to build any more hutches. We used to eat them young cottontails on The Mesa." Jason staked out a small garden so his wife could plant her vegetables and flowers. They enjoyed their new life.

Melissa talked often about taking a trip to The Mesa. "I want to visit Shug, and I ain't never seen Benjy's wife, that little Mormon girl." But Jason could no longer drive in the city traffic, and Mary Belle's free time was taken up with education courses at the university in Tempe. Spider and his wife visited her parents on their vacation. With no transportation, the Herricks' proposed trip to The Mesa was delayed again and again.

During one of Mary Belle's Sunday visits, Jason had a coughing attack. They were getting increasingly frequent. But this time his handkerchief was stained with blood. "This does it," Mary Belle declared. "I am calling up and making an appointment for you with the doctor."

There followed a month of weekly trips to the clinic, One morning several days later, Mary Belle sat in the doctor's private office. "I have the laboratory results," he began. "Mr. Herrick has a growth on his lungs—malignant. The cancer cells have taken over in the lymph glands. Spread up his neck. How do you wish to handle this? Do you wish to tell Mr. Herrick the truth?"

"Yes, Doctor." Mary Belle closed her eyes. "I know them. They would want to know. They are both strong people. My mother has survived a great deal in her life. You tell them. Now."

Jason accepted the news with stoicism. "Thank you, Doctor, for telling me the facts. That's the way we want it—to know. I don't want to take none of them X-rays. None of that radium or cobalt. Just burn you up. Don't do no good. In the end, we all have to go."

Melissa felt faint. Her eyes blurred. She knew that she must not lose control. She came to Jason's side. "We'll make out. Do the best we can. Whatever happens, I ain't gonna let no one force somethin' on Jason he don't want."

Jason grew weaker. Soon he was forced to spend his time in bed. The end came one day when Melissa was alone with her husband. Bringing him a bowl of soup, she found that Jason did not respond. She put her head against his chest, felt the coldness of his forehead. She knelt by the bed, praying silently. Finally she telephoned Mary Belle. "He's been gone for some time. I been sittin' here alone with him for an hour. I needed it—it's our last hour together."

After the funeral, Melissa said, "Funny how you just don't realize some things. I knowed he couldn't stay with us much longer. But I find it hard to believe I won't ever see him again. My darling Jake . . ."

Melissa insisted on staying on in the red brick house. "We worry about you," Mary Belle told her. "You are so contrary. It's not safe for you here alone." But Melissa refused to move. "I don't want to be a burden on nobody. I wanta do my cryin' alone. All the world has woes—without listenin' to mine. I got me some sweet memories of Jason Herrick. He give me more happiness in one day than I got in all those years on The Mesa." Mary Belle continued to worry. As she was leaving her mother's house one Sunday, Melissa stopped her at the door. "Have you got your canteen filled?"

"Mother! There's a service station in nearly every block. And telephones. I'm only driving nine miles to Scottsdale."

"You don't wanta ever go nowhere without takin' water. Mr. Baker always said to take along a piece of balin' wire. Never know when it'll come in handy."

Mary Belle wrote to Hannah. "I haven't heard Mother talk of Papa in years. The doctor says she's in good physical shape for a woman her age. But I see her mind slipping at times. The other day she was talking about making a pallet to lie on in the wagon bed, and hanging the jerky on the clothesline. She was telling Baby about being a bride in Texas, and how handsome Papa was. She said the whole country thought she made a good catch for a girl of fifteen, getting a cattleman with a ranch in Stone Springs. She has not mentioned Jason. Yet I know she suffers the loss. It seems as if she thinks that by keeping quiet she can blot out his going."

On the next visit Mary Belle found her mother with a burned hand. "That blamed pan of water spilled on me. I was tryin' to carry it to wash out my britches." She tightened the cloth around her hand. "I just put me some soda on it."

"That does it, Mother. You're worrying me to death. I'm going to find some woman to stay with you. I know you won't move. Jason spoiled you so, and now you must have your own way. But at least with someone living here we won't have to phone all the time and come over so often to check on you. Jake left you plenty to be independent on."

In the next few years Melissa had many housekeepers. Mary Belle and Baby discussed it. "Mother is so set in her ways. She's hard for anyone to get along with. Wants to save, save, save —as if she had only one dollar left in the world. Wanted the housekeeper to boil the coffee grounds again, said it was wasteful to use them just once. She is irascible. Wants her freedom, she claims, whatever that freedom means. No one will stay with her very long."

In the end, it was decided that Melissa would move in with Mary Belle, in the new subdivision house she had bought outside of Phoenix.

7.

Melissa lay in the four-poster bed, staring at the paisley canopy above her. A morning breeze, carrying with it the scent of orange blossoms, gently fluttered the window curtains.

The sound of a television set invaded the quietness of her bedroom. "This is your sunrise commentator with your daily morning broadcast"

"Mary Belle, turn off that infernal machine. Too much dadgum racket!" The voice was thin and old, but the quavery command carried to the kitchen.

The responding voice was strong. "Mother, just a minute! Soon as I turn off the stove. I thought you wanted to know what's going on in the world. Goodness knows, I try to please you. I don't like it this loud, but I turned it up so you could hear. When you are ninety—"

"I ain't ninety. Eighty-nine. And I ain't deaf. I can hear— more'n I want to lotsa times."

Raising her arms, clad in the long flannel sleeves of her nightgown, the old woman strained to pull herself out of bed. She tugged at the quilts. But the pale hands collapsed, impotent, on the covers. She turned her body and fumbled at the stand by the bedside. She touched a pistol, old and too heavy now for her to lift, the steel marred with specks of rust. Melissa smiled. "Come here, youngun."

A stout woman, well past her middle age, stepped into the bedroom and stood with her hands on her wide hips. Mary Belle prided herself on her control in dealing with her mother "when she was difficult." Now the daughter's voice was even condescending. "What is it, Mother dear? And don't call me youngun. Mary Belle is my proper name."

The old woman opened her mouth, displaying the bare gums. "Help me outa this damn bed."

"Do you have to use profanity?"

A frail hand wiggled above the patchwork quilt. "You don't like my cussin'? I don't like this bed. Bed is where people die."

"And stop talking of dying, while you're at it. You've been saying that for the past ten years. You will outlive me. You are ninety and—"

"Stop right there, you contrary heifer. I'm eighty-nine." The old woman's glee increased the wrinkles in her face. Her eyes narrowed. "Gimme my glasses. My dime-store spectacles. Not them fancy ones you got the doctor to give me."

"Mother, I am taking you to the bathroom. You don't need your glasses. Sometimes you really do exasperate me."

"So-o-o. I exasperate you, Miss Prissy? Cussin' ain't becomin' to me? What is? To hear you tell it, nothin'. I don't give a hootin' holler in hell if it is or if it ain't."

"Please," frustration creased the daughter's forehead,

"Don't say 'ain't'—you know better than that."

"Yessum, Miss-Know-It-All, I know better. But I am a-aimin' to do as I damn well please."

Mary Belle's plump body stiffened. "Yes, you will do as you please. Regardless of my embarrassment. Or my needs. Or my feelings." Placing her hands firmly under her mother's armpits, she lifted her out of bed with a haste born of duty disliked.

"Hurry up, I gotta pee." The tone betrayed urgency.

"I'm hurrying." Supporting the old woman with both hands, Mary Belle took measured steps toward the bathroom. "Mother, let me know when you're finished. Don't try to get off the commode by yourself. You might break your thigh again. Don't be obstinate. Call me. I'm leaving the door open. I can't keep an eye on you and on breakfast at the same time." She walked out.

Melissa sat on the toilet singing a song. The tuneless humming reached the kitchen. "They called him Mustang Gray/He left his home when but a youth/a-rangin' he did go/He joined the Texas Rangers/a cowboy for to be . . ." She stopped. "Youngun, come git me. I'm through." Fumbling, she pushed the handle on the toilet, and the echo of flushing water filled the room.

Mary Belle came to the door, arms folded across her chest. Her mouth was set in a tight line, her eyes shooting accusations. "Why did you flush the toilet? You know the doctor told me to check your stool."

"Doctor?" The high enfeebled voice mimicked. "Doctor, lawyer, merchant, chief. They're all men." Her voice trailed off and for a moment her thoughts floated out with the orange-scented breeze. "Men? Shug said, 'Men is for lovin'.'" Her eyes regained their alertness. "No damn man is going to tell this little froggy how high to jump."

"Yes, I know. I've heard that before. No man is going to boss you." Mary Belle sighed despairingly. "I give up." Buttressing

her mother's delicate shoulders against her own, she helped
Melissa walk to the kitchen table.

As they crossed the living room, Melissa stopped to look at
a picture on the wall. "Whatd' you say the name of that place
was?"

"Taj Mahal. I brought the picture back with me from
India."

"Shore is purty. I'm gonna show that picture to Shug."

Mary Belle caught her breath. Softly she spoke, "Mama, you
remember that we lost Aunt Shug. She's been gone a year."

The old woman's eyes were vacant. She seemed neither to
see nor hear. Her voice rambled. "Shore as tootin', I'm gonna
show Shug that there picture."

Mary Belle gently moved her mother forward, "Let me hold
your arm. We'll go into the kitchen for breakfast."

The old woman snapped. "I want a egg. Fried hard in lard,
not this squashy jumble, soft-boiled mess. I don't like toast.
Makes my belly ache. I gotta have biscuits or corn bread.
Gimme somethin' to gum this old mouth on, like fried salt
pork."

The daughter's large breasts heaved. She waited before she
answered. "Mother, you are going to diet."

"So, I'm gonna die? That what yore tellin' me?"

"I said 'diet.' You're so busy tellin' me what you want, what
you are going to do, and what you're not going to do, that you
don't listen. Your diet stipulates that you are to have no fried
foods. The doctor said the cholesterol—"

"Klo-est-er-all hell! And to hell with the doctor. I'm a heap
sight older'n him. He'll never see the day he's in as good shape
as I'm in. Puny feller. That simpy smile. More'n likely he'll keel
over and die long 'fore I'm dead and buried."

The daughter clasped her hands and raised her eyes. "I do
the best I can with you."

"What is this? Coffee? I don't want this instant stuff outa
that jar. I know—no caf-feen and no acid. I don't want it. I

won't have it. I won't drink it. I want my coffee boiled, as Ben Baker used to say 'strong enough to float a horseshoe on.' On The Mesa we boiled the grounds for a week, just addin' more water and a speck of new coffee each time. This stuff's too damn weak. Tastes like—"

"Mother!" Mary Belle put her hands over her ears. "Don't say that word."

The old woman was not thinking of her daughter. She stared into space. "Coffee. I remember campin' on the Navasota. We run plumb outa coffee, and there come up a squall . . ." Melissa tapped the formica table with birdlike fingers.

"Mother, you are rambling again. I don't know what you're talking about. Time for breakfast."

"I gotta take my physic 'fore I eat."

"Here it is." The daughter spoke decisively. "While you eat this well-balanced, nourishing meal, I wish to discuss with you the day's itinerary."

"Oh, usin' them big words again. If you mean what the hell yore goin' do today, whyn't you say so right out?" The teaspoon shook in the old woman's hand. "Gimme sugar for this." She waved the spoon.

"No more sugar. The doctor said . . . Oh, what's the use? You are impossible. My bridge club meets here today. I want you to wear that new Dacron dress I bought you. Those man's pants you insist on wearing look horrible." Mary Belle put bread in the toaster.

"So. Now I am horrible, huh? I'm a-tellin' you that I am a-goin' to wear my khaki britches. Yore pappy never approved of wimmin wearin' britches and bein' comfortable. He said 'tweren't ladylike." With quivering hands Melissa lifted the coffee to her lips. She sipped and shook her head. "This is weak as p—"

"Mother!"

"I ain't a-gonna say it but I kin taste it."

"Our agenda today—"

"Them big words again? First, it's the i-tin-i-rary. Now, it's the a-jen-da. Yore high-falutin' bridge friends has seen britches before. They wear 'em."

"They don't wear those . . . gruesome men's trousers. They have polyester pants suits, styled women's apparel. And your hair, I'll curl—"

"Curl my hair? I want you should call Baby and tell her to come and cut it. She's the only one what'll pay mind to how I like it."

"Baby's got a job, she's—"

"What do you call her?"

"A photo-journalist."

"I say she's a damn fine barber."

"I will not let her cut it. It's so short now that it doesn't reach to the top of your ears. Why do you want to look that way? Repulsive. I know. Don't tell me why. Shows your release from man's domination. I've heard that before too."

"Watch yore language, young lady. Re-pul-sive? Youngun, my hair's too long. Yore pappy never 'lowed me to cut it. My hair gives me headaches. I say, whack her off. Free me. It itches."

Mary Belle's face tightened. Standing in back of her mother's chair she gripped the wood until her knuckles turned white. When she spoke again, her voice was calm. "The girls will pass by your bedroom before they play cards. I am putting your gun in the bureau drawer. It looks so . . . heathen."

"I'm heathen? Somethin' like a cannibal—that eats hooman bein's? Missy, I want that forty-five left right where it is. Don't know when I might be needin' it."

Mary Belle could not hold back her laughter. "Really, Mother! When we're playing bridge in the other room?" Her tone became determined. "About your cigarettes. Don't smoke those filthy Bull Durhams today. The girls are in my church group. None of them use tobacco."

"I will have my smokes. I am eighty-nine. I'll roll my own

when I want to. Don't you go hidin' my makin's. If yore so-ci-ety friends don't cotton to me, they can go square to hell."

"Mother, please don't talk like that!" Mary Belle clenched her hands. "The girls admire you. They think you have spirit. Independence. They say you are an 'individual.' "

"You mean they say I am a 'character.' And stubborn. And how in the hell do you put up with me, they say."

A smile relaxed Mary Belle's face. The old woman had verbalized her own tightly contained thoughts. "Mother of mine, there's no getting ahead of you. You are never monotonous. Never lacking for a repartee."

The old woman stirred her spoon around and around in the milk toast. "Did you ever listen to the quail just talkin' like the water bubblin' over the rocks in Tonto Creek? I can hear 'em outside right now."

"I'll warm your breakfast for you. It's cold. You are rambling again."

"I 'spose you say I'm see-nile?" The old woman jabbed her spoon at the milk toast. "When's Carter comin' to see me? That boy does beat all."

Mary Belle took her mother's face in her hands and turned it up toward her own. "Mother, you remember, we left Carter on The Mesa."

"Oh," the voice whined. "Carter, my boy, we buried you on the hill with the filaree." The frail hands fluttered and waved toward an imaginary hill.

Mary Belle felt a catch in her throat. She ran her fingers over Melissa's head. "You have lovely hair. Soft. Fine. Natural wave if you would let it grow long enough. Not nearly so gray as mine. If you would let me, today, I could push a wave in it and pull it to one side."

"Want it combed back, slicked back, that's all."

"If that's the way you want it, that way it shall be." Mary Belle's voice was soft now. "You are more important than the bridge girls anyway. I guess I do get a bit fractious with you.

We are confined here day after day by ourselves." The big woman bent down, drawing her mother's infirm body close to her. "I'll never be the woman you are." She pressed her lips against the colorless forehead.

Melissa looked up, her eyes clear. "No, Mary Belle. I'm the one who is cantankerous. You put up with a lot from me. The other children bring me fine presents on Mother's Day. Things I cain't wear. Don't want 'em. Don't need 'em. Don't like 'em. Just put them all away in the dresser drawer. On Easter they send me flowers I cain't smell. You gotta water the flowers and wash out the vases."

The old woman continued, her voice low and gentle. "They bring their passel of younguns for a five-minute visit on Sunday afternoon. They kiss me and cain't wait to git away. Then they feel good 'cause they came to pay their respects to their ma. But you are the one who takes care of this crochety old woman. Cookin' for her. Dressin' her. Listenin' to her complaints and her ailments."

Her mouth opened in a grin, and she blew a kiss from her fingertips. Her voice purred. "You know what? I'm goin' wear that new fancy dotted dress for your bridge party. And I'm gonna put in my store teeth. Daughter, you are all right."

Mary Belle patted Melissa's short-cut hair. "Now, what are your desires?" she asked.

The old woman sucked in her cheeks, bringing her lips together in a withered oval. She mused. "My desires? Let me see. I have a item on my a-jen-da. I want a good shot of Jim Beam, a heavy snort of it. A little toddy 'fore yore gal friends come a-high tailin' it in here, a-cacklin' and a-fussin' over me."

Her eyes grew vague. "Make me a pallet to lie on in the wagon bed." She saw The Mesa stretching before her with its floor of filaree. The breeze careened down the slopes of the Four Peaks and brought with it the aroma of greasewood. Opening her mouth, she savored the spicy air. She heard the hoofbeats. Then he came into view, a lean cowboy riding a stocking-legged bay. His laugh reached her, echoing from the Sierra Anchas to the Mazatzals.

He dismounted and walked toward her. "Howdy, Melissa."

She whispered, "Ike Talbott, you'll do to ride the river with."